FLIRTING WITH FOREVER

A HOT ROMANTIC COMEDY

DIRTY MARTINI RUNNING CLUB
BOOK 4

CLAIRE KINGSLEY

Always Have LLC

Published by Always Have, LLC

ISBN: 9798385637188

Edited by Eliza Ames

Cover Design: Lori Jackson

www.clairekingsleybooks.com

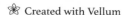 Created with Vellum

To all my readers who waited so patiently for Nora to get her turn. I love your faces!

ABOUT THIS BOOK

He'll break all her rules

Nora Lakes is sophisticated, successful, and happily single. Career problems aside, her life is fine the way it is, thank you very much. Sure, her best friends are all moving into a new season of life—full of husbands and babies and white picket fences. But that's not what Nora wants.

Neither is the gruff, tattooed guy next door.

Tattoo artist Dex St. James has enough trouble on his hands without the distractingly beautiful woman next door. Being a single dad to a teenage girl is no joke. The last thing he needs is a flirtatious new neighbor who makes his blood run hot.

He'll just avoid her. She's not his type anyway.

But Nora and Dex can't seem to stay out of each other's way. Between a pesky nocturnal visitor, Nora's blossoming friendship with Dex's daughter, and their undeniable chemistry, that up-against-the-wall, brain-melting kiss was probably inevitable.

Nora has rules when it comes to men, and she has her

reasons. Dex threatens to break every last one of them. She doesn't want forever. He won't settle for anything less. But when these two collide, the result is fire.

And maybe even forever.

Author's note: opposites attract in this fun, swoony, single dad romcom. A smart, sassy woman meets a rough-around-the-edges tattoo artist with a heart of gold. Daddy/daughter moments, all the banter, neighborly shenanigans, a meddling family, badass lady friendships, and a hero who's determined to fight the heat between them—until he falls first.

Flirting with Forever can be read as a stand-alone.

1

DEX

*M*y new neighbor was trouble.

One glance out the window told me that. I narrowed my eyes at the woman. Long dark hair in a bouncy ponytail. Fitted tank top with a big martini glass on it. Leggings that hugged a set of wicked curves. She clearly knew how to use them. I was surprised the moving guys were getting anything done.

They grinned at her. Flirted with her. Even though she was way out of their league. And she seemed to enjoy every second of it. Ate up the attention.

Yep. Trouble.

My daughter Riley appeared on the stairs, dressed in a unicorn t-shirt and jeans. She'd done her brown hair in two French braids—she was into braiding lately. Without really looking at me, she came downstairs, said nothing, and went into the kitchen.

I let out a long breath. She was a different sort of trouble. Around the age of twelve, my once sweet baby girl had morphed into a hormonal enigma. Turning thirteen a few months ago hadn't improved the situation. She shifted between silent and sullen or talkative and animated and there seemed to be no way to predict which Riley I was going to get. Recently, she'd burst into tears at the dinner table and when I'd asked her what was wrong, she'd sobbed, "I don't know."

Growing up was hard.

So was raising a teenage girl. Especially on my own.

She'd also started developing a body that was incredibly alarming. Thank goodness her cheeks were still slightly rounded, making it clear she was still a kid.

I wasn't ready for all this.

"Hey, Ry?" I inched toward the kitchen, not sure if I should get too close. It was like living with a wild animal—totally unpredictable. "What'cha up to?"

"Tea."

One word answers were pretty common lately, especially during a silent and sullen phase. Of course, she could turn on a dime and suddenly launch into a discussion of the most recent book she'd read or a rant about math homework.

I just tried to roll with it. No idea if that was the right thing to do. For a while, I'd felt like I was rocking this single dad thing. But lately, not so much.

Maybe I could get a few more words out of her. "Looks like someone is moving into the Olsons' old house."

She took out a tea bag and set it in a mug. "Yeah."

I waited to see if she'd say more. Nothing.

Okay, neighborhood news wasn't interesting enough to spark a conversation. I'd try a question. "Do you have any homework this weekend? I forgot to ask after school yesterday."

"Yes."

"Need any help with it?"

"No."

"If you do, let me know."

No reply.

Apparently it was time to roll with it and just give her space. "I have to go into work soon and I'll probably be there late tonight. Are you good? Need anything?"

"I'm fine."

Wow, two words. That was something.

"There's leftovers for dinner, or you can make something."

"Okay."

She poured hot water over her tea bag, picked up her mug, and headed for the stairs.

"Love you," I said, almost under my breath. I didn't expect a reply.

She glanced over her shoulder. "Love you, too."

I felt that deep in my chest. If that was the longest sentence I was going to get out of her, I'd certainly take it.

Sometimes I wondered if she did things like that to keep me from losing my mind. As if a part of her knew that I needed those little reminders that my baby girl was still in there.

I wandered back to the living room and glanced out the window. The woman next door was typing something on her phone and I couldn't seem to look away. It wasn't just her body, although that was certainly nice to look at. She had an air about her, like she was charged with electricity.

Thanks to Phil across the street, I already knew more about her than was necessary. She was single—or at least not married—and lived alone. I didn't know how he'd gotten that information, but that was typical. Phil was always the first to know everything on our street.

Not that it mattered. Single or not, she wasn't my type.

Actually, nobody was my type. I'd taken dating off my agenda a long time ago. Someday? Maybe, but I kind of doubted it. For the time being, I was focused on raising my daughter. Once she was on her own I was looking forward to the freedom of not having to answer to anyone.

Which was why it didn't make any sense that I was staring out the window at the woman next door. She wasn't that hot.

Okay, yes she was.

If you were into that sort of thing.

"Dad?"

I whipped around. "Yeah?"

"What were you staring at?"

Damn it. "Nothing."

"Then why are you standing there looking out the window?"

Great, now she chooses to speak in complete sentences? "Just looking. It's nice out."

Her brow furrowed, as if she were confused. I got that look from her a lot. "Okay."

"What's up? Do you need something?"

She held out a piece of paper. "I need you to sign this for school."

"What is it? A field trip or something?"

"No. I'm failing PE."

I walked over and swiped the note out of her hand. "Failing? How are you failing PE?"

She shrugged but didn't offer an explanation.

I read the note. She was indeed failing PE and her teacher cited a lack of participation as the reason.

"What does this mean?" I asked. "Are you just sitting out and not doing anything during class?"

"I guess."

"You guess? Ry, that's not an answer. You can't fail a class, especially one like PE. That should be a slam dunk for you."

She scowled at the floor. "I won't fail. I'll do extra credit or something."

"Have you talked to your teacher about it already?"

"No."

"But you're going to?"

"Yeah."

"Do I need to talk to her?"

"No."

With a slight shake of my head—seriously, failing PE—I took the note to the kitchen and dug through the junk drawer until I found a pen. I started scrawling my signature across the bottom but the pen didn't work. No ink. Damn it. I found another one and scribbled a quick circle on a discarded sticky note to make sure it worked. It was bright green but it would do. I signed the note and held it out to Riley.

"I'm going to check in with you in a few days and you better have a plan to get this grade up."

She took the paper. "I will."

I watched her go back upstairs, feeling helpless. Instinct told me something else was going on. She'd been in sports her whole life, PE should have been a breeze. All she had to do was show up and participate. But, for some reason, she was shutting down.

It was happening in all areas of her life. Her grades were slipping. She hadn't been to a friend's house in months and she'd stopped inviting kids over. No matter what I tried, our conversations were brief and stunted. Almost awkward. Which was so weird. We'd always been so close.

What had happened to the happy little girl whose favorite place had once been my lap?

A yawn overtook me out of nowhere, reminding me of how badly I'd slept the night before. Insomnia sucked but there didn't seem to be much I could do about it. Sometimes I slept okay but most nights I was up for at least a few hours. Been that way for years.

I headed back to the kitchen and started a fresh pot of coffee. I needed something to wake me up before I had to go to work. As a tattoo artist, I couldn't afford to be drowsy on the job. Mistakes weren't an option when you were needling permanent ink onto someone's body. Tonight, I had a couple of consultations and a client returning to fill in more of his sleeve. I was excited about the sleeve—it was turning out awesome—and I definitely needed to be sharp.

While I waited for the coffee, I went back to the living room and looked outside. The woman was out there, still flirting with one of the movers. He went up the ramp into the truck and for a second, she glanced my direction.

It was like being hit by a jolt of electricity. I felt the zap in my chest. Seemed like a bad omen.

I'd keep my distance. Just because she was right next door didn't mean I had to have anything to do with her. The last thing I needed was more female trouble in my life. I glanced upstairs, toward Riley's closed bedroom door. I had enough of that already.

2

NORA

*M*oving was ridiculous.

I wasn't even the one hauling furniture and boxes. I'd hired movers, which meant I was in more of a supervisory role. But even making sure things were being taken to the right rooms and starting to sort through the mess was a lot of work.

Joey, one of the moving guys, came out of the house and grinned at me as he walked up the ramp into the back of the truck.

He was cute. Not I'd-invite-him-to-stay cute, but we'd been having fun. Flirting with a couple of muscular men certainly made moving into a new house more pleasant.

My new house.

I'd fallen in love with it immediately. The cute two-story on a quiet cul-de-sac had pretty maple hardwoods, new appliances, and a neutral color palette just waiting for someone to make it their own. It had a quaint front porch with just enough space for a little bistro table and chairs and big windows that let in lots of light.

Although now that I was here, with my entire life packed into boxes, I was wondering what I'd gotten myself into.

When I'd picked up my keys the day before, the house had looked like a fresh, clean slate. Now it was a mess—furniture and boxes everywhere.

And the yard. It appeared that the previous owner had stopped doing any sort of maintenance while waiting for the deal to close. The grass was too tall and I had no idea what plants were weeds and what was overgrown landscaping.

I'd never had a yard before. This was going to be interesting. Especially considering all the other houses on the street had lawns that were as well manicured as my nails.

I put my hands on my hips. I'd just have to figure it out.

But first, I needed a place to work. And sleep. And ideally the ability to cook, although takeout was definitely on the agenda for at least the next few days.

My phone buzzed with a text. As if I needed the reminder that work was a thing, I had a text from my boss, April.

What did she want? She knew I was moving.

I decided to ignore it for now and swiped away the notification. I'd get back to her when I at least had a place to sit down. And could locate my laptop.

Joey came down the ramp with a load of boxes on the hand truck. "Just you living here? No husband or boyfriend?"

"Just me."

"Does that mean you're taking applications?"

"Why? Do you think you'd get an interview?"

He grinned, flashing a set of straight teeth. "Oh yeah. My resume has an impressive skills section."

My hands rested on my hips and I gave him a subtle eye roll. "That's what they all say."

With a wink, he rolled the hand truck toward the house.

His counterpart came out with a similar cocky grin. "Don't believe anything he says. He's totally full of it."

"And I suppose I should believe what you say?"

He paused on the ramp and shifted his shoulders so his chest flexed beneath his t-shirt. "Obviously."

"Does that mean the skills section of his resume is lacking?"

"Yeah, my dude in there has trouble finding things. If you know what I mean."

"Too bad. It's nice when a man knows his way around."

"That's why they call me the navigator."

My eyebrows drew in. "Has anyone ever called you that?"

He grinned again. "No, I just made it up. But it sounds good, right?"

"Maybe think twice before you use that line again."

I left him to get another load and went inside to check on our progress.

Chaos. It was chaos.

I sighed at the boxes everywhere. The guys seemed to be doing a good job of putting things in the correct rooms, but the mess was a stark reminder of how much work I had ahead of me. And I couldn't help but wonder, again, what I'd gotten myself into.

Nora Lakes, homeowner. And not just a homeowner, but the owner of a house on a quiet suburban cul-de-sac. This was white picket fence territory. Most of my new neighbors had minivans in their driveways and swing sets in their backyards. It was so different from the urban apartment I'd been living in.

But I'd decided it was time to settle down. All three of my best friends now had husbands and houses, and life in my old apartment hadn't been nearly as fun without Everly and Hazel living in the same building. It had felt like time for a change—time to level up.

Marriage wasn't for me, thank you very much, but a woman didn't have to get married to take her life in a new direction. A more adult direction.

So I'd bought a house.

"Ma'am?"

Joey's voice from one of the bedrooms made my shoulders tighten. Had he just ma'amed me?

He appeared in the hallway and I quickly softened my expression. I didn't want to show that kind of weakness.

I raised my eyebrows. "Sorry, did you call me?"

"Yeah, I wasn't sure if you were out here. Do you want us to put your bed frame together? That way you'll at least have a place to sleep tonight."

"That would be great, thank you."

"No problem." He grinned like he was expecting me to engage in a fresh round of flirty banter at the mention of my bed.

Ma'am? Really?

I pretended not to notice his playful expression and waded through the boxes into the kitchen. It was probably just a slip-up and he used that term with clients all the time.

Then again, the movers were probably both ten years younger than me. At least.

I sighed. When had that happened?

An idea for a column popped into my mind, something exploring the modern woman's experience of aging. From those first realizations that you're no longer twenty-one to navigating the different seasons of life with elegance and grace. It would make an amazing series, especially if I found women of different ages and backgrounds to interview and—

I stopped that train of thought. There was no point. April would never approve it. Not unless I found some way to spin it into a story about sex. That was all they ever wanted me to write about.

Sex at any age? They'd probably approve that. But it was so much less interesting. As if the only way a woman could be happy was to get, and give, regular orgasms.

I loved sex as much as the next person—probably more —but I was getting tired of constantly writing about it. There was so much more to a woman's life than what her vagina was doing.

And there used to be more to my career than writing about blow jobs.

But this wasn't the time for a deep dive into my career woes. I'd just signed a mortgage, so my job was rather important, regardless of how I felt about it.

The boxes in the kitchen were stacked in a haphazard jumble, blocking my access to just about everything, including the fridge. I had a few bags of perishable food on the counter that needed to be put away, so I set to work pushing the boxes into neater rows.

My phone buzzed again, but this time it was Hazel, checking in on my progress. All three of my besties had offered to help but I'd assured them I'd be fine. There was an unwritten rule that after a certain age, you stopped asking your friends to help you move and just hired movers like a grown-up.

I took a picture of the chaotic kitchen and sent it to our group chat.

Me: *Making progress!*

Hazel: *I suspect the exclamation point is meant to insinuate* *a false sense of enthusiasm so we won't worry that you're over-whelmed.*

Me: *Oh no, I'm overwhelmed. But I'll be fine.*

Everly: *Are you sure? We can still come over.*

Hazel: *We could at least help put things away.*

Sophie: *Say the word, and we'll be there!*

I loved my friends so much. They were the best.

Me: *Not yet. But if I can't dig myself out in the next day or so, I'll take you up on it.*

Everly: *That's fair. So excited for you!*

Sophie: *Me too! I can't wait to see it!*

Hazel: *Me too, to all of the above.*

I slipped my phone back into the side pocket of my leggings. I loved that they were so willing to help, and I knew they meant it. But they all had their own lives. Busy ones. I felt like I needed to handle this move on my own.

At least I could walk to the refrigerator—and open it. I put the contents of my old fridge away and decided to go back outside and see how close the guys were to emptying the truck.

They were almost finished, just a few more things to bring inside. I took a deep breath of the cool early spring air. It was quiet, which was going to take some getting used to. But I was going to like it here.

A man came out of the house next door and I did a double take.

Tall, dark hair, square jaw roughed up with light stubble. His thick chest and shoulders gave that t-shirt a workout, and his arms were covered with tattoos.

He was so not my type. The opposite, in fact. I preferred a polished gentleman. A suit was like lingerie for men, as far as I was concerned. Facial hair was fine as long as it was meticulously groomed. I liked men who opened doors and pulled out chairs. Men who smelled good and wore shoes that were every bit as expensive as mine. Men who were professional and refined.

So why was I staring at this one like I'd never seen a real man before?

His jeans were worn and probably dirty. His t-shirt was plain gray. And the tattoos? Why cover up all that skin with so much ink? It was so unnecessary.

He glanced in my direction and his eyes flicked up and down, like he was taking me all in. But his expression didn't change, giving me no indication whether or not he liked what he saw.

Not that it mattered.

Still, he couldn't even smile? Most of the people in this neighborhood had been so friendly. Phil from across the street had stopped by twice, once when I'd picked up the keys and once when the moving truck had first arrived. But this guy didn't offer me so much as a chin tip.

He got in his car—a black sedan that was as boring as his outfit. He looked like he belonged on a motorcycle, not in a family car.

I had to admit, I was mildly intrigued. Who was my mysterious, unfriendly, tattooed neighbor?

Without a second glance, he drove away, leaving me alone with my curiosity.

3

NORA

$\mathcal{I}$ stood up from my desk, reached my arms over my head, and stretched. My home office wasn't completely unpacked, let alone organized, but it was functional. I worked from home about half the time, so this room, along with my bedroom, bathroom, and the kitchen, had been top priority.

The small spare bedroom that I'd turned into an office had a window facing the front, letting in plenty of light. I was going to need more shelving, but I'd have room for it. Once I took care of that, and put up some art on the walls, it would be a lovely work space.

The stretch felt good after sitting for the last couple of hours. Thankfully, my instinct had been right, and April's weekend text hadn't been an emergency. She'd sent me a list of ideas for my next column and we'd reviewed them in our regular Monday meeting. Now it was up to me to turn those ideas into something engaging—and clickable.

Always clickable.

That was becoming more of a challenge, especially

because April seemed to be determined to pigeonhole me as a sex writer.

Sure, I wrote about sex. Some of my most popular articles when I'd been an independent blogger had been about sex. My *How to Give a Great Blow Job* article had gone viral and it was what had put me on Glamour Gal Media's radar. When they'd offered to buy out my blog and take me on as part of their online media empire, I'd been thrilled. It had seemed like my dream come true.

Except now my column, *Living Your Best Life*, had been turned into a shell of what it had once been. Instead of writing about all sorts of things—female friendships, women's empowerment, health and beauty, fashion, and yes, sex—April wanted me to keep finding new ways to give blow job instructions.

Sex sells, she'd say.

And she wasn't wrong. But I was getting tired of it. As if the only professional value I had was in my ability to use the word "cock" without blushing.

I went out to the kitchen to grab something to drink. Although the house itself was older, most of the interior had been renovated. The kitchen was adorable, with white cabinets, light gray counters, and a gray tile floor. I got out a pitcher of iced tea, poured myself a glass, and wandered outside to get some fresh air.

My new bistro table and chairs set was adorable and fit perfectly on the cute front porch. Clouds drifted through the blue sky and the scent of freshly cut grass hung in the air. Phil from across the street was busy trimming the hedge in front of his house, using big shears to cut pieces of the plant, then stepping back to check his work. He noticed me and waved. I waved back.

This was nice.

My other neighbor—the grumpy tattooed one—pulled into his driveway. I'd seen him once or twice since move-in day, but only fleeting glimpses as he came and went. A teenage girl—probably twelve or thirteen—got out of the passenger side. According to Phil, who seemed to know everyone on our street, she was his daughter. I didn't know what had happened to her mom, but I did know it was just the two of them.

Which made the grumpy one a single dad.

That shouldn't have made him more intriguing. I wasn't into dating single fathers any more than I was into dating men covered in tattoos. But for some reason, it did.

Not that my curiosity meant I was attracted to him.

Much.

He got out and headed straight for the front door. His daughter glanced in my direction. I lifted my hand in a wave, wiggling my fingers at her. She smiled back.

Her dad? Not so much. He ignored me and went inside, followed by his daughter.

The buzz of my phone turned my attention from my neighbors. The name on the screen made me pause. Landon. That was interesting.

Landon and I had dated a couple of years ago. For a time, he'd been perfect for me. I liked men who treated me well, could perform in the bedroom, and who preferred to keep things casual while still maintaining a certain level of monogamy while we were dating. Long-term commitment wasn't for me, but neither was being one of many. I wasn't going to sleep with a man who would turn around and shag some other woman the next day, and of course I'd offer him the same courtesy. Landon had fit the bill.

Until he hadn't.

He'd wanted more than I had it in me to give. More

commitment, to be precise. He'd started to get too attached, which was when my flight instinct had kicked into high gear, and the time had come to end it. All things considered, we'd parted amicably.

What did he want now? Another shot? Or just a hookup with a woman who'd once blown his mind?

Landon: *Hey. Been a while. Just wanted to see how you're doing.*

Me: *It has been a while. I'm doing fine. You?*

Landon: *I'm okay. Started a new job a few months ago. It's good.*

Me: *That's great. I just moved into a new house.*

Landon: *Awesome. I'd love to see it.*

I eyed the screen, trying to read between the lines. Was he hoping for an invitation or just catching up?

Landon: *Are you free tonight?*

Me: *Depends. What did you have in mind?*

Landon: *I'd love to see your new place.*

My place? Well that answered that question. He was hoping for an invitation.

I pondered for a moment. Did I want him to come over tonight? We'd been good together, particularly physically. If I invited him here, I knew what I'd get out of it. I could do worse than a night of great sex. Well, good sex at least, let's not be too generous. But good sex was better than none, right? It had been a while.

Still, the thought of sleeping with Landon wasn't really appealing to me. No low swirl of warmth or pleasant tingle of pressure between my legs.

Me: *Sorry, I don't think so.*

Landon: *You sure? We could make it my place.*

Me: *I appreciate the offer but I don't think it's a good idea.*

There was a long pause and I wondered how he'd take

my rejection. I didn't want to hurt his feelings—he was a decent guy—but I wasn't going to let him talk me into something I didn't want to do. Especially if that something involved taking my clothes off.

Landon: *No worries. Figured I'd give it a shot. Take care.*

Me: *You too.*

I put my phone down. That was that.

My body chose that moment to give me a little reminder of how long it had been since I'd taken my clothes off with a man. Longer than I would have liked. Sadly, the last person to touch my lady parts was my gynecologist at my last yearly appointment several months ago—even when you're careful, it's important to make sure you're healthy. Still, I didn't regret turning Landon down.

Grumpy tattooed guy came out of his house and that tingly reminder between my legs flared to life. A rush of heat flooded through me.

What was that about?

Sure, he was very masculine. What woman wouldn't look at that broad chest and thick arms and experience a biological reaction? He looked like the sort of man you'd want to be with if the world ended and you needed a fierce protector to keep you alive. Like he could hot wire a car, hunt wild game for dinner, and keep you sexually satisfied with equal skill and confidence.

But I lived in the real world and that feeling was just hormones.

"Hey, Dex." Phil paused his hedge trimming to wave at my neighbor. "How's it going?"

Dex lifted his hand. "Not bad. You?"

"Can't complain. Have a good one."

"You, too."

So he did have it in him to be friendly. Interesting.

His gaze swung to me and I took the opportunity to smile. *Go ahead, grumpy tattooed guy. Ignore my neighborly smile.*

He did.

Without the slightest acknowledgment that I existed, he got into his car, backed down the driveway, and left.

Rude.

I sipped my iced tea, feeling irritable. What was his problem? I couldn't decide what bothered me more—that he kept ignoring me or that I cared that he kept ignoring me.

But would it have killed him to wave? Tip his chin? Anything? It wasn't like he was rude to everyone. He'd just had a perfectly polite interaction with Phil. That was all I was asking for.

A few minutes later, his daughter came out. She glanced up and down the street, as if looking for any sign of her dad, and I wondered if she was about to sneak away. Her movements seemed tentative, like she was afraid of getting caught breaking some rule.

But she didn't leave, nor did a boy who was probably too old for her arrive in a beat-up car to whisk her away somewhere her dad wouldn't have wanted her to go.

Not that I knew anything about that scenario.

Actually, I very much did. Minus the dad part. Mine would have had to have been around to notice me jumping into a car with a dangerous boy.

The girl slipped earbuds in her ears and looked like she was about to lower herself onto her front step—they could have used a bistro table and chairs, too—but she glanced at me and paused.

I smiled and gave her a little wave. Maybe her dad was a jerk, but that didn't mean she was.

Her answering smile was tentative—almost shy—which made me love her instantly.

"Hi." I waved again. "I'm Nora."

She took out her earbuds. "Um, hi. I'm Riley."

"Nice to meet you, Riley."

"You, too."

"Would you like to join me for some iced tea?" I asked. "I have more inside."

Another little smile graced her lips. She was adorable.

"Okay."

I waved her over and invited her to sit. She pocketed her earbuds and sat down while I went inside to refill my iced tea and get her a glass.

I brought our drinks outside and joined her at the table. "I forgot to ask you if you prefer sweetened. This doesn't have any sugar in it. If I'm going to drink my calories, I prefer there to be alcohol involved."

Her brows drew together slightly, as if she were the tiniest bit confused. "Unsweetened is fine. I don't have much of a sweet tooth."

"Me neither. Salty is my downfall."

"Oh my gosh, me too. I put extra salt on my fries and my dad thinks I'm crazy."

"Look at that, we already have something in common." I lifted my glass. "To new friends."

She clinked hers against mine and we both sipped.

"So, Riley. Tell me about you. How old are you?"

"Thirteen."

"And what grade are you in?"

"Seventh."

"How is it? Do you like school?"

She shrugged. "It's okay, I guess."

I shook my head slowly. "Seventh grade was not my favorite year."

"Really? Why?"

"So many reasons. For one thing, it was the year I got boobs and I had absolutely no idea what to do with them. I went to school without a bra one day and the boys started calling me Nora Nipples."

Riley winced. "That's mean."

"Seventh grade boys leave a lot to be desired. I am happy to tell you that at least some of them improve. But don't hold your breath. It takes at least another decade."

"That's okay. I kind of had a crush on this one boy at the beginning of the year but I decided he was too immature."

"I think that's smart. You'll have plenty of time for that later. What are you into?"

She glanced down with a shrug. "I don't know. Art, I guess."

"What kind of art? Do you draw?"

"Yeah, and paint."

"Do you? That's interesting. Maybe you could show me sometime."

"You want to see my art?"

"Absolutely. But only when you're ready. Art can be very personal."

"Yeah, it is," she said, a hint of awe in her voice, like she was surprised that I understood. "Are you an artist too?"

"Oh, I wish." I waved that off. "I don't have that kind of talent."

"What do you do? Like, for your job?"

"I'm a writer."

"Really? A professional one?"

"Yep. I write a weekly column about, well, women's

issues." I didn't really want to get into the topic of my latest article with a thirteen-year-old.

"I love writing."

"Do you? Look at us, finding all sorts of things in common. What do you like to write?"

"A lot of things. I've written some stories and I always get good grades on my essays. I write poetry sometimes, too."

"I love that. Good for you."

I took another sip of my tea. Riley did the same. I was just about to ask her another question to keep the conversation going when she beat me to it.

"Where did you move from?"

"Just down in Seattle. I had an apartment there and it was nice, but I decided I wanted more space. A place of my own."

"Do you like it here?"

"I do. It's a nice neighborhood and everyone is so friendly." *Everyone except your dad.* "What about you? How long have you lived here?"

"Since I was little. My dad picked it because it seemed good for kids."

Her answer made me wonder about her mother. But I knew better than to ask. Too personal, especially since we'd just met.

"Looks like he was right."

"You don't have kids?"

I laughed, probably louder than I should have. "Sorry. No, I don't have kids. It's just me."

"So you're not married?"

"No." I shook my head. "Definitely not."

"Do you have any pets?"

"I don't. Well, I briefly had a cat, but it wasn't really mine. My friend Sophie moved in with me for a while during a rough patch with her now-husband and she adopted a break-up cat. She took him with her when she moved out. Do you have any pets?"

"No. We had a fish for a while but he died and we didn't bother getting another one. What's a break-up cat?"

"A Sophie invention. She was sad and her solution was to start adopting animals."

Riley smiled. "That's kind of funny."

"It was. Sophie is positively adorable. One of the sweetest women you'll ever meet. Actually, all three of my best friends are."

"You have three best friends?"

"I sure do. Everly, Hazel, and Sophie. I'm lucky that way."

"Are they all really pretty like you?"

Oh my god, I loved this girl. "That's sweet of you to say. And yes, although we're all very different. Most people wouldn't guess we're friends. What about you? Who's your best friend? Or friends?"

She glanced down, her openness receding like flower petals curling in on themselves. "I don't really have a best friend."

The sadness in her tone tugged at my heart. "I didn't when I was your age, either."

"Really?" Hopeful eyes met mine.

"Nope. I had a hard time getting along with the other girls my age until I met Everly and Hazel. That wasn't until eighth grade." I swirled my glass, making the ice cubes clink. "The thing about friendships, and boys for that matter, is that you never want to settle. Having acquaintances or people you can have fun with is fine, but you want to be careful about who you let into your circle of trust."

"So, you mean it's better to have no friends than bad friends?"

I tilted my head, thinking about that for a moment. "Yes. Bad friends aren't really friends, are they?"

"No, I guess not."

"And you never want to compromise who you are so other people will like you."

She nodded slowly, like she was taking it all in. I hoped I was giving her good advice. I was used to having these kinds of chats with women my own age, not kids. But it seemed like something Riley needed to hear.

We kept chatting for a little while—a bit about movies and music and our favorite shows to binge watch. She finished her tea and set her glass down.

"I should probably get home. I have homework."

"Fair enough. Promise you'll come visit me again?"

She smiled. "I promise."

We both stood. She hesitated and my intuition told me she might need a hug.

"Can I give you a hug?" I tentatively held out my arms.

She stepped in and hugged me. What a sweetheart.

"See you later," I said.

"Bye."

She went home and waved at me from her front step before going inside.

Maybe her dad wasn't friendly but he'd certainly raised a lovely daughter. I hadn't exactly been expecting to befriend a thirteen-year-old, but now that I had, I was even more satisfied with my choice of neighborhood.

It felt a bit like it was meant to be.

4

DEX

With some time between clients, I decided to head home and have dinner with Riley. Although I loved my job, the hours weren't always ideal. Tattoo shops tended to open late and stay open later, which wasn't great for a guy raising a daughter on his own. We'd found ways to make it work and things were easier now that she was old enough to be by herself. Still, I didn't like her spending too much time alone.

I'd decided not to text her to let her know I was on my way. Not that I expected to catch her breaking any rules. She was a really good kid, and man, I knew how lucky that made me. She could see me on the tracker app we shared—she called it our spy app—if she checked. But I still liked to keep her on her toes. Remind her once in a while that I *could* catch her breaking the rules.

I got home and stopped at the mailbox. I wasn't great about checking the mail every day and it showed. There was a stack of stuff shoved inside, bending the envelopes at the back. I tucked it all under my arm and walked up the driveway.

And I definitely didn't look to see if the new neighbor was outside.

Okay, yes I did.

To her credit, she was quiet. I'd hardly seen her and there was nothing to indicate she was going to be an annoying neighbor. No loud music or constant guests clogging up the street with their cars. Her yard needed some help, but she'd inherited that problem, so I couldn't really blame her for it.

There was no sign of her, despite the nice weather. She was probably at work.

Pushing her out of my mind, I went inside and set the mail on the counter. Evidence of Riley's after-school snack was on the kitchen table, but I didn't see her downstairs.

"Hey, Ry?"

No answer.

Probably headphones.

I went upstairs and rapped my knuckle on her partially open door. "Riley?"

She sat on her bed, resting against a couple of pillows propped up behind her. School books were spread around her comforter and she had a spiral notebook in her lap. She popped out one of her earbuds. "Oh hey, Dad. What are you doing home?"

"I had some time. Figured I'd come home for dinner."

"Cool. What are we having?"

I opened my mouth, then closed it again. I hadn't gotten that far. "I don't know. Should we go see what's in the fridge?"

"Sure." She closed her book and followed me downstairs.

I opened the fridge and eyed the contents while she leaned against the counter.

"Do you have homework this weekend?"

"Nope. Already got it done."

I raised my eyebrows. "You really came home on a Friday and did homework first thing?"

She shrugged. "Now I don't have to worry about it all weekend."

"How'd you get so smart? Most adults don't have that figured out."

"I get it from Grandma," she said without missing a beat.

I grinned. "That's probably true."

My mom had watched her a lot when she was little.

"How's your PE grade?"

She shrugged. "Okay. I'll probably get a C."

"A C? Come on, Ry, you can do better than that. It's not brain surgery."

"At least I'm not failing."

"Yeah, true." I decided not to push too hard about the PE grade. It was nice having an actual conversation with her. And to be real, a mediocre grade in middle school PE wasn't the end of the world. "Can you live with spaghetti?"

"I love spaghetti."

I took out a package of ground beef. Riley found a jar of spaghetti sauce and a box of pasta in the pantry. I started browning the meat and she set a pot of water on the stove to boil.

She picked through the mail I'd left sitting on the counter and held up a magazine with a woman on the cover. "What's this?"

"I don't know. Reggie probably put the wrong mail in our box again."

"Oh, it's for Nora."

"Who's Nora?"

"The lady next door."

That caught my attention. "The one who moved in last weekend? How do you know her name is Nora?"

"I met her."

"When?"

"The other day after school. She was outside and invited me over."

"Excuse me? You're not supposed to go into other people's houses unless I know about it."

"I didn't. I sat on her porch."

"I don't know how I feel about that."

"Why? I go over and talk to Phil and Donna when they're outside. That's basically the same thing."

I broke up the meat with a spatula and stirred it around as it started to sizzle. I didn't have a good reason for this to bother me. She was right, sitting on a neighbor's porch wasn't against the rules. And there was probably nothing wrong with it. But still, I didn't know this woman and something about her just being there was getting under my skin. I wasn't so sure I wanted her making friends with my daughter.

"Just be careful. We don't know anything about her. People aren't always what they seem."

"Yeah, I know." She shuffled through the rest of the mail. "There's a bunch of her stuff in here. Do you want me to take it over there?"

I glared at the mail, as if it were responsible for being put in the wrong box. "No, I'll take it to her."

She shrugged again and set the mail down. "Okay."

I handed her the spatula so she could keep the meat browning and quickly sorted through the mail, separating mine from the neighbor's. Nora Lakes. Pretty name. I'd have to tell her about Reggie. He'd been doing our mail route for something like a hundred years. Although he was the nicest guy, his accuracy at mail delivery had gotten worse over the years. We were all used to it. It was normal to see a knot of neighbors all exchanging mail, making sure it got into the right hands.

Hopefully he wouldn't keep giving me Nora's.

"I'll be right back."

"Okay." Riley held up the spatula. "I've got this."

"Thanks, kiddo."

I took the pile outside. There wasn't a vehicle in her driveway. Probably wasn't home. That was fine, I'd just leave it on her front porch. It would save me the hassle of having to talk to her.

The street was quiet. Blue sky, a few puffy white clouds. If I hadn't had a client later, I'd have cracked open a beer and sat outside. It was shaping up to be a nice night.

I rounded the end of my driveway, ready to walk up hers, when I stopped in my tracks, my eyes on the most incredible ass I'd ever seen.

Seriously, don't judge. It was right there. Any man would have stopped and stared.

Nora was on her hands and knees, ass in the air, digging up a plant. At least, that's probably what she was doing. All I could see was her amazing backside.

I stood like I was frozen, staring at her.

And didn't move.

How long had I been staring? No idea.

Still staring.

Not moving.

I couldn't stop imagining my hands on those round hips, slamming into her like—

"Hey, Dex. What'cha looking at?"

My back tightened at Phil's voice coming from across the

street and for a second, I hoped to god Nora was wearing headphones.

She was. But she'd still heard him.

Her head whipped around, and the sight of her looking back at me with her ass in the air did nothing to improve the situation.

My jaw hitched and I tore my eyes away from her. "Hey, Phil. Nothing. Just bringing over some mail." I held it up as if to prove my innocence.

"Oh. Well, you were just standing there, so I thought there was something in the yard. Maybe a skunk or something."

"Nope. No skunks." Just a ridiculously hot woman with an ass that men would go to war over.

And said ass was still right there, in front of me. She hadn't moved, just looked at me over her shoulder, her lips curling in amusement.

Lips were nice too.

Who was I kidding. She was fire.

But I was not the guy who was going to get burned.

"Sorry." I held up the mail again. "Some of your mail ended up in my box."

"Oh. That was nice of you." She finally shifted and stood, relieving me of the agony of staring at that magnificent backside. She took out her earbuds and brushed the dirt off her hands. "Thanks."

I handed her the mail and was about to go back inside, but she kept talking.

"I'm Nora," she said and held out her other hand.

I took it in mine. Long, slender fingers. Soft skin. "Dex."

"Nice to meet you. I already met Riley. She's a lovely young lady."

That made me crack a smile. How could it not? "Thanks. Yeah, she's great."

Phil crossed the street, dressed in a t-shirt and cargo shorts with his signature red crocs. The entire neighborhood gave him shit about those shoes but he didn't care. Called them his dad shoes and claimed if we all knew how comfortable they were, we'd wear them too.

I'd given up a lot since becoming a father but red crocs were where I drew the line.

"Looks like you have your work cut out for you," Phil said, gesturing to Nora's untamed front yard.

"I really do," she said. "I have no idea what I'm doing but I figure, how hard can it be?"

"Well, proper lawn care is more complicated than most people think." Phil's tone took on the quality of a wise old sage. "There's fertilization, aeration, weed control, proper watering..."

He kept going but I tuned him out. Phil was immensely proud of his lawn and once he got going on the topic, he could talk your ear off. I'd heard it all before.

Nora's eyes glazed over after about the second or third sentence, but she kept nodding along. I couldn't decide if I was annoyed that Phil had wandered over to discuss lawn care or if I was grateful for the interruption. There was something about Nora that set off every one of my internal alarms.

Trouble.

Her eyes flicked to me with a plea for rescue. Phil was onto the importance of mowing at a diagonal relative to the street.

I patted Phil on the back. "That's some good info. No wonder your lawn looks so great."

"Thanks, Dex. I'm pretty proud of it."

She smiled and I didn't miss the relief in her eyes. "Thanks for the tips. I'll see if I can get the yard in better shape."

"Well, it sure is nice to have you in the neighborhood," Phil said. "We need more young families around here."

"Thanks, although it's just me."

"Sure, I know you're not married or anything." His gaze moved to me. "Hey, Dex isn't married either. Maybe the two of you—"

I slapped Phil on the back again, harder this time. "Good to see you, Phil." I nodded to Nora, but I needed to get out of there. "Nice to meet you."

Her lips curled in a subtle smile and her eyes flicked up and down, like she was sizing me up. For a second, all I could see was the curve of her neck, from her jaw to her collarbone, down to that gorgeous set of tits.

She was stunning.

And I was staring again.

Tearing my eyes away, I turned. I resisted the instinct to adjust myself as I walked back to my house. The last thing I needed was to implicitly admit to the hard-on she'd just given me.

Damn, that woman was dangerous. And I had a feeling she knew it.

5

NORA

*D*ex's strong hands roamed over my body, teasing and tempting me. I tipped my legs open, inviting him in. I wanted those thick fingers stroking me, plunging inside me. His mouth left hot brands on my skin, his teeth grazing as he worked his way lower. My nipples tightened and my body tensed. I wanted to cry out for more, but I couldn't seem to speak.

What was taking him so long?

My breath came in quick gasps as the heat built inside me. *Dex, please.* Why couldn't I get the words out? I needed to tell him what I wanted, guide him. Demand more. He was here, why wasn't he giving me what I needed? Why couldn't I feel his—

A loud bang jerked me awake and I sat up in bed, gasping for breath.

I was covered in a light sheen of sweat and unreleased tension pulsed between my legs. Dreaming. I'd been having a sex dream.

Well that was disappointing.

And what had made that noise? Had it been part of the dream?

Another loud bang rang out from somewhere outside. My sexual frustration disappeared and my heart started racing. Who was out there? Was someone trying to break in?

For a moment, I debated what to do. Stay in bed and hope nothing bad happened? Or get up and check things out?

This was my house. My responsibility.

My heart pounded harder. I slipped out of bed, grabbed my phone, and tiptoed to the door. Why I was trying to be silent, I had no idea. It was my first burglar, I didn't know what I was doing. If only Phil across the street had lectured me about home security instead of lawn care, I might have been better prepared.

Weapon. I needed something to defend myself or maybe scare off an intruder. Half my house was still in boxes, and it wasn't as if I had a baseball bat lying around. I went for the next best thing—a broom I had tucked away in the closet near the kitchen.

The house was dark and quiet. The front door was closed. I crept closer and checked to make sure it was locked. The deadbolt was in place.

With my heart still racing, I clutched the broom handle and moved toward the kitchen. There was a sliding glass door that led to the back yard—also closed and locked. I let out a breath. It didn't seem like anyone had come inside.

Another bang. I jumped, dropping my phone, and grabbed the broom with both hands. Something, or some-one, was definitely outside.

I took careful steps to the glass door and peered into the night, half-convinced someone was going to jump out at me. But I didn't see anything. Just the dark backyard.

Maybe it was nothing.

But I needed to be sure.

I flipped the lock on the glass door and slowly slid it open.

Cool air rushed into the house, chilling me thoroughly. I was wearing nothing but a silky camisole and shorts, but I didn't want to go back inside and grab a sweater. I'd only be outside for a minute, just to make sure nothing was out there.

I stepped out the door and down the two steps to the patio. The concrete was freezing on my bare feet and I kept hold of the broom handle, just in case. It was eerily quiet, just the rustle of the breeze through the trees and the faint hum of a far off car.

My gaze swept from side to side in an arc, but I didn't see anything. The back yard was only fenced at the back—open to my neighbors on both sides—and mostly empty. Just tall grass and a gravel path that led between my house and Dex's.

There could be anything in that grass. I stopped at the edge of the patio, reluctant to step into what looked like a rat-infested jungle in the dark.

A noise behind me made my blood freeze in my veins. My eyes widened and my breath caught in my throat. It sounded like scratching and on the heels of my thought about rats, I turned slowly, expecting to see a giant colony of rodents with beady red eyes, staring at me.

The scratching continued, but I didn't see anything. No otherworldly eyes shining in the darkness. But something was definitely near the house.

Great, whatever it was, it was between me and the back door. Now what was I going to do?

Maybe I could make a run for it. I'd stupidly left the

glass door open, which meant either a burglar or a rat colony could easily slip inside. Now I was going to have to turn on all the lights and search the house from top to bottom before I could go back to sleep.

Something near the corner of the house moved, making a loud enough sound that I did what any self-respecting woman who was in her backyard in the middle of the night with a broom in her hands for self-defense would do.

I screamed.

My scream made everything worse. Something clattered against the concrete patio and I screamed again, my fear addled brain convinced I was about to be attacked.

Out of nowhere, light flooded Dex's yard as his porch light came on and he flew out his back door. I caught a glimpse of all that tattooed muscle hurling through the night toward me.

"What happened?"

My mind chose that moment to remember that I'd been having a sex dream. About him.

A rush of warmth flooded my face it took me a second to answer. What was wrong with me? I never got flustered. Especially around men.

Even men who were walls of muscle wearing nothing but boxer briefs.

"Sorry." I took a quick breath. "I heard a noise and I thought maybe someone was trying to break in."

"And you were going to fight them off with a broom?"

I loosened my grip on the broom handle and lowered it. "Don't judge, I grabbed what was handy. And I really did hear a noise. Are there rats around here?"

"Maybe but I've never seen one. Is your porch light out?"

"I don't think so. Why?"

"Maybe you should turn it on."

I stared at my open door, still irrationally afraid I'd be mauled if I went near the source of the last noise I'd heard.

Dex grunted, and although he was probably annoyed, it gave me a tingly reminder of my dream. He went to the back door, reached inside, and flipped the switch.

The porch light came on, illuminating Dex in all his tattooed majesty.

My lips parted and I stared. He was broad and thick—in every way imaginable. Lean enough to see the lines of muscle but not so ripped that he looked like he lived in a gym. His tattoos covered one whole arm, from shoulder to wrist, and the other had ink up to the elbow.

And he filled out those boxer briefs very, very well.

I stood there, gaping at him, But in the seconds it took my mind to clear, I realized it probably didn't matter, because he was staring at me.

Of course, it was cold and I was wearing a sheer white camisole and shorts. He could probably see just about everything.

I could suddenly *feel* everything. The chill breeze tickling my skin. My hard nipples brushing against the silky fabric of my top. And the remnants of that dream, the tension between my legs suddenly begging to be sated.

That rough, tattooed man could probably destroy my body in a hundred different ways.

And by the way he was looking at me, he was thinking about it.

The scratching sound came back. I jumped away as the plastic lid to my trash can moved on its own. Dex rushed to me, grabbed the broom out of my hands, and held it like a baseball bat.

It was about then that I realized my trash can was tipped

over. There hadn't been much in it, but a few pieces of trash were scattered nearby.

Dex took a step closer, still holding the broom at the ready. "What the..."

The lid popped up and turned over, revealing black and gray fur and a set of beady eyes. I gasped but Dex didn't even flinch.

"It's just a raccoon." He lowered the broom. "Freaking trash panda."

The creature eyed us and I was certain it was about to jump up and attack our faces. I took a step behind Dex, so he'd be between me and the raccoon.

"Don't those have rabies?"

"We're not going to find out." He pushed the broom, brush side down, toward it. "Go on, get out of here."

It sat up on its hind legs and hissed once before scampering off into the darkness.

"There goes your home invader." He turned around and held out the broom.

"Do you think he was alone?"

"Looked like it."

"How did he make so much noise all by himself?"

He shrugged. "Tipped over your trash can."

Reluctantly, I took the broom.

"You're scared of the raccoon, aren't you?" he asked.

"Of course I'm scared of the raccoon." My eyes darted to my still-open door. "What if his buddies went into my house?"

"I don't think he had any buddies."

"How do you know? Are you a raccoon expert?'

He sighed. "Do you want me to go in and look for you?"

I really did. It was the middle of the night and way too much to ask of the neighbor I barely knew. But I didn't want to go back to bed without checking everywhere, and even better if I didn't have to do it alone.

"Please?"

He eyed me for a second, as if deciding what to do about me. Then he swiped the broom out of my hands and went inside.

I followed him in and shut the door while he started turning on lights. The kitchen was mostly organized, although a few stray boxes were pushed into a corner. He glanced around, and I did the same, but there weren't any raccoons.

Or rats. Although it had been a raccoon in my trash, I wasn't convinced that rats hadn't crept into the house while we'd been distracted.

Dex went into the living room and turned on another light. It was more chaotic in there, with several stacks of unpacked boxes and shelves that still needed to be reassembled. To his credit, he was thorough, checking on, around, and behind everything. He even bent down and looked under the couch.

He seemed to be convinced there weren't any furry intruders and left the broom propped up against the wall. But he still checked the rest of the house, with me close behind. We looked in the extra bedroom and the guest bath. My office was clear and finally, we got to my bedroom.

Something about having that man step into my bedroom made my lady parts pulse with tension. I rolled my eyes. What was I going on about? Sure, he had a certain rugged appeal, but that didn't mean I'd let him anywhere near my lady parts.

Although maybe I would.

He bent over to check under my bed. I watched from the doorway, trying to guess by his movements whether he'd found more raccoons. But he didn't react. Just straightened and shrugged his broad shoulders.

"I think you're fine."

That was a relief.

His eyes lingered on me and I was once again aware that we were both barely dressed. And now we were in my bedroom.

I thought about it. We were both up and unlikely to get much sleep after my nocturnal trespasser. He was nothing like men I usually dated, but that didn't mean we couldn't have some fun together. A friend with benefits right next door? That sounded like a win-win to me.

But before I could make even the slightest suggestion as to how I could thank him, he looked away and brushed past me, out the bedroom door.

"Thanks for your help," I said to his back as he headed for the kitchen.

He didn't turn around. "You're welcome. Goodnight."

And just like that, he was out the door.

He hadn't even given me the chance to apologize for waking him.

It was his loss. Although maybe he'd done me a favor. I'd been awakened from a vivid sex dream that still lingered in my mind—and body. That could have been clouding my judgment and I'd have regretted sleeping with him. Or maybe none of that rough manliness translated to prowess between the sheets.

But something told me that wouldn't have been a problem.

I found my phone where I'd dropped it on the kitchen floor and went around turning off the lights. The time on the microwave caught my eye. It was just after three in the morning. I wasn't sure if I'd be able to go back to sleep, but I decided to try. I went back to my room and climbed into bed.

My eyes closed but it was as if Dex had left an aura of testosterone in my house. Turning over, I tried to push him from my mind. But as I drifted off to sleep, the memory of his presence invaded and once again I found myself lost in an erotic dream starring my big, tattooed neighbor.

6

DEX

The coffee in the back room of my tattoo shop was just shy of terrible. I drank it anyway. At least it was hot and filled with caffeine. After last night, I needed it.

I'd already been up when I'd heard Nora scream—insomnia strikes again. Without pausing to think about what I was doing—or put on more clothes—I'd rushed outside. And found my terrified neighbor ready to fend off the neighborhood wildlife with a broom.

She'd also been practically naked.

Apparently her silky tank top and shorts qualified as pajamas but they didn't leave much to the imagination. I hadn't noticed at first but as soon as I'd turned on her porch light, that incredible body of hers had come into focus.

Every bit of it.

Just the memory of those luscious curves was enough to give me a semi.

I rolled my eyes and took another drink of the awful coffee. I needed to think about something else—anything else. My indecently hot neighbor was going to get me into trouble.

Kari poked her head in the back room. She had flaming orange curls and a slight piercing addiction. Nose, septum, eyebrow, bridge, labret, plus several in each ear. And that was just her face. She ran our front desk and was apprenticing under Sonny, one of my senior artists.

"What happened to you?" she asked.

"Nothing."

"Are you sure? You look like shit."

I scowled at her. "I had a rough night."

"Couldn't sleep?"

"Nope. Then there was a raccoon in my neighbor's trash, so that was a whole thing."

"Have you tried hypnosis? I know a guy who swears by it."

"I've tried everything."

It was true, I'd tried everything to cure my insomnia. From normal stuff like low light in the evenings, melatonin, herbal teas, and even prescription drugs, to weirder folk remedies like eating fried lettuce before bed—not something I'd recommend—and turning my bed to face north.

Nothing helped. I'd more or less resigned myself to it.

"Sucks, man."

"I'll live."

"For now. I read somewhere that lack of sleep takes ten years off your life."

"Thanks, Kari. That's helpful."

"I'm just saying. Anyway, your appointment is here. Her name's Alicia."

"I'll be right out."

I downed the last swallow of my coffee and went out to meet my client.

She was young, maybe twenty at the most, with straight brown hair that hung around her shoulders. She wore a loose t-shirt, distressed jeans, and a pair of hot pink Converse low-tops that Riley would love.

Which made me realize, she had to be closer to Riley's age than mine.

I resisted the urge to ask her if she was old enough for a tattoo. She had to be—Kari always checked ID before booking—but I had the weirdest urge to ask her if she was sure about this.

Was this what happened when your kid hit her teens? Women under twenty-five started to look more like daughters than peers?

"Alicia?" I asked, giving her a warm smile.

She shifted from one foot to another—clearly nervous—and smiled. "Yeah, hi."

"I'm Dex." I offered my hand and took hers in a gentle handshake. "Nice to meet you. If you're ready, I'll take you back to my station and we can talk about your tattoo."

"Thanks."

I led her to my station at the back of the shop and offered her a seat. Her eyes darted around and she fidgeted with a bracelet on her wrist. Over the last couple of years, I'd replaced most of the posters and stickers on the walls with Riley's art. She loved to paint and I loved being surrounded by her work.

I kept my posture casual and expression friendly. I was well-practiced at altering my demeanor to suit each client and make them comfortable. I'd be gentle and soothing with someone like Alicia. Tougher with a guy getting ink for the tenth time.

"Tell me what you have in mind," I said.

She tucked her hair behind her ear. "I'd like a flower on my upper back or shoulder blade. I've looked at lots of pictures but it's hard to decide."

"That's okay, I can help you narrow it down. Right or left side?"

"Right."

"Do you want just the flower or another design element, like text with it?"

"Just the flower. Or multiple flowers. It doesn't have to be just one."

"Okay. Are you thinking something with color or black and gray?"

"I'm pretty sure black and gray. I heard that colors fade faster."

"Some do, especially reds and lighter tones, like light blues and greens. It also depends on how well you care for the tattoo, especially when it's new. Colored tattoos generally require more aftercare and take longer to heal. I can definitely do both, but I'll be honest, my favorite is black and gray. I can create designs that are beautifully realistic and detailed."

"That sounds amazing."

"How about I show you some options? You point out what you like, and don't like, and we'll go from there."

She nodded and I noticed she wasn't fidgeting anymore. I got out a binder with samples of my work and we flipped through the pages. She gravitated toward roses with both blooms and leaves, and as we chatted, a few designs began to solidify in my mind.

Climbing roses with a leafy vine. A couple of open blooms and another still closed. Hints of growth, change, a young woman becoming who she's meant to be. Mid-back to shoulder. Lots of shading and depth.

It would be gorgeous.

When we finished, I took her to the front desk to get on my schedule for her tattoo. I'd have several design options to show her and could make any alterations she wanted before we got started. Then I went back to my station to jot down a few impressions and ideas while they were still fresh in my mind. It wouldn't take me long to sketch out her designs. I'd done a million flowers. Which was fine. It meant I knew what I was doing and most importantly, she'd love the final result.

Kind of important when you were talking something permanent.

Alicia was my last appointment of the day, so after taking care of some bookkeeping in the back office, I headed home.

Nora's garage door was open and her Jeep was inside. The memory of her perky tits flashed through my head. *Damn it, Nora.* Why couldn't she have at least worn something dark to bed last night? Then I wouldn't have the image of her gorgeous body burned into my mind.

The minivan in my driveway helped dispel the image. My mother had that effect on me. I parked next to her and went inside.

I found her sitting in the kitchen with Riley, each with a mug of tea. My mom was on the tall side, with a short silver bob and skin that was still bronzed from her recent trip to Hawaii with my dad. She glanced at me with a smirk that made me nervous.

Then again, my mom had at least eight hundred looks that made me nervous for various reasons.

"Hey, Mom. Hey, Ry."

"Hi, Dad." Riley's tone was bright. Probably the grandma effect. They'd always been close.

"I didn't realize you'd be home so early," Mom said.

"Sorry if I interrupted your plotting."

"Who said we were plotting?"

I went into the kitchen and leaned against the counter. "You're always plotting something."

Riley laughed.

Man, I loved hearing that sound. She could plot with Grandma all she wanted if it made her laugh like that, although she'd been in a pretty decent mood for the last week or so.

"I'm sure I have no idea what you're talking about," Mom said.

"Yeah, I bet you don't. What are you up to today?"

"Oh, you know, grandma taxi. Today was preschool pickup and gymnastics."

Mom drove a minivan, despite the fact that her children were all adults, so she had ready transportation for her growing brood of grandchildren. Dad still worked but Mom had retired, and now she spent her free time helping her kids with their families. I had a brother and two sisters, and they had a total of ten kids between them, all nine and under. I was the odd man out with an only child.

Then again, I was kind of the black sheep of the family. My older brother, Dallas, practiced law in the same firm as my dad. So did his wife, Tori. Our oldest sister, Angie, was married to Mike, a software engineer, and she stayed home —and homeschooled—their five kids. Like a boss. Sometimes I wished I could send Riley to my sister's school. Maggie was the baby of the family and she'd popped out two kids, alongside running a successful home decor shop with her husband, Jordan.

Me? I was the only one who'd never been married—not even to Riley's mom—I was a single dad to just one kid, and I'd dropped out of law school to open a tattoo shop.

That had been an interesting conversation with my parents.

But I couldn't complain. My family wasn't perfect, but we'd always been tight.

Riley handed me a flier for her school's spring art show. "Can you come?"

"For sure." I might have to move an appointment around, but I'd make it work. "Are you displaying some of your paintings?"

"Yeah, three of them I think."

"That's awesome."

"We'll be there, too." Mom sipped her tea and the way she met my eyes over the rim of her mug was very suspicious. "I've been thinking, the weather has been so good, it would be fun to get everyone together for a barbecue."

"Yeah?"

She set her mug down. "Normally, we'd be happy to host, but your father decided the backyard needed to be torn up and redone."

"And?"

"And Angie doesn't really have a good backyard, and of course Maggie's family lives in a condo, so they're out."

Here it came. "Mm hmm."

"Dallas and Tori have been so busy with that big case they're working on. I'd hate to impose on them."

"But you have no problem imposing on me."

"You have that lovely backyard. We should use it more often."

"We?" I asked with a laugh.

"Yeah, Dad," Riley said. "It would be fun."

That clinched it. "All right. Barbecue at our place. When?"

"Does two weeks from Saturday work?" Mom asked.

I grabbed my phone and swiped to my calendar. I had an appointment that day—working on a client who already wore a lot of my work. But I'd be done by the afternoon. I'd just have to tell Kari to keep the rest of my day clear.

"I have to work but we could do it after."

"Good."

I met her eyes again. There was something in her tone. "You already invited everyone over, didn't you?"

She batted her eyelashes, as if she were innocent. "You kids are all so busy. It's hard to schedule anything."

That was my mom for you. I didn't really mind. We all had busy lives and it had gotten harder over the years to get together regularly. I hadn't seen Maggie in almost a month, which was weird.

"What would you have done if I'd been too busy?"

She stood and patted my cheek. "We would have worked it out."

"Sure, Mom."

"I have to get going." She took her mug to the sink and gave it a quick rinse. "I need to swing by the store before I go home. Riley, honey, thanks for spending a little time with me. Love you."

"Love you too, Grandma."

"The bounce house will be delivered that morning but as long as they have access to a power outlet, I don't think you need to be here. I'll make sure they know where to put it."

"Bounce house?"

She picked up her purse. "The kids are going to love it."

"I'm sure they are. Any more deliveries I should know about?"

"No, but can you handle the grilling?"

"That I can do."

"Perfect. Thanks, honey." She placed a quick peck on my cheek.

I gestured toward the front door. "I'll walk you out."

Mom and Riley exchanged a goodbye hug, then I followed her out to her van. I opened the driver's side door for her.

"How was Ry when you got here?"

"She seemed fine. Why?"

I glanced away. "I don't know. There's been a lot of teenage stuff lately."

"That seems pretty normal, considering she's thirteen."

"Maybe. Did she say anything about school or her friends or..." I didn't want to say it but I couldn't pretend it wasn't a possibility. "Boys?"

"No, just the art show. And she was in a perfectly cheerful mood. I didn't get the impression that anything was wrong."

"Cheerful? Are you sure you're not mixing her up with someone else? One of Angie's kids, maybe?"

"Positive. She wasn't even holed up in her room when I got here. She was outside."

"Was she really?"

Mom nodded. "Chatting with your neighbor."

My brow furrowed. "Which neighbor? Phil?"

"No, the one next door." She got a dangerous glint in her eyes. "The very attractive woman next door. What's her name? Nora?"

"Mom, don't."

"You should invite her to the barbecue."

"I don't think so."

"Why not? Knowing our family, we're going to wind up spilling into her yard anyway. We might as well feed her."

"Mom, please tell me you didn't already invite her."

"No, I didn't get a chance to talk to her. But you should."

"No."

"She seems nice. And Riley sure likes her."

"How do you know she's nice? You just said you didn't talk to her."

"She waved and it was a very nice wave."

"I'm not inviting her to our family barbecue." Although it did occur to me I should probably warn her about it.

"You're so stubborn." She slipped on a pair of sunglasses. "Love you."

"Love you, too."

She got in the van and I shut her door, then watched her back out. We waved one last time before she took off down the street, off to her next errand.

I glanced at Nora's house before I went back inside. Had she gone back to sleep after I'd left last night? I certainly hadn't. Insomnia might have kept me up anyway, but Nora hadn't helped. There was no way I was inviting her to my family's barbecue. I needed to make sure I limited my exposure to her.

That woman was dangerous.

7

DEX

I hated being late, especially for school stuff. I'd moved one of my clients so I could make it to the art show, but my earlier appointment had gone long. You just couldn't rush a tattoo. That led to awful tattoos, and I didn't do shoddy work. Ever.

It also meant sometimes I ran late. And even though there hadn't been much I could have done about it, I still felt bad.

Dad-guilt was a thing.

I parked and followed the handmade signs pointing the way. The spring art show was being held in the school gym and the side door was wide open.

Inside, tables were set up in rows to display the students' art. At a glance, there were sketches and paintings of various sizes, plus all sorts of pottery and sculpture. A lot of talent in the room, especially considering they were all young teens.

My eyes swept the crowd of kids and their families until I spotted Riley. She was with my mom and dad on the outskirts of the action, so I headed their direction.

Mom wore a blue dress with a brown leather belt and

Dad looked like he'd just come from the office in his button-down and slacks. No jacket, but he did wear a blue on blue striped tie.

I was a carbon copy of my father. Same build, although I was thicker from years of lifting weights, same square jaw, same eyes. We even had similar hair, although his was shot through with gray.

"Son," he said with a nod.

"Hey, Dad. Hi, Mom." I grabbed Riley in a hug. Her stiffness reminded me we were in front of her peers and maybe a hug from Dad wasn't considered cool. I didn't care—hugged her anyway. "Hey, Ry. Sorry I'm late."

She stepped back. "It's okay. It's open house style, so people have been coming and going."

"Just wait until you see Riley's paintings," my mom said. "They're beautiful."

My dad patted her on the back. "Our girl is very talented."

"Thanks, Grandma and Grandpa."

"I can't wait," I said. "Show me the way."

"We actually have to get going," Mom said, checking her watch. "Dinner reservations."

"Yeah, no problem. Thanks for coming."

They hugged Riley and was it my imagination, or was she a lot less stiff? She even hugged them back.

Maybe it was still cool to hug grandparents.

Her hair was in braids again, but she'd left a little bit loose around her face. She tucked a piece behind her ear and opened her mouth as if she were about to say something, when her eyes widened and a smile lit up her face. "Oh my gosh, you came!"

I looked over my shoulder and almost choked on my own tongue.

Nora?

"Of course I did," Nora said with a dazzling smile. "I told you I would."

Riley practically ran into her arms. Nora's eyebrows lifted in surprise, but she gave Riley a long hug.

She was dressed in an outfit that was somehow sexy as hell without being inappropriate for the setting. Form-fitting black shirt, high-waisted jeans, and red heels. Her dark hair cascaded around her shoulders in waves and when she flashed that smile again, it made something tighten in the pit of my stomach.

Fuck me, she was beautiful.

Riley stepped out of her long embrace. "Oh, sorry. Grandma and Grandpa, this is Nora. She lives next door."

Nora turned that million-watt smile on my parents. "So nice to meet you. I'm Nora Lakes."

"Joel St. James," my dad said, offering his hand. "My wife, Gillian."

"It's so lovely of you to come to Riley's art show," my mom said, her eyes flicking to me with a not-so-subtle eyebrow lift.

"I was thrilled to be invited."

"I wish we could stay and chat," my mom said. "But we were just on our way out."

"Another time," Nora said.

"I'm going to hold you to that," Mom said. "By the way, did Dex tell you about the barbecue?"

Nora's gaze moved from my mom, to me, then back again. "No, I don't think he did."

"Dex, I taught you better manners than that."

I crossed my arms. "Really, Mom?"

She ignored me. "He's hosting a barbecue at his place a week from tomorrow and we'd love to have you."

"You should totally come," Riley said.

"How could I refuse?" Nora said. "I'd love to."

"Wonderful." Mom tucked her hand in the crook of Dad's arm. "You three have a nice evening."

"You too," Nora said.

Mom stepped in for a hug and kissed my cheek. I gave Dad a hug, then we said the last of our goodbyes and they left.

Riley fidgeted with her hands. "So, do you want to see my paintings?"

I was about to say yes, I absolutely wanted to see her paintings, when I realized she wasn't asking me. Her eyes were on Nora.

"Yes," Nora said. "Which ones are yours?"

"This way."

I followed behind, trying not to feel left out. But Riley was so animated and enthusiastic. It was like seeing my baby girl again. Taller, and not very baby-like anymore, but I recognized that bounce in her step and sparkle in her eyes.

She led us to the end of one of the long tables where there were several paintings set on easels. I recognized Riley's style immediately. One was a woman with long dark hair, wearing a black dress. She stood in an empty field, looking down, as if sad. Most of it was gray and black, except for the faintest hints of orange, red, and purple on the horizon, like the sun had just set behind her. Or was rising, depending on how you wanted to interpret the scene. It was gorgeous.

Another was completely different, although I could still see the stamp of Riley's imagination. It was a landscape with mountains in the background and a little cabin with a creek running in front of it. She'd added a single blue bird on the branch of a tree, the bright color drawing the eye in a way that added interesting depth to the painting.

Finally, the largest canvas was a signature Riley St. James. A unicorn with its front legs in the air, mane and tail streaming behind. But the scenery around it was stark and foreboding, with a streak of lightning in the sky. The animal had eerie red eyes and the rainbow colors in the mane and tail gradually turned gray and colorless at the ends.

It was beautifully creepy.

Nora gazed at the paintings, her full lips parted. "Riley, these are amazing."

"You like them?"

"I don't just like them, I love them. They're absolutely stunning."

"Thank you." Riley turned to me and lifted her eyebrows.

"She's right, they're stunning." I pointed to the painting of the woman. "Your use of color here is perfect. The perspective and use of light are spot on. And the gradient on the unicorn's mane and tail is so smooth. You made it look like the color is bleeding right out of it. Well done."

"Thanks, Dad." She fidgeted with her hands again, glancing around the gym. "That's it for mine but if you want to look around, you can."

"Lead the way," Nora said.

We followed Riley around the tables. She pointed out a few pieces, but mostly just let us look. It was neat to see what the other kids had done, and slightly awkward to walk around with Nora at my side.

Especially because she drew attention.

It was subtle, but I could see it happening. Gazes followed her, eyes lighting up with interest.

Were they curious about *her*, or curious about *us*?

Not that there was an us, but walking side-by-side at a middle school art show kind of gave a certain impression.

I didn't blame people for noticing her. Hell, every time I caught a glimpse of her out the window, I stopped and stared. She was gorgeous, well-dressed, put together. But that wasn't the entire story. Her poise drew the eye, made you stop and take notice.

There was just something about her.

"That's about it," Riley said when we'd made our way around the gym. "I hope it wasn't too boring."

"Not at all. This was really fun," Nora said and something in her tone made me wonder if that surprised her a little.

"It was fun," I said. "Although your paintings are the best ones in here."

"You have to say that because you're my dad."

I shrugged. "I still mean it."

"I agree," Nora said. "And I'm not your dad."

Riley smiled and it brightened her whole face. "I guess we can go whenever. I just need to get my stuff out of my locker."

"Your call, kiddo," I said. "I'm ready when you are."

"I'll be right back." She headed for one of the gym entrances.

A mildly uncomfortable silence followed her departure —uncomfortable for me, at least. Probably because I kept thinking about Nora dressed in those sheer pajamas when the raccoon had been in her trash.

Not exactly appropriate for the setting.

Or any setting.

I took a quick breath to clear my head. "Thanks for coming. This means a lot to her."

"I was so touched that she asked. I wouldn't have missed

it." She glanced around the gym, her eyebrows drawing in. "I haven't been inside a middle school since I went to one. Those were not my best years."

My brow furrowed. That surprised me. "Really?"

"I guess it took me a while to come into my own. Plus the boys were annoying and the girls were mean. It was pretty awful. At least until I met my best friends."

"Sounds about right." Maybe that was why Riley seemed to be struggling. Just the normal trials of middle school.

"What about you? Did you get through middle school unscathed?" she asked.

"Not really. I was a late bloomer, so I was one of the smallest in my class. That sucked."

She looked me up and down. "You're kidding."

"Nope. I grew five inches over the summer before ninth grade. Hurt like hell but I was a new man going into high school."

"I bet the girls were falling all over you."

I chuckled at that. "There was an increase in female attention."

Her lips turned up. "Who could blame them?"

There was a hint of flirtatiousness in her voice. Playful rather than aggressive.

And damn it, as much as I wanted to deny it, I liked it.

Trouble. So much trouble.

She glanced around. "Can you point me in the direction of the ladies' room?"

I gestured toward the side of the gym. "It should be over there."

"Thanks."

With a seductive twitch of her lips, she turned and walked away.

Walked was not the right word. Nora Lakes didn't walk

like a mere mortal. But she didn't strut or saunter, either. Her movements were more subtle than that, as if sexiness was simply baked into who she was, rather than something she was attempting to exude.

Trouble.

But damn, that ass.

Tearing my eyes away, I looked around for Riley and found her near the gym entrance. She had her backpack slung over one shoulder and stood talking to one of her classmates.

"Hey, Dex."

My internal alarm blared at the voice behind me. Oh shit. I turned, my back tensing.

Aimee Bachman's dark hair was up, highlighting the fact that her shoulders were bare. She wore a bright red tube top and tight jeans, which was not the most provocative outfit I'd seen on her at a school function.

I suppressed a shudder. Some women got divorced and went on being normal moms in the neighborhood. And I was the last guy to judge anyone for getting a divorce or being a single parent. But Aimee had taken a different route, turning into a predatory man-eater who seemed to be interested in only one thing—sleeping with every unmarried man she could get her hands on.

She'd been after me for years.

"Hi, Aimee. Enjoying the show?"

Her eyes flicked to my crotch. "Definitely. So much talent."

I rolled my eyes. Somewhere along the way, she'd lost all ability to be subtle. It wasn't a good look. "Yeah, well, I need to find Riley."

She stepped closer. She smelled faintly of mint gum, cheap perfume, and cigarette smoke. "I'm sure she's fine.

What about you?" She touched my arm. "How have you been?"

"Fine."

"Are you sure? You seem lonely." She lowered her voice. "I could help with that."

"Sorry honey." Nora appeared out of nowhere and hooked her arm in mine. "I didn't mean to take so long. Hi, I'm Nora."

Aimee looked like she'd just been slapped. She stepped back, eyes wide, lips parted.

Nora went on, as if this wasn't insanely awkward. "What a great show this was, don't you think? This school must have an excellent art program."

Aimee's cheeks flushed red. "Who are you?"

"Nora Lakes." She slid her hand down my arm and twined our fingers together. "Dex, we should probably get going. We promised Riley ice cream."

I glanced down at her, trying not to laugh at how she was playing this so flawlessly. "We did promise her ice cream, didn't we? Let's go."

She squeezed my hand as we turned away from Aimee. I squeezed back.

"Night," I said, half over my shoulder as we walked off.

"Sorry if I read that wrong, but you looked like you could use a little help."

"You read that exactly right. Thanks."

I dropped Nora's hand before Riley caught sight of us. I didn't need those kinds of questions. She hitched her backpack higher up her shoulder and met us at the door.

"Dad, can I spend the night at Katie's?"

My brow furrowed. "Which one is Katie?"

She pointed to a girl wearing a boxy t-shirt and jeans. Like Ry, she wore her hair in two French braids and she had

purple Converse to Riley's turquoise. I recognized her and
her mom, standing nearby. Riley had spent the night at her
house before, but it had been a while.

"Sure, I suppose."

Riley smiled. "Thanks, Dad. If you can't drive me over
there, Katie's mom said she can pick me up. They're
ordering pizza and we're going to make root beer floats."

"Sounds awesome. I can take you." I turned to Nora.
"Give me a second."

I walked over to confer with Katie's mom—her name
was Kristin—and solidified the plan. I'd take Riley home to
get her stuff, then bring her to their house. Kristin would
drive her home tomorrow afternoon. Pretty standard stuff.

"Thank you so much, Dad, you're the best." Riley waved
at her friend. "Bye, Katie. I'll see you in a little bit."

Man, it was great to see her happy.

Riley practically ran out to the car. Apparently getting to
Katie's in a hurry had become her biggest priority.

"I guess we'll have to do ice cream another time," Nora
said as we crossed the parking lot.

"And it sounded good, too. Thanks again for coming.
And for fending off the horny mom."

She laughed. "Happy to help."

We stopped and I felt a strange pull, as if we were
connected by a taut rubber band. If either of us slipped, it
would snap us together.

That wouldn't end well. It never did.

So I resisted the urge to hug her goodbye. "See you
later."

"Bye, Dex." Her eyes lingered on mine, then she turned
and waved to Riley. "Bye, Riley. Have fun."

Riley waved from inside the car, then motioned for me
to hurry.

"Yeah, yeah, I'm coming." I avoided eye contact with Nora and tried to be as non-flirtatious as possible. "Drive safe."

Without looking back, I got in my car. I felt like I needed to get away from her. Like we'd crossed a line—even though we really hadn't—and if I didn't leave now, I'd wind up in serious trouble.

I really couldn't let that happen. Yeah, she was gorgeous and I even kind of liked her. But at the end of the day, I barely knew her. And the last thing I needed right now were the complications of a woman in my life.

I already had one and I could barely handle that.

Nora was tempting, but that was what made her so dangerous. As I headed home, I resolved to keep my distance. It was nice that Riley liked her so much. That was fine, they could be friendly across the fence, as it were.

But I needed to stay away.

8

NORA

*W*hoever had remodeled this house had picked the perfect bathtub. It was freestanding and luxuriously large. I settled into the warm water and closed my eyes, breathing in the lavender scent of the bath bomb I'd added.

Perfect. Just what I'd needed. It had been a week.

The master bath had a spa vibe, with wood cabinets, dark tile, and contrasting white countertops. I'd added my fluffy white towels and small white ceramic vases with sprigs of dried eucalyptus for a minimalist, natural look.

I picked up my long stem wine glass and sipped the chilled white. Light and refreshing. Also just what I'd needed.

The sound of a car outside caught my attention. I knew without looking that it was Dex. His car made a distinct knocking sound when he turned the engine off. I wondered why he didn't get it fixed. Maybe he just didn't notice.

That man was an enigma. Rough around the edges but still hugged his mother. And his father. That had been a fascinating dynamic to witness. I tried to picture my brother,

Jensen, hugging our father, but that was an image I couldn't conjure. My father didn't hug me, and I was his daughter. Granted, I rarely saw him. He was very settled with his wife, Jensen's mom. In London. Made it hard to pop by for a visit.

And Dex was hosting a family barbecue. I wondered what that would be like. Apparently I was going to find out.

Was all of this typical for neighbors on a suburban street? First, Riley had asked me to come to her art show, which had been nothing short of adorable—both the invitation and the event itself. And now I was invited to a family barbecue next door.

Although that clearly had the stamp of a matchmaking mother.

It was cute, really. Flattering in its own way. Not that I was wife material, something Mrs. Gillian St. James would figure out soon enough. But I wasn't worried about that. Dex didn't strike me as the type to pay much heed to his mother's promptings.

My phone buzzed with a message. It was an email from my boss and against my better judgment, I opened it.

My eyes slid over the brief note, letting me know the final copy of next week's column was attached, and they'd made a few minor changes.

I took a healthy swallow of wine and opened the attachment.

Minor changes? That was laughable. My piece had been shredded. It still sounded like me, for the most part, but exaggerated. Like they'd taken my voice and turned up the volume.

With a roll of my eyes, I put my phone down. I already knew there wasn't anything I could do about it. Once April had deemed an article final, it was final. I'd pushed back before and she'd refused to budge.

And there was something to be said for picking your battles. If they wanted to edit more drama and slang into my tone, fine. I'd let it go in the hopes that I'd win the larger war —the war over the content of my column.

A car door shut outside, dragging my thoughts back to Dex. I didn't even know if it was him and yet there he was, at the forefront of my mind.

Maybe it was because I kept dreaming about him. The first had been nothing but a warm up. That man had invaded my nights and in my erotic nocturnal imagination, he was larger than life.

So much larger. Especially in the ways that really counted.

Granted, from what I'd seen, my imagination wasn't far off.

I sank back into the water with a sigh. I'd been single for too long. That was my problem. I wanted—not needed—a man who'd take me out, show me a nice time. Someone who could be a gentleman in the streets and an animal in the sheets.

But I hadn't met anyone interesting lately and I rarely went back to past flings. I wasn't anyone's fuck buddy, thank you very much.

Of course, there was another potential option. And he was right next door. He might not fit my usual criteria, but there was something undeniably tempting about him.

I soaked for a while longer, relaxing in the luxurious warmth. The candles I'd lit flickered. It was so quiet here. No hustle and bustle of city streets below, no constant hum of traffic or blare of horns and sirens. Just the occasional sound of a car or a barking dog to break up the relative silence.

I liked it.

When I was suitably languid, I blew out the candles, then got out of the bath and dried off. I undid the claw clip holding my hair up and shook it out as I walked into my bedroom, the scent of lavender clinging to me. I traded the towel for a silky pink robe that matched my current toenail polish.

Something loud was going on outside, like the sound of a motor. I went to the window and peeked out through the sheer curtain. Dex was out there, mowing his lawn.

He was dressed in a shirt that wasn't just sleeveless, it looked like he'd ripped the sleeves off himself. Jeans and sunglasses completed the picture. Casual, just shy of messy. He was probably sweaty and smelled like freshly cut grass.

Interestingly, that appealed.

I watched him for a long moment as he pushed the mower in a straight line, then turned and did another row.

On a whim, I grabbed my phone and sent a message to our group text.

Me: *I'm watching a man mow his lawn and I'm oddly turned on. What's that about?*

Sophie: *I love it when Cox mows our lawn. It's so sexy.*

Me: *Really?*

Sophie: *Well sure, he usually takes his shirt off and gets all sweaty. What's not sexy about that?*

Cox was an attractive man, objectively speaking. I could see why Sophie enjoyed watching her husband work.

Hazel: *I'd say it represents competence and reliability.*

Me: *Do you want to jump Corban's bones when he mows the lawn?*

Hazel: *Certainly. Even better when he fixes something.*

Everly: *We don't have a lawn but I love it when Shepherd fixes things. Or when he backs up the car.*

Sophie: *Oh yes. Backing up the car with his arm over your seat? The best.*

Everly: *YES*

Hazel: *I concur.*

I had to agree. There was something innately sexy about the way a man backed out of a parking spot with his arm draped over your seat. I glanced out the window again. Competence and reliability. I could see why women would be drawn to that in a man. And Hazel would know. She was a psychology researcher and a certified genius.

And if a man was competent at some things, maybe he'd be competent in others.

He certainly was in my dreams.

Sighing, I grabbed my wineglass out of the bathroom and took it downstairs. I was debating whether or not I wanted a second glass when something that sounded like a drip of water caught my attention. The sink was off but maybe the faucet was leaking a little. Tilting my head, I watched. Nothing.

Drip.

That hadn't come from the sink. Drip. Drip. Why was I hearing water? That couldn't be a good sign.

I crouched to check beneath the sink but it was dry. The drips kept coming. There was definitely water somewhere. The sky was clear today and it didn't sound like rain pattering against the window. What was going on?

Drip.

That one hit my head. I touched my hair, and sure enough, there was a small splash of wetness.

Oh no.

The drips kept coming, faster now, and I slowly lifted my gaze to the ceiling.

Water beaded in several places above me, seeping

through the ceiling and collecting into larger and larger drops, until they broke free and fell with a splash onto the floor.

Or my hair.

"Oh my god."

I needed a plumber. But what was I supposed to do in the meantime? Clearly my bathwater had somehow drained into the space between the upstairs floor and kitchen ceiling. And that bathtub held a lot of water. I had a sudden vision of those beads of water growing larger and merging into a single, enormous bubble that would pop with the weight of all the lavender scented liquid and flood my kitchen.

Without second guessing myself, I tightened my robe around my waist and hurried next door.

Dex seemed to have finished mowing. His garage door was closed and I didn't hear the roar of the lawn mower. I knocked and waited, hoping he'd answer.

I heard his heavy footsteps a second before the door opened. He was still dressed in that sleeveless shirt, his jeans had bits of grass on them, and his feet were bare. His mouth opened as his eyes swept up and down my body. To his credit, they came quickly back to my face.

"I have a problem."

"You... What?"

"There's water leaking in my kitchen. Through the ceiling."

"Oh. Shit." He stepped away from the door and slid his feet into a pair of battered army-green flip flops. "Let me take a look."

"Thank you."

We walked next door and I tiptoed on the cold concrete. I hadn't noticed it on my way over but now the chill in the early evening air blew right through my robe. My skin prickled and I shivered slightly.

I probably should have put some clothes on first, but oh well.

Inside, Dex went to the kitchen and stood with his hands on his hips, looking up. "Yeah, that's not good."

"It must be from the bathtub. The master bathroom is right there and I just took a bath."

He glanced at me and there were those eyes again, running up and down from my head to my toes. "I can see that."

"So what do we do?"

"Call a plumber."

"I know that, but what do I do about all the water that's about to flood my kitchen?"

He turned his attention back to the ceiling. "I'll be right back."

Water continued dripping. Were there more spots beading moisture or was that my imagination? So far they hadn't collected into one super drop, but I wasn't discounting that as a possibility.

A couple of minutes later, Dex came back with a battery powered drill or electric screwdriver or whatever those things were called. Tools weren't exactly my area.

He dragged a chair from the dining room into the kitchen. "Do you have any buckets?"

"Why? What are you going to do?"

"Drain the water." He pulled the trigger on the drill and it buzzed a few times.

I looked up. "You're going to drill holes in my ceiling?"

"Holes are easier to fix than a bunch of water damage. We need to get the water out of there."

I didn't have any buckets but made a mental note to get

one. Or several? How many buckets did a homeowner need? Instead, I rooted through the cupboards and found some mixing bowls.

"Will these work?"

"Hope so." He climbed onto the chair. "But you might want to get some towels too. I'll drill next to the spots where it's dripping so just put the bowls where you see water splashes."

I tried not to wince as he placed the bit against the ceiling and started drilling. I set a bowl on the floor to catch the water and sure enough, as soon as he'd drilled through, a stream of water poured into the bowl.

It wasn't going to be big enough, so I stood by with a fresh bowl, ready to replace it when the first one got too full.

Dex got down and moved the chair a few feet to the left.

"Do you have to drill in more than one place? Won't the water just drain right here?"

"It's pooling across too wide of an area." He climbed on the chair and aimed the drill. "There's no slope in the ceiling to get the water to run to one spot."

I grabbed another bowl and set it beneath him just in time to catch the stream of water. "Lovely."

I replaced the first bowl and dumped the water in the sink while he drilled another hole. Water continued streaming from the ceiling while he drilled two more.

"How much water was in there?" he asked as he climbed down from the chair.

"It's a big tub."

"It looks like it's starting to slow down, but I should go check and make sure it's just from the tub and you don't have a broken pipe or something."

He went upstairs and I made sure the bowls didn't overflow, but the water seemed to finally be running out. The first hole had slowed to a drip and the second wasn't quite such a steady stream.

"I'm going to test a few things," he called from upstairs. "Yell if the leaking gets worse."

I waited, my eyes on the ceiling. Another of the holes stopped streaming water and the first one barely dripped. I heard the sound of the sink upstairs. Nothing happened.

"Still good down there?"

"I think so."

The toilet flushed and I winced at the thought of *that* water leaking through the ceiling. Especially into my kitchen. I might have to move out.

But nothing happened.

"Still okay?"

"Nothing changed."

He didn't answer, so I went upstairs to see what else he'd found—if anything. He stood with his hands on the sides of the tub, bent over at the waist. Not a bad view.

"Well?" I asked.

"I can't tell much without ripping up the floor." He straightened and turned. "But it looks like it was probably just the tub. Is the water stopping?"

"It seems to be."

"That's good at least. Just don't use the tub again until you get a plumber out here."

"Fair enough." I brushed my hair over one shoulder. "Thanks for coming over. I guess it looked more alarming than it was."

"No problem."

His drill was sitting on the counter but he didn't move to pick it up. He just stood there with his eyes lingering on my mouth.

This was interesting. Not a precise reenactment of any of

my sex dreams, but it certainly brought them to mind. The heat between us was undeniable and my body lit up at the possibilities.

A night with Dex? Yes, please.

"I should go." He grabbed the drill and stepped toward the door. "Riley's um... sleeping at a friend's house."

"You could stay for a bit." I lifted one shoulder with an air of casual indifference. "Have a glass of wine."

"I need to get back."

"Dex." I stepped closer and met his gaze. "You should stay."

His eyes ate me alive—deep blue and simmering with lust. He wanted me.

The feeling was mutual.

My lips curved in a smile and I inched closer, tilting my chin up, inviting his kiss.

For a second, I was convinced he was going to take me up on my offer. My nerve endings tingled with the anticipation of those big hands and all that rough stubble. But instead of dipping his head to put his mouth on mine, his body stiffened and he moved back.

"Look, I don't want to make this awkward, but I'm not um... not interested."

Stepping away, I blinked in surprise. Although I wasn't insulted. I was curious.

Because he was lying.

My ego wasn't so large that I assumed every man I met would want to take me to bed. That wasn't why I knew he was lying. I could see the deception in his eyes. He was working just as hard to convince himself as he was to convince me.

I brushed my hair back from my face. "Sorry, I must have misread the situation."

"I can give you the name of a good plumber if you need one." His voice was gruff and he brushed past me, giving me a tantalizing whisper of his scent. Deliciously male.

"That would be great."

He was already halfway down the stairs.

Why are you running, Dex?

I followed him down. Tension snapped off him like jolts of static electricity and he headed straight for the front door. He'd done the same thing the night the raccoon had been in the trash—left abruptly once the problem had been solved.

"What am I supposed to do about the holes in the ceiling?"

He stopped but didn't turn around. "I can come by another time and patch them."

I paused in the living room, making it obvious I wasn't some psycho who'd follow him home and make a scene because he'd turned me down. "Okay. Thanks again for your help."

"No problem. Night."

And just like that, he left, shutting the door behind him.

I stared at the door for a long moment. His rejection did sting a little. I could admit that. But I wasn't upset by it. Disappointed, certainly. But mostly I just didn't understand it.

I knew men well enough to know when one wanted me —wanted me so much he'd already fucked me a dozen times in his imagination. I'd have bet anything that Dex had done just that as soon as he'd opened the door for me. His daughter wasn't home, so the opportunity had been perfect. Hell, I was naked under this robe and I knew he'd noticed.

Tightening the tie on my robe, I turned for the kitchen. Dex St. James wanted to convince himself he wasn't interested? That was fine. I certainly wasn't one to chase a man.

But I wasn't going to let him get away with the lie, either.

Not without teasing him, at least.

Oh, he could run. And I certainly wasn't going to force the issue. That wasn't a good look on a woman any more than it was on a man.

But I was right next door. And he was about to find out just how often his new neighbor could be in his line of sight. Teasing, tempting, flirting? I was an expert at those.

I'd been training my whole life for this.

9

NORA

I walked out of the conference room after our regular Monday meeting feeling typically frustrated. There had been a time, when I'd first started working for Glamour Gal Media, that I'd come out of these meetings energized and excited for the week ahead. A new topic to research, a new article to write, a new angle to explore—all with the backing of a large multimedia company, giving me access to an unprecedented audience.

I'd essentially stumbled into my career. I'd started as a blogger, when blogging had still been the big thing, and morphed that into an online business as a writer and influencer, specializing in topics of interest to women. As the audience for my blog, *Living Your Best Life,* had grown, so had the sponsorships and endorsements.

It had been a lot of fun but also a lot of work. So when an article I wrote, about giving sexy blow jobs of all things, had gone viral and caught the attention of Glamour Gal Media, I'd been thrilled. I'd thought signing on with them would be just what I needed. They could take care of things like graphic design and all the back-end technical details. I could focus on what I enjoyed—research, interviews, and pulling it all together for a fun, informative read.

While they did take care of the aspects of the business that I'd wanted to outsource, they'd also taken control of the content of *Living Your Best Life*. I'd been under the impression that I'd still have creative control.

I'd been wrong.

I didn't have control of anything. Not even the final product that went under my byline.

But it wasn't all bad. I went back to my office and took a seat at my desk. I could work from home as much as I wanted. I really could focus on the things I enjoyed—the research, the interviews, the writing. They paid me very well. My shoe collection, not to mention my new house, were testaments to that. My career afforded me a life I enjoyed living.

I just had to write yet another article about sex.

After the dozens I'd already written.

With a sigh, I crossed my legs at the ankles and opened my laptop. April wanted my next piece to be about sex in public. Parked car, restroom, that sort of thing. I'd had to hold back from rolling my eyes at her bathroom suggestion. Sex in a public restroom? Gross. No thank you.

But I knew she was right. People would love reading about it. Even people who'd never in a million years have sex in a place where there was a high risk of being caught.

Especially people who'd never have sex in a place with a high risk of being caught.

I opened a new document and jotted down a few notes. Sometimes I felt like I was writing fiction more often than not. How was I supposed to research this? Wander down to Pioneer Square and do person-on-the-street interviews? Ask random passersby about their experiences having sex in risky places?

I couldn't drum up much excitement about the idea. Maybe I'd just ask my besties. It wasn't like April wouldn't make sure the article was exaggerated and embellished before it was published anyway.

"Hey," Tala poked her head in my door.

"Morning."

Tala Reyes was about my age and all five feet of her was nothing but gorgeous curves. She had thick black hair, big dark eyes, and excellent taste in fashion. She'd started with Glamour Gal shortly after me and worked in the editing department.

She came in and plopped down into one of the extra chairs. "Mondays, am I right? Is it just me or do you dread our weekly meetings?"

"I didn't used to but yes, there's always some dread involved." I sighed. "Sex in public. Riveting topic."

"It could be worse."

I tilted my head. "Could it?"

"Sure. April has me working on a piece from Jenna about *alternative beauty treatments*," she said, making air quotes. "At least you don't have to get a snail facial."

"Is that what it sounds like?"

She nodded. "Snails crawling on your face. Do snails crawl? Or do they slither? I don't know, whatever word you use, it's a facial involving snail slime."

I winced. "That's disgusting."

"See? Could be worse. And at least you know your article will be clickable. Gotta love our bonuses." She grinned.

That was what it was all about. Clicks. Racy topics and provocative headlines, all to get as many eyeballs as possible. Clicks meant advertising revenue for Glamour Gal and bonuses for us. That was one thing I couldn't complain about. The bonus structure was generous for everyone.

And Tala was right. A sex in public article by yours truly would generate plenty of clicks.

"Anyway," she said. "How was your weekend?"

"It was fine. Still unpacking." And plotting ways to show my strangely reluctant neighbor what he was missing. "What about you? Wait, didn't you have a date? How did it go?"

She sighed. "I don't know. I've been out with Pete a few times now and I'm just not sure."

"Not sure about what?"

"For one thing, he's always late. And I know we're all glued to our phones nowadays, but he was texting all through dinner."

"Oh, hell no." I sat up straighter and brushed my hair over my shoulder. "Darling, when a man is out with you, you should be his focus. There's nothing on his phone that's better or more important than you."

She nodded along. "Yeah."

"You have to know your worth. A high value man knows how to treat a woman well, in public and in private. If he can't be bothered to pay attention to you now, when you're just getting to know each other, what's he going to be like down the road? Or in bed?"

"That's such a good point. I love talking to you. You're like the guru of dating."

I smiled. "I just hate seeing women sell themselves short for a man who isn't worthy of them."

"What about you? Have you met a man who's worthy of you lately?"

An interesting question. Was Dex worthy of me? My

body certainly thought so. "My new neighbor is inexplicably hot but I don't see anything happening there." I shrugged, maintaining an air of casual disinterest. I wasn't about to admit to a coworker, even a friendly one like Tala, that he'd turned me down. "At least he's nice to look at. And he has the sweetest thirteen-year-old daughter. I just love her."

"Ooh, sexy single dad next door? That is hot. I bet you could spin that into an article."

"Maybe, although I don't think April would be impressed with an article about the surprising things one finds sexy in a neighbor. Like watching him mow the lawn."

"Also hot."

"It really was." I tapped my finger against my lips. "And he's not even my type."

"When it comes to raw physical attraction, I don't know if type matters." She stood and smoothed out her blouse. "I should get back to Jenna's article. And thanks for the advice. I'm not going to bother seeing him again. I'll wait for a man who's worthy. And who'll love Frannie and Freddie."

"I'm sorry, who?"

"My ferrets. They're my babies. I'm so glad I hadn't introduced them to Pete yet. So much less awkward this way."

I nodded slowly. I wasn't quite sure what to say to that.

"Chat with you later," she said with a smile, then turned and left.

I spent the rest of the morning at the office, trying to find ways to make the article interesting. I did some research on the psychology of exhibitionism, although I had a feeling that wasn't the angle April was going to want. Whatever I wrote was likely to be edited into something like the top ten ways to have sex in public without getting caught.

Lunchtime rolled around and I closed my laptop. I was meeting my besties for lunch and I didn't want to be late.

The restaurant was a short drive from my office. I found a parking space a block away and went inside.

I pulled off my sunglasses and smiled at the hostess. "I'm meeting friends. Ah, there they are."

My three best friends were already there, at a table in the bar. Sophie's face lit up when she caught sight of me and she waved, as if I needed her to flag me down so I'd go to the right table. Her mass of blond curls were a little wild—as usual—and she had a slight flush to her cheeks. She'd recently found out she was pregnant with her first baby and she and her husband, Cox, were thrilled.

Hazel's straight brown hair was down and she pushed her glasses up her nose as she turned around. The two of us couldn't have been more different if we'd tried but we'd been best friends since we were fourteen. She was scholarly and brilliant, if a little bit literal. It was hard to believe she'd been married to Corban Nash, her former enemy, for two years already.

Where had the time gone?

Everly stood and I caught her in a hug, kissing each of her cheeks.

"I'm so glad to see you," she said.

I basked in her sunshine smile. Everly was one of the happiest people I'd ever met. Even back when her dating life had been a total disaster, she'd always found the bright side.

Now she didn't have to look very far. She'd married the very stoic, but also very hot and extremely wealthy, Shepherd Calloway. Their daughter, Ella, would be two this summer and she was every bit as sparkly and happy as her mommy.

Once in a while, when I was holding little Ella, I'd experience the strangest twinge in the region of my ovaries. It was the oddest thing.

Although Ella Calloway was the prettiest, most pleasant child I'd ever heard of. She'd make anyone's ovaries ache a little.

"Where's our baby?" I asked.

"I was going to bring her, but Richard and Dahlia came by and asked if they could take her to the park. Obviously I couldn't say no to her grandpa and grandma."

"That's okay, I'll get my Ella fix another time." I pulled out my chair and sat. "Soph, you look amazing. How are you feeling?"

"Really good," she said with a smile. "Except in the morning when I spend an hour throwing up. And then in the afternoon when I'm so tired I can't keep my eyes open. But other than that, great."

"I'm sorry you're having morning sickness," Everly said. "That's no fun."

"It's not so bad," Sophie said. "Those crystallized ginger candies you got me have been helping a lot."

"Oh, good!"

"The presentation of ginger is important to the effectiveness of nausea prevention," Hazel said. "The active ingredients vary in their bioavailability, depending on the processing method and most studies have found that ginger powder, followed by fresh ginger and ginger tea have the most bioavailable ingredients, hence are likely to be the most effective."

Sophie blinked. "Wow. How do you know so much about ginger?"

"I did a little reading."

Everly's eyes widened. "Why? Is it because you're—"

"Oh." Hazel fixed her glasses again. "No, I'm not pregnant."

Sophie and Everly both slumped in their seats, clearly disappointed.

"But I think I'd like to be," Hazel said, her tone matter of fact.

All three of us gasped.

"What?" Hazel asked.

"Are you and Corban trying for a baby?" Sophie asked.

"It's been a topic of discussion."

"Aw," Everly said, her eyes misting. "I'm so excited for you."

"I'm not pregnant yet," Hazel said. "Although I have determined it's in my best interest to give up alcohol, just in case."

"Good plan," Sophie said. "You never know when it will happen."

I smiled at her. "Says the woman currently pregnant with a broken condom baby."

She sighed dreamily and rested her hand on her belly. "Yeah."

How things had changed. Not so long ago, our conversations had revolved around things like careers, dating, and sex. And they'd usually taken place at night, over martinis. Now we typically got together for lunch, rather than Friday or Saturday night drinks, and my friends' lives were full of husbands, in-laws, and babies. It was all very cute and domestic.

But I couldn't help but feel a little left out. I didn't have anything to add to a conversation about a long-term, deeply committed relationship, because I wasn't in one. Nor did I want one. And babies? I was more than happy to live vicariously through Everly and Sophie, and hopefully soon,

Hazel. But I didn't see babies in my future any more than I saw a husband.

I just wasn't the type.

Everly reached over and touched my arm. "How is everything at the new house? When can we come over and see it?"

My friends had come with me to look at the house before I'd bought it but they hadn't been there since I'd moved in. "I love my house. Come over any time. There are still boxes lying around but who cares."

"We won't judge," Hazel said.

"Of course not," Sophie said. "I think it took me and Cox six months before we unpacked the last box when we moved into our house."

"Have you met any of your neighbors?" Everly asked. "Are they nice?"

Had I ever. "Well, there's Phil across the street. He's obsessed with his lawn. And there's a very sweet couple a few doors down. I can't remember their names but they have two kids. Or maybe it's three. Actually, most of the people on my street have kids. There are a lot of minivans."

"Cute," Everly said. "What about the hot lawn mowing guy?"

"Dex St. James," I said, letting his name roll over my tongue like a piece of candy. "He's big and burly and not very friendly and he has way too many tattoos. I love his daughter, though. You all need to meet Riley, she's an absolute doll."

"That's sweet," Sophie said. "Is she little?"

"No, thirteen," I said. "I went to her school art show the other night and it was impressive. She paints and she's so talented."

"You went to her art show?" Hazel asked. "That's an interesting development."

"Why is that interesting? She invited me. Obviously I went."

"I wasn't aware you were getting to know them," Hazel said. "I thought you were simply watching him through the window while he did yard work."

I arched an eyebrow. "Thank you for making me sound creepy. And yes, I've gotten to know them. I'm even invited to his family barbecue."

"Wait, are you dating him?" Sophie asked.

"What? No. What makes you say that?"

"He invited you to a family barbecue."

"To be fair, his mom invited me."

"His mom?" Sophie asked, her mouth dropping open like I'd just said something incredibly shocking. "Nora, why have you been hiding this from us?"

My three friends stared at me as if I'd just announced I was moving to Australia and would never see them again. "What are you talking about? I'm not hiding anything. I've run into Dex a few times and I've chatted with his daughter and yes, I went to her art show. And met his parents. And he helped me when my bathtub was leaking and the water was dripping in the kitchen last Friday. And also when I had a raccoon in my trash and I thought someone was breaking in. But really, there's nothing going on."

Hazel leaned closer, peering at me through her glasses like I was a subject in one of her psych experiments. "You're lying."

"I'm not lying. That was all true."

"Then you're omitting something."

"Are you okay?" Everly asked.

With a slight roll of my eyes, I took a deep breath and held out my hands. "Circle of trust."

Everly clasped my hand on one side and Hazel took the other. They both held hands with Sophie, creating our sacred circle. What was said in the circle of trust stayed in the circle of trust.

"It's possible that I'm mildly attracted to Dex," I said, adding a hint of flippancy to my voice so they would know this wasn't a serious problem. "He's not my type in any way but he is very rugged and manly and despite the fact that he probably wears the same jeans every day, he smells good. But he turned me down."

"I'm sorry, what did you say?" Sophie said. "Because it sounded like you said he turned you down and I'm assuming you mean you suggested sex and he said no and I don't see how that's possible."

"That is difficult to picture," Hazel said.

"I don't think I could have turned you down if you'd ever used your magic on me," Everly said, and the four of us dropped hands.

I leaned in and kissed the air near her cheek. "This is why I love you so much. Apparently I don't have the right kind of magic for him. We were alone, in my house, and his daughter was away for the night, so it was the perfect opportunity. But he said he wasn't interested."

"Not interested?" Hazel asked, her brow furrowing.

"I'm suddenly calling into question everything I thought I knew about the world," Everly said. "How could he not be interested in you? You're Nora Lakes. That's not possible."

"My ego thanks you but it's not the first time a man has turned me down." I paused, tapping my lips with my finger. "No, wait. Maybe that is the first time a man turned me down."

"He probably has an understandable reason," Everly said. Always the optimist. "Maybe he just got out of a relationship."

"Do you know what happened to the mom?" Sophie asked.

I shook my head. "I don't know anything about her."

"But if his reason was a recent breakup, wouldn't he have said so?" Hazel asked.

"It would make for a softer rejection if he said he'd just gotten out of a relationship," Everly said. "Just saying he's not interested is a little harsh."

"At the risk of sounding more conceited than usual, there's no way he wasn't interested in me. That's what he said, but his entire body said otherwise. I know when a man wants me and he was working very hard to hold himself back. I'd just gotten out of a bath and was naked except for a robe, for fuck's sake."

"Was it that pretty pink one?" Everly asked.

"Yes. It's my favorite after a bath. And not only did he walk away, he stomped out with hardly another word. Just, sorry I'm not interested. And that was it."

"This is very perplexing," Hazel said.

"I'm glad it's not just me," I said. "I keep trying to tell myself this isn't a big deal, and it really isn't, but I also keep thinking about it. Why do I keep thinking about it?"

"Any of us would think about it," Everly said. "I'd probably be over-analyzing every word I'd ever said to him along with every outfit I'd ever worn in his presence, trying to figure out what was wrong with me."

"Oh, same," Sophie said, nodding sagely.

"I have to agree," Hazel said. "It makes sense that this would be a blow to your confidence."

I fiddled with one of the buttons on my blouse. "I

wouldn't say it's a blow to my confidence. That might be too dramatic. But he did nudge it off balance a little."

Plus, I kind of liked him and it stung that he didn't like me.

"At least neighbors aren't too hard to avoid," Sophie said.

"Oh, I'm not going to avoid him."

"You're not?" Everly asked.

"Don't get me wrong, I'm not about to throw myself at him." The corners of my mouth lifted. "He claimed he's not interested but he was lying. So I'm going to tease him. Show him what he's missing."

"Dex, you have no idea what's coming for you," Sophie said with a laugh.

I lifted my glass and they all followed. "A toast. To Dex St. James and the power of flirtation. May living next to me be sweet, sweet torture."

"Cheers!"

I took a sip. Sophie was right. Dex had no idea what was coming for him.

10

DEX

The text on the page blurred. I moved the book a few inches further from my face and the lines sharpened. Better, except now I was uncomfortable. Holding the book at this angle, I couldn't rest my arm on the chair. The reading glasses sitting on the side table next to me would fix that problem. I knew this, but I stubbornly ignored them.

I wasn't even forty. Too young for fucking reading glasses.

Bending my elbow, I tried to get comfortable. The words blurred again, the letters softening around the edges just enough that I had to squint. That was going to give me a headache.

Fine.

I grabbed the reading glasses and slipped them on. The tension around my eyes eased as the page came into comfortable focus.

It was a thriller I'd read before. I knew the twists and could pick out the clues, but that was the appeal. I didn't have to concentrate too hard. Worked out well when I'd been reading since four in the morning because I couldn't sleep.

I did that a lot.

And re-reading a book was a hell of a lot better than staring at the ceiling, thinking about Nora.

I did that a lot, too.

Obviously I'd done the right thing last Friday night when I'd walked away. She'd made it crystal clear what she wanted, and to be honest, I respected that. She wasn't playing games, pretending like she wasn't interested in order to get me to make the first move. Her suggestion had been straightforward—assertive, but not overly aggressive.

But there was no way I could take her up on it.

So I'd spent the week doing what any man would have done in my shoes. Pretending she didn't exist.

I was pretty good at it, too. Except in the middle of the night, when I'd lie awake, picturing the way she'd looked in that slinky robe. Those big, expressive eyes and pouty mouth offering me a night in paradise.

Still, I'd done the right thing. Even if the more animal side of me thought I was an idiot.

Maybe I was an idiot.

I turned the page, the paper crisp beneath my fingers. I hadn't read the last few paragraphs, but I knew the story well enough that I didn't worry about it. I'd been reading for hours, waiting for the rest of the world to wake up. Or at least for Riley so I could see if she wanted breakfast before I had to go to work. It was after eight, but it was Saturday, so she might not emerge for hours yet.

She'd have to get up eventually. The family was coming over for my mom's barbecue later.

So was Nora. Possibly.

And there she was again, flooding my mind.

Maybe I should have just fucked her and got it over with.

Who was I kidding? That wasn't my style. I was kind of old-fashioned. I wanted sex to mean something. Granted, I'd let my dick do most of the thinking for a while when I was younger. And I knew all too well how dangerous it could be to fuck someone you weren't in love with.

That was how I'd wound up with Riley.

I'd never, ever regret having my daughter. She was the best thing that had ever happened to me. But if I'd known how useless her mom would be at parenting, I might have chosen my sexual partners more carefully.

That was it. I was careful. I had to be. It wasn't just me who could get hurt if—or when—things went wrong. I had Riley to think about. And I had no idea how she'd feel about me getting involved with someone. Seemed like it would be weird.

Besides, relationships ended. Or mine always did. I couldn't shield Riley from everything but I didn't have to put her through that.

Slow footsteps on the stairs caught my attention. I took off my reading glasses and twisted in the armchair. "Morning, Ry."

"Morning." Her hair was loose and wavy from her braids and she was still in her pajamas.

"Do you want some breakfast?"

She rubbed her eyes. "Not yet."

"I have to go to the shop at eleven. I'll try to be back before everyone gets here, but I can't guarantee it. You know how it is."

She paused at the bottom of the stairs. "Yeah, I know. Start times are more like vague suggestions in our family."

I smiled. She had that right. Having the family over for

dinner meant people started showing up right after lunch. With appetizers.

The St. James clan knew how to eat.

Riley shuffled into the kitchen. It sounded like she was heating up water for tea. I thought about going in there but I was always torn between wanting to smother her and not wanting to smother her. She'd been quiet all week in a way that worried me. Her sleepover with Katie seemed to have perked her up—for about a day. But as soon as Monday had rolled around, she'd been back to silent and sullen.

Hell with it. I put the book aside and went into the kitchen. Without a word, I grabbed my daughter and pulled her in for a hug.

For a second, she was stiff, like I'd caught her by surprise. I probably had. But she relaxed and put her arms around me, hugging me back.

There was my girl.

I let her go and stepped back, acting casual, like hugging my little girl wasn't oxygen to me.

She played it cool, getting a mug out of the cupboard. "Is Nora still coming today?"

Well, shit. I had no idea if Nora was still coming because I'd worked very hard to avoid her. I'd even kept the curtain on the front window closed when I was home so I wouldn't catch a glimpse of her coming or going.

I shrugged. "I'm not sure. Haven't seen her. But don't be disappointed if she doesn't. A family dinner is a lot to ask of someone who's just a neighbor."

"She's not, though."

"What do you mean? She lives next door. I think that's the definition of neighbor."

"No, she's not *just* a neighbor."

My brow furrowed. What did she mean by that? She

couldn't know what had happened between me and Nora. She hadn't even been home that night.

"She's a friend," Riley continued, her tone matter-of-fact.

Right. Riley's friend. Good. That could work. "Yeah, I know she's your friend."

She rolled her eyes. "She's your friend too, Dad. Quit being weird. I know about the thing."

My jaw hitched. How the hell did she know? I decided to play stupid. "What thing?"

"I saw you guys but it's not a big deal."

If I'd have been drinking something I would have spit it all over the kitchen. She'd seen us? What? How? "Ry, I think you have the wrong idea."

"What do you mean I have the wrong idea?" Her eyes met mine but I couldn't tell if she were alarmed or excited. "Are you guys actually together? Because I thought you were faking."

Now I was really confused. "What are you talking about? We're not together."

"Yeah, I know. That's what I mean. You guys were holding hands at the art show but it was just to get away from Mrs. Bachman. That's totally a thing a friend would do, not someone who's just a neighbor."

Okay, that was making sense. I let out a long breath. She wasn't talking about seeing me with an almost naked Nora. "I get what you're saying. I didn't realize you'd seen that."

"Mrs. Bachman tries to make out with all the dads. I'd hate to be one of her kids. So embarrassing."

"I feel sorry for her kids, too." And the dads who were dumb enough to take her up on it.

The teapot came to a boil and Riley poured the hot water over her tea bag. "After I get dressed, I'll go next door and make sure Nora's still coming."

So much for pretending she didn't exist. "Okay, kiddo."

"Just don't fake hold hands with her in front of Grandma. You know what would happen. She'd be taking me shopping for a flower girl dress by next weekend."

I laughed a little too hard, trying to cover the sudden shock. Flower girl dress? Oh, shit. "Yeah, she would."

With a little smile, she picked up her mug and went back upstairs.

I took another deep breath. Felt like I'd dodged a bullet.

Except another one was coming for me if Riley made sure Nora was coming over tonight.

No, that was fine. I couldn't avoid her forever. And my family was overwhelming as hell. Big, loud, and nosy. If she did brave the chaos, she'd probably stay just long enough to be polite and then get her hot ass back home.

I could handle it.

The doorbell rang and I looked at the clock. Damn it, if that was my sister, I was going to tell her to go the fuck home and come back around lunchtime like a normal person with family dinner plans. It wasn't even nine in the morning.

I opened the door but it wasn't either of my sisters. It was a couple of twenty-something kids—there I went again, thinking of adults as kids—wearing bright blue Party People Rentals t-shirts.

"Hey," the first guy said. "We're here with a deluxe pirate ship bounce house."

"Right. You guys can bring it around back. Let me get some shoes on and I'll meet you out there."

Both dudes gave me a chin tip and headed for their truck. I forced myself to not look toward Nora's house and went back inside to find my shoes.

I met them in the backyard and let them pick where to

set up the inflatable monstrosity. They spread it out, hauled an extension cord to an electrical outlet and told me to just turn it on when we were ready. I thought they might have tested it first or something but they took off before I could ask.

It was my mom's deal, so I decided not to worry about it.

I turned to go inside and almost ran right into Nora.

A very sweaty Nora.

Fuck.

Her hair was up and she was dressed in nothing but a sports bra and shorts that were an inch away from being underwear. Her tan skin glistened with a light sheen of sweat, just as if I'd spent the last hour fu—

"Hey." She flashed me that gorgeous smile—all full lips and white teeth. "Sorry, I was out for a run and saw the party truck outside. What's that?"

She pointed toward the bounce house but I couldn't take my eyes off her. I wanted to lick the sweat off her neck.

Better yet, off those unbelievable tits.

No, I didn't. I was not getting involved with Nora Lakes.

I tore my gaze away and glanced over my shoulder. "It's a bounce house. My mom ordered it."

"Of course, big family barbecue. I can't wait."

"Look, you don't have to come. My family is pretty obnoxious."

"Are you uncomfortable with me being there?"

"No." I crossed my arms. "No, it's not that at all. You don't make me uncomfortable."

She smiled and despite the fact that she hadn't moved an inch, it felt like she kept getting closer. "Good. I wouldn't want that."

"I just wouldn't want you to be uncomfortable."

"You don't make me uncomfortable, Dex." She batted her eyelashes, just once.

God, she was good, her sex appeal somehow simultaneously subtle and right in my face. A woman like Aimee Bachman would have been running her fingers through her cleavage sweat to pull my attention to her boobs or licking her lips while eying my crotch. Nora did none of those things. It was like she wasn't even trying to be the sexiest fucking woman on the planet. She just was.

"Nora!" Riley came running out the back door, still in her pajamas. "Hi."

"Hi, beautiful." Nora beamed at my daughter and it just about broke me. "Don't hug me, I'm all sweaty."

"I don't care." Riley barreled into her and flung her arms around her. "Can you still come tonight?"

"Of course I can."

Riley stepped back and tucked her hair behind her ears. "Good. I haven't seen you so I thought maybe you forgot and made other plans."

"Not a single plan in sight. And come visit anytime, sweetie. I missed you this week."

She gazed at Nora, as starry eyed as if her favorite rock star had just offered her a back stage pass. "You did? I missed you too. Um, that sounded weird. Sorry. I'm going to go upstairs and figure out what to wear."

"See you tonight." Nora wiggled her fingers in a wave.

"Bye." Riley's cheeks flushed and she almost ran into the sliding glass door trying to get back in the house.

"She is the cutest," Nora said.

"I know, she really is." I let my eyes linger on Nora for a second while she was still watching the back door.

So damn sexy.

Maybe I was an idiot.

"I'll let you get back to your preparations," she said. "Can I bring anything?"

"No, we'll have enough food to feed my entire family for a week. It's how these things go."

"Let me at least bring a bottle of wine. I want to contribute."

"Won't say no to that."

"Great." Her eyes sparkled and the corners of her mouth twitched in the barest hint of a smile. "I'll see you later."

"Bye." I did my best to keep my eyes on her face instead of her deliciously sweaty body as she turned and walked toward her house.

Of course, once she turned, I couldn't take my eyes off her ass.

I'm only human.

She paused, glancing over her shoulder, an amused smile crossing her lips.

Busted.

With an annoyed growl, I stomped my way back inside.

That woman was going to be the death of me.

11

NORA

I didn't know if Dex had been avoiding me or if it was a coincidence that I hadn't seen him all week. No lawn mowing. No yard work. I hadn't even caught a glimpse of him going to or from his car.

Couldn't the man at least have the decency to let me torture him a little?

I went inside to get some water, pleased with myself for opting to run in my sports bra and a pair of tiny shorts. To be fair, it was unseasonably warm for April and I'd decided on a longer, hence sweatier, run. The outfit had been comfortable and appropriate for my workout. Truthfully, I hadn't even put it on for Dex's benefit.

Running into him outside had been a happy accident.

It had also confirmed what I already knew. Dex was interested. Very interested.

He could deny it all he wanted. I saw the way he looked at me.

I went upstairs to shower and ponder what to wear this afternoon. Nothing too provocative. I wasn't going over there to throw myself at him. But girl next door wasn't really my look either. I needed something classy, yet approachable.

In the end, I picked a ruffly white tank top, ankle length jeans, and wedge sandals. Big gold hoop earrings would add a little flair.

Perfect.

As I got into the shower, I nursed a pang of regret for not offering to help Riley pick out her outfit too.

I'D BEEN under the impression that the barbecue was a dinner function, but the noise began around two. I glanced out my bedroom window into Dex's backyard. The bounce house was inflated and there seemed to be kids everywhere. Adults were putting food out on tables and setting up chairs, and I recognized Gillian, talking with another woman, both with drinks in their hands.

An unexpected surge of nervousness swirled through me. I didn't usually mind social situations with strangers. I liked meeting new people and I was comfortable with small talk.

But something about the intimacy of a family barbecue was oddly intimidating.

Maybe I'd make an excuse and cancel. It wasn't like they'd miss me.

What was wrong with me? I wasn't meeting my boyfriend's parents, desperately hoping they'd approve of me. It was just Dex and Riley. And I'd met his parents already, so what was I worried about?

Still, I second-guessed my outfit, trying on different combinations, until I finally circled back to the clothes I'd already chosen.

No one had told me what time to come over, but the party was clearly in full swing. So I grabbed a bottle of wine —my favorite, a dry Riesling from Salishan Cellars—and headed out the back door.

The shrill laughter of children filled the air and a few women milled around Dex's backyard. My stomach tightened with nervousness but I tousled my hair and pushed the sensation aside. This was just a casual get-together at a neighbor's house. Nothing to fear.

Riley came out the sliding glass door, looking adorable in a cropped t-shirt and ripped jeans. Maybe it was my imagination, but she looked straight at me, as if she'd come outside specifically to see if I was on my way over yet.

She smiled and ran to meet me. "Hi. You made it."

It hadn't escaped my notice that she always seemed surprised when I showed up, as if she hadn't been expecting me to follow through. "Sorry if I'm late. I thought this was a dinner."

"Oh, yeah." She glanced over her shoulder. "My family seems to think dinner starts right after lunch. I guess they just like to hang out."

That was rather endearing. "I love that. How was your sleepover with your friend last weekend?"

She shrugged. "It was okay."

"Just okay?"

"Yeah, it's fine." She grabbed my hand. "Come on, I want to introduce you to everybody."

I recognized the way she'd said *fine*. It meant something was wrong but she wanted to avoid the topic. As much as I wished I could stop and dig into it with her, she led me to her backyard, right into the middle of her family.

"Grandma," Riley called. "Nora's here."

Gillian was dressed in a blue floral blouse and trouser

jeans. Her chin-length bob was exquisite on her, high-lighting her eyes and cheekbones perfectly.

"Nice to see you again." I held up the wine. "Should I give this to you, or go in search of your son?"

"I can take it for you." She took the wine with a smile. "I'm glad you made it. I hope we're not too intimidating for you."

"Not at all," I lied. It felt like everyone was watching me. "I'm excited to meet everyone."

"These are..." Gillian hesitated, gesturing vaguely at the hoard of small humans running around. "My grandchil-dren. I'm hoping the bounce house will be a good outlet for their energy and they'll calm down by dinner."

"Yeah, right," Riley said. "My cousins are cute but they're all crazy."

Two women approached, both with a striking resem-blance to Gillian, although they had eyes like Dex.

"My daughters, Angie and Maggie." She pointed to another woman standing outside the entrance to the bounce house, apparently supervising. "That's my daughter-in-law, Tori."

"The men are all inside," Angie said. She had long hair in a simple ponytail and wore a black t-shirt, jeans, and flip-flops. "I'm sure they'll be out soon to stand around the grill and talk about cars and football."

"And pretend the kids don't need supervision in that thing," Maggie said, gesturing to the bounce house. "Are your boobs real? Because you're stunning and I'm wondering how much it costs to look that good."

Riley put a hand over her mouth to cover her giggle.

Angie rolled her eyes. "Oh my god, Maggie."

I just smiled. "They're all mine. Good genetics. My mom has a fantastic rack."

"You're so lucky." Maggie cast a rueful glance at her own chest.

"You'll have to excuse my daughter," Gillian said. "Being the youngest makes her think she can get away with saying anything."

"We were all thinking it. I'm just the one brave enough to say it. And no offense, Mom. It's not your fault my boobs are sad."

"You can blame your grandmother St. James," Gillian said. "The women on my side of the family are well endowed."

"It's really more about how you dress them." I stepped closer to Maggie and unfastened two of her buttons to show a bit more skin. Her shirt was too baggy, so I reached around and cinched it at the waist behind her. "See? Your boobs look better already."

"She's right," Angie said. "That shirt just got about ten times cuter."

A man in a polo shirt and cargo shorts came outside with a beer in his hand. He paused, his eyes on Maggie, and blinked a few times. "Wow, babe. Were you wearing that earlier?"

Maggie looked down at herself. "Yeah."

He licked his lips and shook his head before coming down the steps onto the patio.

"How did you do that?" Maggie whispered. "He hasn't looked at me like that in months."

I wanted to tell her to come next door and give me thirty minutes and I'd have him hauling her out to the garage to fuck her up against the wall. But Riley was standing too close and that didn't seem like something I should say in front of her.

"Sometimes we have to change things up a little to remind men of our best attributes." I let go of her shirt.

"I like her," Maggie said.

A few more men came outside, including Dex's father, Joel. One of the others had to be Dex's brother. He was a sleeker, more polished version of Dex. The same tall frame with a slightly slimmer build, neatly trimmed hair, and he wore a fitted short-sleeved button down and casual slacks.

Dex came out behind them, dressed in a t-shirt from a band I'd never heard of and jeans with holes in the knees.

If you'd paraded those two men in front of me a few weeks earlier and asked me which one I'd prefer, I would have unhesitatingly chosen the brother.

But now? It wasn't the fact that the mention of Gillian's daughter-in-law told me he was married that made my eyes pass right over him. It was Dex. All that rough, tattooed, messy charm made my mouth water.

He was mid-conversation, laughing at something one of the other guys said. He wore those ugly battered flip flops and had a beer in his hand. One of the kids ran over and latched herself onto his leg. Still talking, he patted her head. She squeezed his leg, then ran off again.

That was so not good for my hormones.

Gillian had just said something. Eyes were on me, expecting a reply. I mentally backtracked, hoping a part of my brain that hadn't been occupied with salivating over her son had heard her.

"I'm a staff writer for Glamour Gal Media." I was pretty sure she'd asked me what I did for a living. "My column is called *Living Your Best Life*."

"It's so cool that you're a real writer," Riley said.

I smiled at her. Her admiration was so touching. "It has its ups and downs but most of the time, it's great."

"Nora, I'm sorry, we're being rude," Gillian said. "Would you like a drink? I can open the wine or get you something else."

"How about I go open it." I offered to take the bottle and she handed it to me. "That way you can keep chatting with your daughters. Would anyone else like a glass?"

"I'm fine for now," Gillian said. "Angie?"

"If I start drinking now, I'll wind up in that bouncy house. I don't think my bladder would appreciate it. But maybe later."

"I'd love one," Maggie said. "Although I don't know if Dex owns wine glasses."

"I'm sure I'll find something. Or I can run next door."

I didn't know where Dex had gone; he wasn't in my line of sight as I headed for his back door. A child ran by, brushing against my legs as he darted into the house. Angie yelled for him to say excuse me but it didn't seem like he'd heard her.

Dex's house was similar to mine, with a sliding glass door leading into the kitchen. His had stacks of food and drinks ready to be put on ice covering the counters. He had said his family knew how to eat.

I paused. It occurred to me that I hadn't been inside Dex's house before.

Curiosity ate at me. I wanted to tiptoe around and see what was inside. Nothing creepy. I didn't feel the need to check his medicine cabinet or go through his dresser drawers. But I would have loved the chance to wander through the house, see what sort of space he lived in.

I resisted the urge. It would be too tempting to sneak into his bedroom and smell his pillow.

Instead, I started poking around his kitchen, searching for a bottle opener.

"Looking for something?"

Dex stood just inside the open door, his beer still dangling from his hand. Why was that so sexy?

"Wine opener."

He pointed to one of the drawers I hadn't tried yet. "Should be in there."

"Thanks." I found the opener and removed the capsule from the neck, then started twisting the corkscrew into the cork.

"I guess you met my sisters."

"I did. They're nice. Maggie asked if my boobs are real."

He groaned. "Damn it, Maggie."

"It's okay, I didn't mind."

"Are they?"

I lifted my eyebrows.

He groaned again. "I don't know why I just said that."

The cork came out with a light pop. "Yes. They're real."

"Sorry."

I just smiled. "Do you have wine glasses? Maggie wasn't sure."

"Yeah." He moved to open one of the cupboards. "In here."

Instead of letting him get them down, I sidled up next to him and reached for a glass. Just a little closeness, a slight brush of my hip against him.

I was supposed to be messing with him but the physical proximity flooded me with warmth. How could he possibly smell so good? It wasn't cologne, he just smelled like man.

But I was in control of this game. I didn't shy away from the light touch of our bodies. Just took two stemless glasses off the shelf and put them on the counter. "Would you like any?"

He cleared his throat. "No. I'm good."

"All right." I poured two glasses, then looked at the cork. Knocking it onto the floor so I could bend over and pick it up was such a cliché. I decided to do it anyway.

I shifted so my backside would be right in front of him and took my time bending at the waist. I didn't look back to see if he was watching. I knew; the feeling of his eyes on me was almost palpable.

Glad I'd worn those jeans, I straightened and replaced the cork, my demeanor nonchalant. Nothing to see here, Dex. Just the woman you're not interested in.

From the corner of my eye, I saw him swallow hard, his Adam's apple bobbing in his throat.

Pleased with our little interaction, I picked up the wine glasses. "Thanks, Dex."

"Yeah. Sure."

Without another word, I went back outside. I brought Maggie her glass of wine and noticed Riley, sitting by herself. Her attention was on her phone and she had an obvious look of concern. Her brow was creased, her lower lip caught between her teeth. Was she trying to keep herself from crying? I had the sudden urge to sharpen my claws. Who'd hurt that sweet girl?

I headed her direction, grabbing a chair along the way, and set it next to her. She looked up, her features relaxing.

"Mind if I join you?" I asked.

"Sure." She sniffed.

I lowered myself into the chair. "What's going on?"

"Nothing. Just, you know, family get together."

"No, honey." I pointed to her phone. "What's going on there."

"What do you mean?"

I leaned back and crossed my legs. "I realize we haven't known each other very long so I should probably tiptoe around the fact that you're obviously upset and hope you decide to open up. But that's not really my style. What's going on? Is it a boy?"

She shook her head. "No."

"Friend troubles?"

"Sort of." She hesitated, her eyes on the phone in her lap. "Katie took a picture of me sleeping when I was at her house. And somehow this other girl got it and posted it."

"And you're embarrassed," I said, my voice soft.

"Yeah. It's a bad picture. Now all these other kids are adding stuff to it and making it worse."

I wanted to find out who this girl was and launch a campaign to ruin her life. Then I remembered that she was just a kid. Not that it excused her behavior. Besides, retaliation was so rarely the right answer.

"Do you want to know what I think you should do?"

She nodded, her eyes hopeful.

"Own it."

The hope in her expression melted into confusion. "What? How?"

"This kind of cruelty won't last very long if you don't react the way they want you to. Sure, they'll laugh and say terrible things. But you're better than that. You walk into that school with your head held high. Don't spare them a single glance. They're not worth your time."

"I'm not sure if I can do that."

"Sure you can. Do you like any of these kids who are making fun of you? Are they people you'd share your secrets with?"

"No," she said vehemently.

"See? Keep that in mind. You're beautiful and talented and they only matter if you let them. Don't give them that power. They don't deserve it."

A little smile played across her lips. "Own it?"

"Yes."

She met my eyes. "What if I wear the pajamas I was wearing in the picture? To school, I mean."

I laughed. "That's brilliant. You strut your beautiful self down those hallways. They won't know what hit them."

"Okay. I'll do it. I think it'll actually be funny."

"It'll be badass." I winked.

"Thanks, Nora."

"My pleasure, sweetie. Can I offer one more suggestion?"

"Yeah, please."

"Ignore your phone for a while. Don't look at the things those kids are posting. It'll just make you feel shitty. Don't give them that power."

She glanced at her phone and nodded. "Okay."

"And sorry for swearing. It's not my most ladylike habit."

"That's okay, my dad swears sometimes." She got up. "I'm going to go put this inside."

I stood. "Good for you."

She hesitated for a second, then threw her arms around me. I lifted my wine glass so it wouldn't spill and hugged her back with my other arm.

I watched her go inside, then Dex caught my eye. He nodded in acknowledgment.

And that felt even more satisfying than any teasing I could have done.

12

DEX

*R*iley laughed as she jumped in the bounce house with her cousins. It was music to my ears.

The sound of one of my nephews puking in the bushes, not so much.

"I know, honey," Angie said. It was one of hers and she rubbed his back in slow circles. "I told you not to jump after eating all that watermelon."

Frankly, I was surprised there weren't more puking kids. We'd all spent the afternoon snacking, followed by a big dinner of burgers, hot dogs, chips, and tons of watermelon. All that food plus wild jumping seemed like a dangerous combination.

I took a sip of the wine Nora had brought. I'd put it in a blue plastic cup so she wouldn't notice that I was drinking it. Why? Hell if I knew. The wine was good, why was I worried about whether Nora saw me with it?

That woman had me all tangled up.

She'd practically set my blood on fire when she'd brushed up against me in the kitchen earlier. And when she'd bent over? Kill me.

But that wasn't the worst of it. Seeing her with my family —and with Riley—was making my chest ache in ways I couldn't explain. And didn't particularly like.

There was an easiness to her presence. A familiarity. She mingled with my family and chatted with Riley as if she'd been a part of our clan for years. The women in my family all seemed to like her. I would have heard about it already if they didn't, they weren't shy. And although the men hadn't said much about her, they'd all given me looks that said yeah, we don't believe for a second that you're not into her.

They were right. But they didn't get it.

Dallas came up next to me and glanced into the bounce house. "Mine in there?"

"Yeah, both of them."

"Good. I told Tori I'd make sure they weren't barfing up their dinner."

"Nope. So far, only one little man down."

"Not bad, all things considered." He took a drink of his beer. "How's work?"

"It's good. Busy. The shop's fully booked almost seven days a week."

"Awesome. That's great."

"How about you?"

"Oh man, the case we're working on is really complex." He said that with excitement in his voice, rather than stress or dread. Dallas had always loved practicing law. "I've been putting in a lot of hours lately, so this has been good. Nice to get away and let the kids go nuts with the cousins."

"For sure."

"So what's the story with her?"

I didn't need to ask who *her* meant. "There's no story."

He grunted his disbelief. "Right. You think you're being subtle with the way you look at her, but I know you."

"Come on. Can you blame me?" My eyes flicked to where she stood chatting with Tori and Angie. "Look at her. She's gorgeous. But there's nothing going on."

"Uh huh."

He didn't continue and I hoped he'd drop the subject. One of the kids in the bounce house shrieked and I shifted to get a better look.

Nothing to worry about. It had been a happy shriek.

One of my nieces came barreling out of an opening at the top of the slide. I tilted my head. I hadn't noticed it before, but it kind of looked like—

"Oh my god, that thing looks like a vagina giving birth," Maggie said behind me. "Mom, what the heck?"

Another kid squeezed through and slid down to the bouncy surface below. She was right. It looked exactly like vagina lips. How had I not noticed that before? Apparently I hadn't really looked because now it was all I could see.

Mom came over. "What's the matter?"

Maggie gestured to the bounce house. "What is that?"

"It's a pirate ship," Mom said, clearly confused.

"No, that." She pointed to the opening as one of the kids slid out.

"Wow, you really can't unsee that, can you?" Dallas said.

"What's the matter?" Tori asked.

"Mom rented a vagina slide for the kids," he said.

She put her hands on her hips. "It's not a vagina slide, it's a pirate ship."

The rest of the adults gathered around and the kids responded to what they thought was parental attention by lining up to go down the slide, one by one, each squeezing through the inflatable vagina lips.

Riley looked up at the staircase, like she was about to join her cousins.

I didn't want to see my daughter squeeze out of that thing. "Hey, Ry, maybe don't use the slide, okay?"

"Oh, I won't," she said. "I'm too big to fit."

Dallas chuckled. "That's what I said."

"That's what they all say," Tori nudged him with her elbow.

"Hey."

Nora stood nearby, her lips turned up in amusement. I didn't know whether it was the horribly designed pirate ship —seriously, someone approved that—or my brother's attempt at a dick joke. But she laughed along with the rest of us and for a second, I couldn't see anything else. Not even the vagina slide.

Just her.

I tore my eyes away before she could catch me gazing at her like an idiot.

"That's our cue to go," Angie said. "It's past the little ones' bedtimes anyway."

"Yeah, we better get them home." Her husband, Mike, motioned for the kids to get down. "Let's go, turkeys."

Riley knew the drill. As the oldest of the cousins, she got out first and encouraged the little ones to follow her.

Goodbyes in my family always took at least thirty minutes. Conversations developed over hugs, tentative plans were made, my mom confirmed schedules with me and my siblings. Nora hugged everyone, even giving light cheek kisses.

I had to give it to her, she'd survived the entire evening.

She didn't follow us into the house, where the goodbyes would have to be said again at the door. She pulled Riley aside and whispered something in her ear, gave her another hug, and walked back to her place.

I watched her go while my siblings filed into my house

or searched for missing socks and shoes. She paused at her door and met my eyes. It was hard to see her expression in the low evening light. I wanted to imagine her look was an invitation—still open, even though I'd told her I wasn't into it.

Not that I'd take her up on it. I couldn't.

She disappeared inside and I let out a breath of regret.

13

DEX

*M*y music blasted while I waited in the school pickup line. My evening client had to cancel, so I figured I'd swing by and pick up Riley so she didn't have to endure the dreaded bus. She was a trooper about it but I knew she liked it better when someone could come get her and bring her home.

The bell rang and seconds later, kids streamed out of her school, anxious to get out of there. I waited, tapping the steering wheel to the music, watching for her.

When she came out, I barely recognized her.

She didn't look different, really. Her hair was down and she wore a t-shirt and jeans. Normal stuff. But she walked with her head up, chin lifted, almost strutting away from the school, like she owned the place.

It was badass.

"Hey," I said when she got in the car. "How was your day?"

She shifted her backpack onto the floor between her feet. "Good. Ask me what I got on my math test."

"What did you get on your math test?"

"Guess."

"You just told me to ask. You're supposed to tell me the answer."

She laughed. "Guess anyway."

"Fine. B plus."

"Way to have faith in me, Dad. I got an A."

I held out my fist and she bumped hers against mine. "Nice work."

"Thanks."

Was it her grades that had her in such a good mood? Whatever it was, I'd take it.

"I think an A on a math test demands celebratory ice cream," I said. "What do you think?"

"I think yes."

"Done."

As soon as the cars in front of me moved, I left and headed for a local ice cream place. We stopped and grabbed waffle cones to go—chocolate brownie with walnuts for me and lemon cheesecake for her.

She didn't talk much on the way home. But at least it was due to the ice cream, not a bout of teenage brooding.

We pulled up to the house, still licking drips off our cones.

"I'll get this." I grabbed her backpack for her before I got out.

"Thanks, Dad."

I followed her inside and set her bag on the bench near the front door. The zipper was partially open and something pink stuck out. It looked like clothes but I didn't recognize it. That was weird. I pulled it out and held it up. It was a tank top.

"Ry, is this yours?"

She glanced back. "Oh, yeah. It's part of my pajamas."

My brow furrowed. "Why did you bring pajamas to school? Was it a spirit day or something?"

"No, I just did a thing."

"Did you wear them?" I pulled out the bottoms. It was a tank top and shorts set—pink with white stripes. Fine for sleeping but I wasn't sure how I felt about her wearing them in front of all those pubescent boys.

"Yeah, just for a little while."

"I don't think pajamas are allowed at school."

"They're not."

I brought them into the kitchen where she was finishing her ice cream. "But you wore them anyway? Should I expect a note or a phone call?"

"Neither. I'm not in trouble."

"But why did you wear pajamas at school in the first place?"

"It was Nora's idea. Actually, I guess it was my idea—technically. But she helped."

"Wait, what?"

She sighed. "I wore them to get back at Ryan. I knew I couldn't have them on all day, so I put them on at lunch, did my thing, and changed back into my regular clothes. It wasn't a big deal."

"Get back at Ryan for what? Who's Ryan?"

"Dad," she said, her voice tinged with exasperation. "I told you, it wasn't a big deal. I didn't get in trouble at all. And it worked." She hopped off the stool. "I have homework. Thanks again for the ice cream."

I watched her go, completely baffled. She wore pajamas at lunch to get back at Ryan? Who the fuck was Ryan and what had the little punk done to my baby girl?

Leaning against the counter, I let out a breath. I needed to calm down. Riley was clearly fine. She'd been in a great mood and the way she'd looked coming out of the school today—so confident—whatever Ryan had done, she'd dealt with it herself.

That was good. I couldn't protect her from everything—damn it—and she needed to learn to deal with problems. Instead of worrying about what the hell she was talking about, I probably just needed to be proud of her.

My phone buzzed in my pocket. I dumped the rest of my ice cream cone in the trash and answered. It was my sister, Maggie.

"Hey, Mags. What's up?"

"Did you find a dinosaur lying around somewhere?"

I picked up the little tyrannosaurus rex I'd found in the lawn. "Yup."

"Oh good. My kids haven't stopped asking where Rexie went."

"Do you want me to bring it over?"

"No, it's not that important. Just hang onto it for me and I'll get it next time I see you."

"Sounds good."

"Great barbecue the other day, yeah? Other than the vaj slide."

"Mom's never going to live that down."

"We have to torture her somehow."

"True."

"Nora was sure awesome. You need to thank her for me."

"For what?"

"For the mind-blowing sex Jordan treated me to. I know, you don't want to hear about it, so I'll spare you the details. But I was checking out her column and oh my god, she's brilliant. I tried out like three tricks she suggested and it's basically changed our entire marriage."

"What are you talking about?"

"Her sex column. It's amazing. Like, seriously, if you ever think you're going to have sex again, read everything she's ever written first. That will be one lucky woman."

I had no idea what to say to that. "This is not a conversation I want to have with my sister."

"I know, I know. But seriously. Next time you see her, tell her I owe her like a hundred martinis."

"Yeah, yeah. Bye, Mags."

"Bye."

I ended the call. Sex column? That was what Nora did for a living?

On the one hand, why not? Sex was great and there wasn't anything wrong with writing about it.

On the other hand, Riley worshiped the ground Nora walked on. Was she reading her sex articles? Did they have anything to do with the pajama stunt?

What was the pajama stunt, anyway?

I was well aware that kids her age were doing things that, as far as I was concerned, they were way too young to do. But Riley wasn't doing any of that. Right? She wasn't all that into boys. She still said kissing scenes in movies were gross. I had a little more time before I had to worry about that stuff. Didn't I?

Except her new idol was basically sex on a stick.

I googled Nora Lakes and quickly found her column, *Living Your Best Life*. The more I scrolled through her articles, the more my overprotective dad instinct grew.

Give, and Get, the Best Orgasms Ever
Ten Ways to Drive Him Wild—Before You Hit the Sheets
Shower Sex: Keeping it Steamy
The Ultimate Vibrator Review: Nora's Top Picks

Oral Sex for Beginners: He'll Think You're an Expert
Be a Tease and Make Him Love It
Take Control: Five Ways to Initiate Sex

I CLICKED on the last one and skimmed over the first few paragraphs until the word *pajamas* hit me right between the eyes.

A SET of sexy pajamas can be the perfect segue. Wear them at an unexpected time to give him a little glimpse and remind him of the bedroom. Choose a set that shows as much skin as possible and allows him easy access. There's nothing wrong with a little finger-play before he gets you fully undressed.

FINGER PLAY IN PAJAMAS? Okay, fine, that sounded awesome —for adults—but what the fuck? Had Riley read this?

Even worse, had Nora suggested she read it?

I couldn't ask Riley. If she had read it, she'd either be mortified or lie about it. If she hadn't, bringing it up would just make her curious and she'd go read it later. On the off chance Riley didn't know about *Living Your Best Life*, I wasn't going to be the one to bring it to her attention.

But I needed to know what the fuck Nora had been telling my thirteen-year-old kid.

A voice in the back of my head told me to take a breath and slow down.

I didn't listen.

14

NORA

*T*he loud knock startled me. It wasn't just a knock. Someone was pounding on my front door. It reminded me of the time one of my college boyfriends had done too many tequila shots and decided I was cheating on him—which I was not. He'd come to my dorm in the middle of the night, thinking he was going to catch me in the act, and banged on the door so hard, he'd woken up half the floor.

I was a paragraph or two away from finishing this article, but apparently that would have to wait. I got up from my desk and went to the front door to see who it was.

With a fleeting thought that I should make sure it wasn't an axe murderer before I opened the door, I glanced out the front window.

Dex.

He was dressed, as usual, in a t-shirt and jeans, all those tattoos on display. My heart did a funny little jump at the sight of him on my front porch. Almost like I'd been missing him since Saturday and I was excited to see him again.

Not sure what to make of that, I opened the door right as he was about to knock again.

His brow furrowed, forming a deep groove between his eyes. He lowered his hand but didn't unclench his fist and his entire body thrummed with tension.

"Is something wrong?" I asked.

He stared at me for a second before answering. "Can I talk to you?"

I stepped aside and gestured for him to come in. He swept past me and stalked into the living room.

He was angry about something but I couldn't fathom what.

"Is Riley okay?" I asked.

"Fine. Doing homework." He waved vaguely in the direction of his house. "Were you going to tell me what you do for a living at some point?"

"Excuse me?"

"The sex articles. Were you going to mention that?"

I crossed my arms, my defenses springing up. "What are you implying? I never lied to you about my job and I certainly wasn't hiding it from you. It never came up in conversation."

"Yes, it did."

"When?"

He opened his mouth as if to reply but closed it again.

"We've never had a conversation about what we do for a living," I said. "I only know you're a tattoo artist because Riley mentioned it. Have you been hiding your profession from me?"

"No. I don't have anything to hide."

"Neither do I. I write adult content for an adult audience. I would have told you exactly what I do if you'd have asked."

"What did you tell Riley?"

"About my job? That I write a column."

"Did you share it with her? Tell her to read it?"

Anger bubbled up from the pit of my stomach making my cheeks flush. "No, I did not tell your thirteen-year-old child to read my column."

"Then why the fuck was she parading around school in skimpy pajamas today?"

Oh my god, she'd done it. "Was she?"

"See." He pointed an accusatory finger at me. "You do know what's going on. What did you tell her to do?"

"I didn't tell her to do anything other than stop giving power to kids who aren't worthy of her."

"Wait, what?"

"If you want to know what's going on in her life, you'll have to ask her. It's not my story to tell. But the pajamas were her idea."

"Fuck," he said through gritted teeth. "She talks to you and the next thing I know, she's sneaking a tank top and short shorts to school so she can wear them in front of some little shit named Ryan. And then I see your article talking about using sexy pajamas to initiate sex. My kid is too young for fingering, Nora. Way too fucking young."

I had no idea what he was talking about. "You actually think I was trying to help your daughter get some kid to finger her?"

He winced, turning away like I'd just held up a piece of rotten meat and told him he had to eat it.

"Don't say that."

"I didn't bring it up, you did. I didn't encourage Riley to do anything sexual. We weren't even talking about boys. How do you know Ryan is a boy?"

"It's a boy name."

"I used to work with a girl named Ryan." I stepped closer. "And let me reiterate, I did not encourage Riley to do anything sexual. That's not what we were talking about."

"Then what the fuck were you talking about?"

"Someone made fun of her and hurt her feelings. I told her to own it. Show them they couldn't hurt her."

He stared at me, his mouth slightly open. Without a word, he turned, as if he were going to walk out.

But I wasn't finished.

"You can think whatever you want about what I do. It doesn't matter to me. I write about sex hoping to make a difference in women's lives. To give them a vocabulary to talk about their wants and desires with their partners. To help them take charge of their sexual lives and give them ways to become happier and more fulfilled in their relationships."

He opened his mouth to reply but I kept going.

"I'm not offended if you think what I write is trash. But I am offended that you think I'd push it on your thirteen-year-old. Just because I don't have kids doesn't mean I don't realize there are boundaries you don't cross with other people's children."

"She's my daughter and it's my job to protect her."

"Of course it is. But you don't have to protect her from me."

He shook his head, like he didn't believe me, and stormed out.

I gaped at the partially open door. Had he seriously just come over here to accuse me of giving his daughter inappropriate sex advice?

Unbelievable.

Up until now, I'd thought Dex and I were becoming friends. Despite my resolution to tease him mercilessly, I'd been starting to like him—to see him as more than my hot neighbor.

Now I didn't know what to think.

AN HOUR LATER, I gave up on trying to finish working. I was too distracted. Too angry. I couldn't decide if I wanted to march next door and tell him off or never see his gorgeous face again.

And I was worried. Was he going to tell Riley she couldn't see me anymore?

I didn't know what hurt more. No longer being friendly with Dex or with Riley.

Or both.

Another knock on my door—softer this time—interrupted my thoughts.

Was it Dex?

I hated how much I hoped it was—how desperately I craved reconciliation with him. I was all tangled up inside and I didn't like a man having that kind of power over me.

Putting on my best *I'm fine and I don't need you* expression, I answered the door.

But it wasn't Dex. It was my brother, Jensen, holding a bouquet of flowers.

I let out a breath. This could either be exactly what I needed or a ruinous end to an already shitty day. You never knew with him.

The corners of his mouth curled in a smile. "Nora, my sweet sister."

"Hi, Jensen."

Jensen Lakes, son of my father and his British mistress-turned-wife, was the definition of a playboy. Devilishly handsome, well-dressed, charming, witty—and well aware of his gifts and the effect they had on women. He'd grown up in the UK and used his accent to his full advantage now that he lived here in the States.

"Did I catch you at a bad time? Maybe I should have rang first."

He never called first. I was used to it. Especially since he'd moved to Seattle a few years ago. At first it had been odd, having him around. It was like he wanted to be a part of my life, which had surprised me. Jensen had always struck me as only being concerned with himself—particularly his money and his women, both of which he had in abundance.

But he didn't have anything to gain from a relationship with his half-sister—at least not that I could see. He never tried to use me for networking or business contacts and, despite flirting shamelessly with my friends, he'd never slept with any of them. Now they were all married and, in his words, devastatingly unavailable. Still, he kept in touch, showing up to take me to lunch or dinner regularly.

Despite his ridiculousness, it made me like him.

"I was working but I might as well be done for the day." I opened the door wider and stepped aside so he could come in.

He pushed the flowers at me, his attention already on my house. "So this is the new abode. I was surprised you moved out of the city but I suppose I can see the appeal."

I headed for the kitchen. "Do you want a tour? Or a drink?"

"Why not both?"

I poured us each a glass of wine and took a moment to put the flowers in water before taking him on a tour of my house. He nodded appreciatively and complimented my design choices as we went from room to room. I showed him the back yard through the glass door but he didn't seem terribly interested. Just glanced outside and put his half-empty glass down on the kitchen counter.

"How about dinner?" he said. "My treat."

"What's the occasion?"

"A new house seems like a reason to celebrate."

I smiled. "Do you have somewhere in mind?"

He scowled. "Well, you had to go and move out to the suburbs. I have no idea if there's anywhere decent to eat within a ten mile radius."

"Such a snob." I grabbed my phone and did a quick search. I hadn't lived there long enough to know the local restaurant scene. "There's a wine bar that looks good. Great reviews."

"We'll give it a try. I'll drive."

"Give me a few minutes to change."

I went upstairs and chose a black halter top, skinny jeans, and snakeskin heels. When I came down, Jensen was looking at the photos I'd put up on a shelf in the living room —photos from each of my best friends' weddings.

"Always a bridesmaid," he said with a mischievous lilt to his voice.

"Thank goodness for that."

He sighed, placing the photo of Everly's wedding party back on the shelf. "My one regret in this life is that I never got my hands on any of your delicious friends."

"And my one triumph is that I kept you away from them."

He clicked his tongue. "Nora. You could have trusted me."

"I love you, Jensen, but no woman should ever trust you."

With an amused smile, he headed for the door. "Shall we?"

I grabbed my purse, tucked my phone inside, and followed him out. He offered me his arm, walking me out to his car, and opened the passenger side door.

"Pretending to be a gentleman today?"

"I'm always a perfect gentleman."

I laughed as I got in his car. The wine bar was only about ten minutes away and he found parking on the street. The entrance was almost hard to find, giving it an air of exclusivity. Inside, we found modern decor and low light. Classy and simple. Jensen practically had the hostess's phone number before we were seated but I stopped him before he could get his phone out.

"Do you have to try to pick up every woman you meet?" I asked once we'd taken our seats.

"I don't."

"Yes, you do."

He shrugged. "It's nice to have options."

"You're ridiculous."

"I know." He grinned.

We chatted about work while we perused the menu. I didn't have a clear idea of what he actually did for a living. He seemed to have his hands in a variety of businesses and often traveled for work. After the server took our orders, I shared a bit about my professional frustrations. He was sympathetic, although he didn't have any advice I hadn't thought of myself.

But I did remember how nice it could be to have a one-on-one conversation with him—where he wasn't showing off for one of my friends.

Our dinners came and we talked a bit about our father. Jensen had seen him more recently than I had, on his last trip back to London, but I'd talked to him on the phone shortly after my house had closed. It had been a friendly, if not exactly deep, conversation. Typical for my dad.

Then he asked the question I'd been hoping he'd avoid.

"How's your mother? Has she been by to see your house?"

I took a bite so I could collect my thoughts before answering. My relationship with my mother was complicated.

"No. She hasn't." I poked at my food a few times. "That's probably because she doesn't know I moved."

His eyebrows lifted. "Any reason for keeping her in the dark?"

"Her scathing judgment of all my life choices comes to mind."

"You don't think she'll be happy for you?"

I sighed. "My mother doesn't understand me. She can't fathom why I'm not already on my third marriage, trading up each time so I get the benefits of a divorce settlement and a wealthier man. She's going to look at my house as a sign of failure."

"What husband is she on now? Fifth? Sixth?"

I laughed. "Fourth."

"Oh well, that practically makes her a saint."

"She'd say it makes her smart. I'm surprised she's kept this one around for so long. It's been ten years, I think."

"My guess? A jolly prenup."

"I'm sure. He's a smart man. He'd know better than to marry her without one." I took a sip of my wine. "She's also currently in Greece, I believe, so it's not like she's around for a housewarming party."

"If it helps, my mother has no idea what to do with me."

"I don't think anyone knows what to do with you."

He grinned.

"How is your mother?" I asked.

"She's well," he said with a slight shrug, as if there wasn't much to tell. "Apparently she's taken up gardening. Loves flowers. Dad hired a professional to design a proper English garden. He did always love indulging her."

"I'm glad to hear it."

I'd spent a few weeks every summer with my father and stepmother. I wouldn't have called us close, but we'd always gotten along. She'd at least been kind to me and spending time with them had been a counterpoint to the venom my mother spewed about both of them. Granted, my father had been cheating—cheating on both of them, essentially. There was a reason Jensen and I were only a month apart in age, and it wasn't because my father had been a faithful husband or lover to either of them.

I had complicated feelings toward my father because of his infidelity. I had complicated feelings toward my mother as well. But I'd made peace with it. I wasn't close with either of my parents and I never would be. We didn't have that sort of family.

So I'd made my own family instead.

When we'd finished our dinner, Jensen put his cloth napkin on his plate. "I have to admit, this was ace."

"It was." I did the same. "Thanks for dinner."

"My pleasure, love. It's good to catch up."

It was nice to catch up. And nice to be reminded that there was a good man under all Jensen's bravado.

True to his promise to treat me to dinner, he paid the bill. By the time we drove back to my place, the sun had gone down. Streetlights winked to life and clouds had rolled in, adding a chill to the evening air.

He parked in my driveway and still playing the part of

the gentleman, opened my door and walked me up to the front step. Wrapping his arms around me, he gave me a big hug.

"Take care, love," he said.

"Thanks. You too."

He went back to his car and I couldn't help but glance at Dex's house. His car was out front and his porch light on. The curtains were shut but I could tell he was home. I hoped he hadn't taken out any of his misguided anger on Riley. Although he'd always seemed soft with her. I couldn't imagine him yelling at his daughter, regardless of how upset he was.

Still, I'd make a point to check in on her tomorrow. Particularly if I could catch her when Dex wasn't around.

I let out a long breath and went inside. No matter how much I tried to convince myself that I didn't care what Dex thought of me, the truth was, I did. I wanted him to trust me to be friendly with his daughter.

More than that, I wanted him to like me.

Caring what a man thought—especially a man who'd already rejected me—was so unlike me. I didn't understand where this urge was coming from. It scared me a little, probably because I'd felt it before. And that relationship had been an absolute disaster.

So perhaps it was best that Dex had blown up at me. I couldn't go down that road because I knew exactly where it led. Heartbreak. I'd promised myself never again. And I was going to keep that promise.

15

DEX

a car pulled up outside Nora's house. The same car she'd left in with the same motherfucker who'd taken her out. I parted the curtains just a crack and watched him open her car door. She took his arm and he walked her to her front door.

Don't you dare go inside.

I was fully aware that I had no right to be angry that Nora had a date. What the hell did I expect? She'd offered, I'd said no. What was she supposed to do, take a vow of chastity because even though I couldn't, I didn't want anyone else to have her either?

And what was that about, anyway?

He hugged her. My eyes narrowed. It looked like a good-bye, not a come inside. My heart hammered in my chest and I clenched my fists, waiting to see if she'd invite him in. And if he'd accept.

She didn't. Or he was as big of an idiot as I was and had turned her down. He walked back to his car.

I let out a long breath and stepped away from the window. What the hell was I doing? Talk about being a creepy neighbor. I was spying on her through a crack in my curtains, fuming over her personal life.

Crazy. The woman was making me crazy.

"Dad?"

I tried not to jump but she'd startled me. "Yeah?"

"What are you doing?"

Why did she always catch me when I was staring out the window at Nora? "Nothing. Just heard a car, so I was looking to see who it was."

"Who was it?"

I shrugged. "Someone next door."

Without another word, she turned for the kitchen.

Frustration bubbled up inside me as I followed her. I was tired of feeling like I lived with a surly roommate, not my daughter. Tired of her clipped answers and refusal to tell me what was going on in her life.

"Ry, I need to know what the pajama thing was about."

The look she gave me was just shy of a glare. "Why?"

"Because I don't understand what's going on with you. And I'm concerned about your friendship with Nora."

The glare melted into alarm. "Why? Nora's so nice. Why would you be concerned?"

"Because I don't know what she's telling you." I let out a breath. "Can you just tell me what you two talked about?"

She looked down. "Katie took a picture of me sleeping when I spent the night at her house. Somehow Ryan Hutchison got it and she drew drool on my face and a fart cloud coming out of my butt and posted it online everywhere."

"She?"

"What?"

"Ryan is a she?"

"Yeah. She's super popular and pretty and it's so dumb.

Katie worships her even though she's mean. So I told Nora and she told me it doesn't matter what they say about me. It can't hurt me if I don't care, and why would I care what a bunch of jerks think? She told me to own it, so I thought the best way to own it would be to wear the same pajamas in front of everyone. You know, show them I don't care about the stupid picture."

I stared at her. No wonder she'd walked out of school like she owned the place.

"Damn it, Ry, that's fucking awesome." I grabbed her and pulled her against me. "Sorry for swearing."

Her little body shook with her laugh. "It's okay."

"Seriously, that's some next level badassery. I wish I could have done that in seventh grade."

She pulled away. "It made so much sense when Nora said it. I don't even like those kids so why do I care if they make fun of me?"

"What did they do when you came out in the pajamas?"

"At first they tried to laugh at me but I ignored them. Nora was right, once they realized they couldn't hurt my feelings, they stopped."

"Assholes."

"Permission to swear?"

One corner of my mouth lifted. "Granted."

"They are assholes."

I hugged her again. "Damn right. I'm proud of you."

"Thanks, Dad."

"You know, you can tell me this stuff."

"I know. But it was embarrassing."

I nodded. "Yeah. I get that. I'm glad Nora helped."

"Yeah, she did." She pointed to the fridge. "I'm just going to get a snack."

"Go for it."

Now I really felt like an idiot.

Not only had Nora not had an inappropriate conversation with my daughter, she'd given her great advice. She'd helped her navigate a shitty situation and come out on top. As much as I wanted Riley to feel like she could confide in me, would I have told her to own it? To show those little shits they couldn't hurt her? Maybe, but maybe not. I didn't know what I would have told her, but it wouldn't have been as good—or helpful—as what Nora had said to her.

And even if I had, Riley wouldn't have listened to me the way she'd listened to Nora. She'd needed a woman to talk to.

My deep seated resentment toward Riley's mother briefly flared to life. Unfortunately for both of us, Riley's mom sucked as a parent.

I grabbed a beer out of the fridge. Nora's back porch light was on, illuminating a circle in her backyard. Damn it. I'd screwed up.

Although could anyone blame me? I was flying blind, here, trying to parent a teen girl on my own. So what if I'd jumped to the wrong conclusion and chewed out Nora when I should have been thanking her? Seeing Nora's column had freaked me the hell out.

And because I was really good at being stubborn, I didn't go over to apologize.

～

Guilt ate at me.

Every glimpse I caught of Nora reminded me that I'd been a dick to her and she hadn't deserved it. That I not only owed her a thank you for helping Ry, I owed her an apology.

A big one.

Stubbornness won for a few days. I ignored her, doing my best to pretend she didn't exist. I took Riley to school. Went to work. Focused on my clients, my business, my art. I cooked dinner and made Riley do the dishes and helped with her homework. And I didn't watch through the windows, looking to see if Nora had another date—if she invited him in this time.

Didn't want to know.

I wasn't thinking about it. But if I had been, I would have hated the thought of some other guy's hands on her.

So I didn't think about it.

Much.

By Thursday, I'd almost convinced myself that I had nothing to feel bad about. It hadn't been a big deal. I'd wave to Nora next time I saw her. Show her we were cool.

By Saturday, I hadn't seen her, so I started glancing out the window again, looking for her.

Sunday rolled around and still no sign of her. I wondered if she'd gone somewhere. A work trip? A vacation? Was she with that guy who'd taken her out?

I thought about asking Riley if she'd seen her this week. But how could I do that without sounding suspicious? And Ry had been unusually chatty. Every time I thought I might bring it up, she had something to tell me. And the last thing I wanted to do was stop her from talking. If she wanted to tell me about the experiment they were doing in Earth science or how she jump-roped during her entire lunch period to get extra credit for PE, I was going to listen.

Finally, on Monday the suspense ended. After dropping off Riley at school, I came home in time to see Nora leaving.

She didn't look my direction. In fact, I would have bet anything that she was ignoring me on purpose.

Not that I blamed her.

One glimpse of her and my stubbornness crumbled. I needed to apologize and I needed to do it right.

I went to work and while I tattooed a portrait of a guy's late grandmother on his arm, I pondered what to do. Simplicity was probably best. But walking over there, knocking on her door, and telling her I was sorry didn't seem like enough. I'd put it off too long.

And then I got an idea. Maybe it was stupid, but I decided to run with it. After I finished with my client—the portrait was stunning, if I did say so myself—I headed out to get what I needed, hoping Nora wouldn't get home before I was ready for her.

16

NORA

*I*t had been a day.

April had shredded my sex in public article, taking what I'd thought was a compelling piece and turning into clickbait nonsense.

Adding insult to injury, traffic on the way home had been brutal. My one consolation was that I could work from home tomorrow, saving me the hassle of the commute.

I turned onto my street and narrowed my eyes. It looked like someone had mowed my lawn. I'd let it get fairly long— probably longer than I should have. It made the difference obvious, even from a few blocks away.

Had it been Phil? Was the unruly grass across from his pristinely manicured yard too much for him to take?

If it had been Phil, I wasn't sure whether to be grateful or insulted.

But it wasn't just my lawn. When I pulled into the drive-way, I realized the bare spots on either side—where I'd pulled up what I'd assumed were weeds—were filled with colorful flowers.

Either Phil took this yard care stuff way too seriously or

someone had done something nice for me. But who would have mowed my lawn and planted flowers?

It could have been my friends. I'd complained about not knowing how to take care of a yard now that I was in a house. Had one of them come over while I was at work—maybe with her husband—to spruce things up for me?

I got out of my Jeep and wandered down the driveway toward the street. The pop of color looked great—a small change but it had big impact.

"You'll need to water those if it doesn't rain again soon."

Dex walked over with his hands in his jeans pockets. His expression held a hint of sheepishness that made me want to nibble on him. The urge was so strong, I had to remind myself I was mad at him.

"Did you do this?"

"Yeah."

"And you mowed my lawn?"

He nodded and rubbed the back of his neck. "I thought I should do something to, you know, apologize."

My eyebrows lifted.

"Riley told me what was going on at school. You were right, Ryan's a girl. She put shitty stuff about Riley online. Mean girl stuff, I guess. But you helped Riley handle it. So, thank you."

"You're welcome."

"And I'm sorry I blew up at you. Sometimes I get a little overprotective."

For a second, I wondered what my life would have been like if I'd had a father who was a little overprotective of me.

Between that and the sweet gesture, I couldn't stay mad. "Apology accepted. Is Riley home?"

"No, she's with her grandparents."

Disappointment that Riley wasn't home mingled with a

warm flood of desire. Under different circumstances, this would have been the perfect opportunity to be alone. To find out what that rough body of his could do.

Alas, he was holding onto his claim that he didn't want me.

Still, company sounded nice, even if it was just a friend from next door.

"Do you want to come in for dinner?" I asked. His eyes widened slightly and I continued before he could say no. "Just dinner. I've had a crappy day and a friendly face wouldn't be terrible."

"And my face is friendly?"

"Not really. But it's either you or Phil, and I'd rather not spend my dinner listening to another lecture about diagonal lawn mowing."

The corners of his mouth lifted. "Sure. Why not."

He followed me inside and I set my keys and purse down. "Would you like a drink?"

"That would be great," he said. "Whatever you're having is fine."

As I got out a bottle of wine, I thought about staying in my work clothes. My fitted cashmere sweater hugged my curves nicely and did great things for my boobs, especially when I left the top two buttons undone. My slacks highlighted my assets and heels always make a woman look polished and sexy.

But I really wanted to change into loungewear. And why not? It was just Dex.

"Give me a few minutes." I handed him a glass. "I'm going to run upstairs and change."

"Take your time."

I went upstairs to my bedroom and traded my office attire for a simple black tank top and a pair of flowy, wide-leg yoga pants in a pretty moss green. I went back to the kitchen feeling more relaxed already.

"Better." I fished a hair elastic out of my purse, flipped my hair upside down, and tied it in a ponytail. "And better still."

He pushed my glass of wine toward me. "This should help too. Rough day?"

I took a sip. "Kind of the usual for a Monday. Sometimes I wonder why my boss hired me if she's just going to rewrite half of what I turn in. Then there was traffic, although that's typical."

"Traffic is the worst."

"Do you have much of a commute or is your shop close?"

"It's not far from here. What's up with your boss? She doesn't like your writing?"

I poked around in the fridge and started pulling out random ingredients. I didn't exactly have a plan but that was typically how I operated in the kitchen. "She claims she does but the way she shreds my articles, you wouldn't think so."

"That must be frustrating."

"Incredibly." I got out a cutting board and a knife and pushed them toward Dex, then handed him a zucchini. "Cut that into quarters and then dice, if you don't mind."

He started slicing while I cut up an onion.

"It doesn't help that she won't let me write about anything other than sex," I continued. "I used to cover all sorts of topics but apparently I'm now their dedicated sex columnist. It gets old."

"Kind of like when the sorority girls all come in wanting matching butterflies on their ankles."

I laughed. "How many butterflies do you think you've done?"

"More than I could count. Although I don't mind them if the client is open to something original. It's when I get a group who all want them to be identical that I get a little bored."

He finished with the zucchini so I handed him the cheese grater and a block of mozzarella.

"Do you have any?" he asked.

I didn't miss the touch of heat in his voice. It almost made me wish I had one in a naughty place just so I could offer to show him. "Tattoos? No."

"Virgin skin."

"There's nothing virginal about me, Dex."

He laughed. "Have you ever thought about getting one?"

"I don't know." I got out a pan and started browning some ground beef. "Once in a while I see someone with an amazing tattoo and it makes me think about it. But it's so permanent. I guess I have commitment issues."

We chatted more about tattoos while we cooked. Preparing a meal with another person was surprisingly pleasant. Everly, Hazel, and I had cooked together often when we'd lived in the same apartment building downtown. It had been a while since I'd needed to cook for anyone other than myself and sharing the kitchen with Dex was nice.

What started as a vague idea as I'd looked over the ingredients in my kitchen turned into a rich smelling skillet lasagna. Ground beef, onion, zucchini, mushrooms, marinara sauce, and a healthy topping of mozzarella. I finished it off, letting the cheese melt, then dished up two plates.

"This smells incredible," Dex said as he took his plate to the table. "Were you going to make this for yourself?"

I brought my dinner and wine and sat across from him. "Who knows. I tend to buy random things and hope I can make a few meals out of them."

"At the risk of sounding like a dick, I'm surprised you cook."

"I'm full of surprises."

He took a bite and closed his eyes, moaning with enjoyment. That growly sound in his throat made all the effort worth it. I had to recross my legs to smother the burst of heat.

"This is so good," he said.

"Thank you. And yes, I can cook. My friends and I used to get together and make up recipes all the time. What about you? Can you cook or are you mostly a man of the grill?"

"Both, although I'd grill everything if I could. With Ry, I kind of had to learn. Single dad skills."

My curiosity about Riley's mother surged to the surface. I couldn't stop myself from asking. "Can I ask about her mom?"

He poked at his food for a moment before answering. "Brooklyn and I were kind of dating but mostly just sleeping together. At the time, I thought that was great. All the sex, none of the commitment. Then she got pregnant. She didn't want kids, so I said I'd take the baby. It was like, as soon as I knew Riley existed, I couldn't imagine it any other way. She agreed and even said she wanted to be involved. Turned out what she really wanted was access to Riley when it was convenient for her but none of the responsibility of being a parent."

"Does Riley see her?"

"Sometimes. The last time Brooklyn came around, she took Riley out to lunch and then they got manicures. She promised her she'd come to a bunch of her school functions, maybe be here for Thanksgiving or Christmas. Then, nothing. Just didn't show up for any of it."

No wonder Riley had seemed surprised when I came to her art show and family barbecue. "Poor thing. I know what it's like to have a complicated relationship with your parents. It's not easy."

"It breaks my heart for her." He took a sip of wine. "What are your parents like?"

"Divorced. My dad was having an affair with a woman in London when my mom was pregnant with me. My half-brother and I are only four weeks apart."

He winced. "Yikes."

"Not ideal. My father married his mistress and they're still together. My mother doesn't think it's possible to get marriage right until at least the third try."

"Maybe that's why you've never been married?"

"I'm sure that's a part of it. It's hard to look at marriage as having much value when you didn't exactly have a positive example to learn from. Plus, my mother likes to push marriage on me as if it's a financial investment, not a lifetime commitment that really ought to have something to do with love. You should have seen the fit she threw when she found out my best friend Everly was marrying a wealthy man. Apparently that should have been me and she couldn't fathom how I could have let that opportunity pass me by."

"Did you even know the guy?"

"Only through Everly. And they're perfect together. But to hear my mother tell it, I gave him up so Everly could have him."

"Do you think you ever will get married?"

"No." I answered easily.

"Just, no?"

I shook my head. "I'm not interested in marriage."

He nodded slowly as if he were taking that in. "Not even with the guy from the other night?"

"What guy?"

"I kind of saw you leave with a guy. Looked like a date."

The corner of my mouth turned up. Was that jealousy in his voice? Dex acting jealous over me was delicious. "No, that was my brother, Jensen. I actually haven't dated anyone in a while."

"Oh." He glanced away but not before I saw relief in his eyes.

Very interesting.

"Sorry, I just assumed."

"That's all right. What about you?" I was fine with answering his question about marriage but I didn't want to dig any deeper into my reasons why. "It obviously didn't make sense for you to marry Riley's mother. But have you considered it?"

"Not really. Brooklyn wasn't the first crappy relationship I had, so my track record isn't great. And now it doesn't just affect me. I have Riley to think about. So I haven't been with anyone in a while, either. A long while."

Another woman might have been dismayed to learn Dex St. James didn't want to get married.

It only made me want him more.

But somehow my standard moves to catch a man's attention seemed silly with him. I could take slow bites of my food to draw his gaze to my mouth, touch my lips or my neck. I could shrug slightly so the strap of my tank top slipped off my shoulder or reach across the table and initiate contact by stroking his knuckles.

With any other man, I would have tried. Tested the

waters to see if there was enough chemistry—see where things went.

But with Dex, it felt like he'd see that as an attempt at manipulation.

And if I was being honest, if anything was going to happen between us, I wanted him to initiate.

Which was so unlike me. I loved being in charge of my sex life. If I wanted a man, I let him know. And without fail, men appreciated my directness and honesty.

Dex was a different creature entirely.

Instead of turning up the heat, I let the conversation flow to easier topics as we finished our meal. When he offered to help clean up, I simply did the dishes alongside him. I didn't flirt or brush up against him—not on purpose, at least.

He thanked me again for the meal and we said goodnight. Despite the fact that I could see the hesitation in his eyes, the tension thrumming through his body, I didn't push. Didn't even invite. He knew where I stood and if he wanted anything to change between us, he'd have to make the first move.

But when I went to sleep that night, it was Dex who invaded my dreams.

17

DEX

The heavy metal music blasting from my Bluetooth speaker filled my garage. I was in the zone. The day was overcast but I'd been lifting for almost an hour and sweat beaded on my forehead and dripped down my back.

I grabbed the hem of my shirt and lifted it to swipe the sweat off my brow. This chest workout was wrecking me in the best way. I'd needed it. Lifting weights had always been my go-to for stress relief.

Now I was using it to work off more than stress.

I wondered if Nora had any idea how close I'd come the other night to tossing her over my shoulder, hauling her upstairs, and fucking her senseless.

So close.

Having dinner with her had tested my resolve. I kept looking for reasons not to like her and finding none. Against my better judgment, I liked her a lot.

Which was precisely why I'd resisted. Too many feelings. Too complicated.

I hadn't slept well all week, and while that wasn't unusual, it had left me on edge. Lifting helped.

I did a set of dips, pumping out reps until my arms burned in protest. Dallas liked to joke that I couldn't ever quit lifting weights or all my tattoos would deflate.

He probably had a point.

Outside, I saw Phil wave at someone and walk across the street in his red crocs.

Oh damn. It was Nora.

Poor girl.

She had her hair up and was dressed in a tank top and leggings. Looked like she was about to go for a run. Or had been before Phil stopped her.

I paced around the garage to keep my heart rate up and tried not to think about her. After the other night, I needed to keep some distance between us. Give myself a chance to cool off and stay in control.

But man, Phil could talk a person's ear off. I hated leaving her out there to fend for herself.

I did another set of dips and my arms almost buckled on the last rep. Phil was still out there talking to Nora. Because of course he was. He was probably just getting started.

Go inside, Dex. Take a shower. Nora will be fine.

Nope. Couldn't do it.

Telling myself I had no ulterior motives—I just wanted to save her from Phil—I turned off the music and went outside.

Relief washed over Nora's face when she saw me approach. Then something else. A flash of heat and desire, her tongue darting out to wet her lips.

The woman was going to kill me.

"Hey, Phil." I was a sweaty mess but maybe if I smelled, it

would get Phil to cut his lawn lecture short. "How's it going?"

"Good. Getting in a workout, I see." He lifted his t-shirt sleeve and flexed his nonexistent bicep. "I started a new routine myself. I was just telling Nora about it."

Her eyes widened. "Yes, he was."

"I bought this thing years ago but hadn't tried it out and what a mistake," Phil said. "It's called a shake weight. Heard of it?"

My brow furrowed. "Don't think so."

"It's great. Seems so simple but it works a lot of muscle groups." He held his hands in front of him, as if he were gripping something, and pumped them up and down. "The weight shakes, like this, while you hold on."

Phil mimed his workout, which really just looked like he was jacking off—if he'd had a dick the size of a horse's. Nora bit her lip to keep from laughing.

"Glad it's working for you," I said, trying to keep a straight face.

He kept going. "It sure is. Even Donna noticed a difference. You could probably get rid of half of the equipment in your garage with this one thing."

"Maybe I'm old fashioned, but I'll stick with what I have. You keep doing your thing, though."

He grinned.

"Nice to see you, Phil," Nora said. "But Dex and I need to get going."

I raised my eyebrows. *Get going where?*

"What are you guys up to on this fine Saturday?" Phil asked.

Her mouth curled in a wicked grin. "We were just about to go for a run."

A run? Oh hell no.

"You know, the shake weight takes care of your cardio too." He mimicked the jack-off motion again with both hands. "Really gets your heart rate up."

"Thanks for the tip," Nora said, a laugh leaking through.

Her eyes locked with mine, full of challenge. I could almost hear her saying, "Come on, Dex, go running with me. I dare you."

Fuck it. I was not a runner. But I couldn't resist the dare.

"Let's go."

With a chin tip for Phil, I fell in step with Nora and we jogged away.

"Thank you." She tossed a look over her shoulder. "That could have taken a while."

"He's a nice guy, he just doesn't know when to stop."

"I've noticed."

"So, I can turn here and go around the block. Let you get in your run."

"I don't think so, big guy. You're coming with me."

I groaned. "I just lifted for an hour."

"Good, then you're all warmed up." She picked up the pace, pulling ahead of me.

I ran faster to keep up. This wasn't going to end well for me. I'd been telling myself for months that I needed to work on my endurance. Strength, I had down. I was all muscle and it wasn't just for show. But I could already tell Nora was going to run circles around me.

"Unless you're up for carrying me home, you might want to slow down."

She laughed. I let her pull ahead and took the opportunity to check out her ass. It looked fantastic in those leggings.

"Stop looking at my ass and keep up."

"I wasn't."

She glanced over her shoulder. "I have a hot ass. Of course you're looking."

Damn right.

I sped up to get alongside her. "How long is this torture going to last?"

"Only three miles."

My lungs were already starting to burn. "You're not even breathing hard."

"We just started. Frankly, I thought you'd have more endurance."

"I do when it counts."

"Mm hmm."

This was really making me look bad. I decided I was going to keep up with her, even if it killed me.

Ten minutes later, I thought it might.

I gave up all attempts at conversation when we hit our first hill. Okay, hill was too dramatic of a word for the slight incline. But my legs and lungs claimed otherwise. It felt like I was running up a mountain.

The road descended again and stayed flat for a while. I started to get into a groove, my breathing becoming more regular. At least I didn't feel like I was going to die anymore. Nora ran easily, like it was effortless, although I could see the sheen of sweat forming on her forehead and neck.

It made me want to lick it off. Taste the salt on her smooth skin.

Get her naked and find out if she really didn't have any tattoos.

How my mind could still fixate on sex when I was struggling to survive, I had no idea.

She knew the route, so I let her lead the way. She turned down another residential street. A dog barked from a window and a gray cat ran across the road in front of us. A guy who could have been Phil's brother stood in a yard, hand watering his lawn. He even wore crocs, although his were a more subdued shade of navy blue.

We turned down another street and I figured we were well past the halfway point. And I wasn't dead. Felt pretty good about that.

Until a sharp pain in my calf made me pull up short.

"Shit." I hobbled a few steps but my lower leg had suddenly contracted into a giant ball of pain.

Nora stopped and looked back. "Are you okay?"

I reached down to rub my calf. It hurt like hell. "Cramp in my leg. It's fine, I'll just walk it off."

"We should probably stop and massage it out."

"No, I've got it. We can keep going."

She rested her hands on her hips and tilted her head. "You sure?"

"Yeah." I was already scoring way behind on man points. I wasn't about to admit to any more weakness and make this worse. "You keep going. I'll walk a little and catch up."

Gritting my teeth, I took a few steps. The knot in my calf was so tight, it felt like I couldn't bend my ankle. Nora didn't run ahead. She stayed with me while I limped forward, trying not to groan in pain.

"Stay here. I'll run home and come back to pick you up."

"No." My voice was strained as I tried to take another step. "I'm fine."

"Dex, you can barely walk. You're not fine."

I reached down to knead my knotted muscle again. "Just a cramp. No big deal."

She sighed and came alongside me, slipping her arm around my waist. "Come on, big guy. I think if we turn left here it'll get us home faster."

I put my arm over her shoulders but I certainly wasn't

going to lean on her. I'd break her like a twig. "I'll be okay if I—ow."

There was no point in pretending this didn't hurt like hell. Especially when I couldn't walk without limping. Heavily.

This was not making me look good.

Then again, why was I worried about how I looked to Nora? She didn't need to be impressed with me.

She kept her arm around me and I only leaned on her a little as I limped home, hoping Phil wouldn't be outside. That was the last thing I needed.

"Still hanging in there?" she asked as we turned onto our street.

The sight of my house, and the promise of sitting down, was enough to help me power through. "Yeah."

But damn, it hurt.

She walked me all the way up my driveway, the knot in my leg still burning with every hobbling step. We went inside and I flopped onto the couch, breathing out my relief.

"Well, that was embarrassing." I hoisted my leg onto the couch to stretch it out.

She lowered herself onto the floor next to me and took my calf in her hands. "Here, let me."

"It's fine, you don't have to—" I stopped short, groaning as she dug her fingers into my aching muscle.

Fuck that felt good.

It hurt, but it was a good hurt. Necessary. She kneaded the muscle, stroking it up and down, digging in with her fingers. I winced and breathed hard but I didn't want her to stop. I could feel the fibers loosening, the tension easing.

Plus there was something about her hands on my skin, even though it was just my calf.

I did not need an erection right now, but apparently my body was going there.

Breathing through the pain, I flexed and extended my foot while she kept massaging. Her touch was like magic, easing not only the tension in my leg, but in the rest of my body as well.

Except my dick. I just hoped she wouldn't notice that.

Encircling my calf with her hands, she rubbed up and down a few more times. "Is that helping?"

"Yeah." My voice was rough and low. "So good."

Her lips twitched in a smile and I saw her eyes flick to my crotch.

So much for her not noticing.

Thankfully, she did me the favor of pretending she didn't see it.

"You should drink some water." She stood. "Dehydration can cause muscle cramps."

"So can being an idiot who lifts but skips cardio," I grumbled to myself.

She went into the kitchen and came back with a tall glass of water. I downed it like I'd just spent a month in the desert.

"Thanks. Sorry I screwed up your run."

"That's all right. I mostly do it so I can drink all the martinis I want without guilt."

I laughed and shifted on the couch so I was sitting up, then flexed my foot a few more times. Better. "Clearly I could use a similar habit."

Was it my imagination, or did her eyes dart to my crotch again?

I certainly couldn't get enough of her in her running clothes. Her curves were out of this world. The slight flush in her cheeks and shimmer of sweat on her neck and chest made me think about licking her again.

I bet she tasted amazing.

Our eyes locked. The pain in my calf was almost gone. I was pretty sure I could make it up the stairs, even if I had Nora flung over my shoulder like a cave man.

There it was again. The dare. Her lips twitched and her eyes blazed with heat.

The front door flew open and Riley came in. "Hi, Dad. Nora! Oh my gosh, hi."

I bit back a groan of frustration. Of all the moments for her to come flying through the front door.

"Where's grandma?"

She set her backpack on the floor. "She had to go. She said to tell you hi and she loves you. What are you guys doing?"

"I talked your dad into going for a run," Nora said.

Riley burst out laughing. "A run? Seriously?"

My brow furrowed. "Hey."

"He got a cramp so we had to cut it short."

"Dad, running?" She kept laughing. "That's hilarious."

"Why is that so funny?"

"It just is. Look at you." She gestured to all of me. "You're not a runner."

"Thanks, kid."

"He did fine," Nora said. "The cramp was my fault. I talked him into coming with me and didn't give him a chance to get any water."

"You definitely need to stay hydrated," Riley said. "And make sure you get enough electrolytes."

"Who told you that?"

"I learned about it in PE."

I raised my eyebrows. "The class you're failing?"

She put her hands on her hips. "I'm not failing. I told you, I got it up to a C."

"Still not sure I should take fitness advice from someone getting a C in PE." I grinned at her.

She sighed with a playful roll of her eyes. "Whatever, Dad. Can I go to the dance tonight?"

"What dance?"

"The dance at my school."

My first instinct was to say, *No fucking way*. I remembered school dances. There were always kids sneaking off to make out in unlocked classrooms or closets. Or I'd heard stories. I'd never been sure if they were true or kids making shit up to sound cool.

"I don't know."

"Why not? Katie's going. And so are my other friends."

"Would you hate it if I was there as a chaperone?"

She eyed me with suspicion. "As long as you don't do anything embarrassing."

"I never do anything embarrassing."

"Yeah, right."

Nora was watching our exchange with a hint of amusement in her expression. She thought this was funny?

"What if Nora comes with me?" I asked. "We could chaperone together. I'm sure she'll keep me from embarrassing you."

"Could you come?" Riley asked, her eyes brightening. "That would be so cool."

"Unless you have plans," I said, keeping my voice nonchalant. I hit her with my best *I dare you* look.

She met my gaze, as if to say, *Bring it on*. "I'd love to help chaperone."

I grinned at her. "I'll call the school and let them know."

"Oh my gosh, I'm so excited." Riley clasped her hands

together and practically jumped up and down. "I need to figure out what to wear."

"I can help with that," Nora said.

"Really? It's just casual. I don't need to wear a dress or anything."

"Even a casual event requires some thought and planning."

"Kiddo, she might want to go home and shower first," I said. "We got all sweaty."

Nora shrugged. "I don't sweat, I glisten. Let's go see what we have to work with."

I watched her go upstairs with my daughter and something about it made my chest ache.

18

NORA

*D*eciding what to wear to a middle school dance was proving to be more difficult than I'd anticipated.

I'd helped Riley choose her outfit earlier—a black shirt with a unicorn, distressed jeans, and her favorite turquoise Converse. Later, I'd gone back to their house to do her hair and makeup. I'd kept everything very natural and age-appropriate, showing her how to do a no-makeup look with neutral eye shadow, a hint of eyeliner, mascara, and a very pretty pink watercolor blush that doubled as a lip tint. Then I'd done her hair in beachy waves and made sure she felt great about how she looked before we'd gone downstairs to show her dad.

Dex had approved. He'd tried to hide it but he'd gotten a little misty eyed.

Now I was back at my place, rejecting half my closet.

What did one wear to chaperone a dance? Nothing too sexy. I needed subtle and classy. Most of my work wardrobe fit the bill but I wanted something more fun than a blouse and slacks.

In the end, I chose a caramel colored mini-dress with a wrap front and long, flowy sleeves. I added a belt, beige heels, and gold hoops in my ears. Flirty and fun without being over the top.

Satisfied with my choice, I fluffed my hair, sent a selfie to my friends, and went next door.

Riley came out before I had the chance to knock. She looked so cute, I could have died.

"I can't get over how adorable you are," I said. "You look so fresh and sweet."

"I wish you could do my hair every morning. And you look so pretty."

"Thank you, darling."

Dex came out dressed in a black t-shirt and jeans, with slightly damp hair like he'd recently showered. His eyes swept up and down, taking me in. "Wow."

"I hope this works." I plucked at the skirt. "I'd hate to get in trouble for violating the dress code."

"No, you're... that's... yeah."

Riley glanced at her dad. "Why are you being weird?"

"I'm not." He cleared his throat. "Let's just get going."

We walked to his car and Riley offered me the front seat. I got in and my phone buzzed with a text.

Everly: *You look great! Date night?*

Sophie: *Who's the lucky guy?*

Me: *Not a date. I'm chaperoning a middle school dance.*

Hazel: *That is not what I expected you to say.*

Everly: *Me neither.*

Sophie: *How fun! But how did that happen?*

Me: *It's Riley's school. Dex asked if I'd help chaperone with him.*

Sophie: *So it is a date.*

Me: *I'd hardly call this a date.*

Everly: *Either way, you look gorgeous.*

Hazel: *This is so interesting. I wish I could come and observe.*

Me: *Observe what? A bunch of awkward teenagers?*

Hazel: *No, you.*

Me: *Why?*

Hazel: *This is such a departure for you. Chaperoning a dance is a very parental activity.*

Me: *And I can't be parental?*

Everly: *Of course you can. I'm sure she doesn't mean it like that.*

Hazel: *You can certainly be parental. I'm simply interested in this new dynamic.*

Me: *No, you're right, I'm not very parental. A middle school dance is the last place I would have thought I'd spend a Saturday night.*

Which was true. There had been a time when I'd spent almost all my Saturday nights on dates or out with my friends—always with cocktails involved. It was only recently that things had started to change.

Everly: *You'll be a great chaperone.*

Sophie: *I agree. And you look fabulous.*

Hazel: *I continue to admire your ability to choose outfits that are so stylish and appropriate for any occasion.*

Me: *Thanks, my loves.*

We arrived at Riley's school and parked near the gym. Dex paid for Riley's ticket and conferred with the parent volunteer until she found our names on the list of chaperones. They waved us through.

The lights were low and a deejay was set up on a stage. Huge speakers pumped out pop music and multicolored lights flashed around the gym. A mass of kids danced, jumped, and bounced to the beat, while others mingled around the edges or sat on the bleachers. Parent and teacher chaperones stood alone or in pairs, keeping an eye on the kids.

Riley waved to a friend and ran to join her. I smiled in satisfaction. The other girl was clearly complimenting Riley's styling.

As she should. She looked fabulous.

Dex and I wandered deeper into the gym. The lights and loud music were reminiscent of a club—just one where most of the people were shorter than me. Some of the kids looked so young, especially the boys. I seemed to recall that boys often went through puberty later than girls and that differential was on display here.

Not that the boys needed to have hit their growth spurts to start noticing girls. That was also on display. No wonder the school needed chaperones. There were enough pubescent hormones in the room to start a riot.

I leaned closer to Dex so he could hear me over the music. "Have you chaperoned one of these before?"

"No. There was a back-to-school dance but Riley didn't want to go."

"I'm glad she decided to come tonight."

He eyed the crowd of kids with skepticism. "I guess. As long as she has fun."

His protective streak was so hot.

Really, everything about him was hot. I'd reminded myself that he wasn't my type too many times to count. But apparently I had a new type and it was rough, muscular, and tattooed.

Adding insult to injury, he smelled amazing. Clean and manly.

"How's your leg?"

He looked down at me, his lip twitching in a grin. "Fine. Thanks for reminding me of my humiliation."

I nudged him with my elbow, letting my arm brush against him. "It wasn't that bad."

"It was pretty terrible." He nudged me back. "But I did get a leg massage out of the deal, so I have that going for me."

"Only because I felt guilty for giving you a leg cramp."

"If that's what it takes, it was worth it."

My eyebrows lifted. Was Dex flirting with me? "I'll make a runner out of you, yet."

"I wouldn't go that far. Although I could just trail behind and watch you in those leggings."

I leaned closer. "I knew you were looking at my ass."

He turned to speak in my ear, his breath hot against my skin. "Can you blame me? It's a very nice ass."

"Honey, you have no idea."

He growled low in his throat. Sparks shot through my veins, exploding between my legs. If we weren't careful, the other chaperones would be pulling us apart, as if we were the hormonal teenagers.

A woman across the gym waved to Dex.

"That's Kristin, Riley's friend Katie's mom. I should go see what she wants."

"I'll be right here."

Dex walked over to Kristin and I took the opportunity to check out his ass. It was thick enough to bite into and his thighs were magnificent. It had been hard to resist the temptation to slide my hands up his legs while I'd been massaging his calf.

I caught sight of Riley with a small group of girls, giggling together. She grabbed one of them by the wrist and gestured to the dance floor. A moment later, all four girls were running to dance with the rest of the crowd.

There was something satisfying—even a little exhilarating—in watching her have so much fun.

Dex started back toward me but before he'd gone two steps, he was intercepted by a woman in a leopard halter top and fake leather pants that cut into her round hips in just the wrong spot. Her hair was up and it was embarrassingly obvious the ponytail was fake. The color didn't match the rest of her hair.

She was the horny divorced mom who'd been all over Dex at the art show.

Poor guy. She blocked his way, standing in front of him and moving to the side when he tried to go around her. His discomfort was so clear but she seemed to have no idea. If she was delusional enough to think those pants were doing anything for her, she had to be delusional enough to think Dex was attracted to her.

Part of me wanted to whisk her out of here and take her shopping. She probably had a cute figure but she had no idea how to dress it properly. And the fake hair was just too much.

Dex met my gaze, his eyes pleading with me to save him. I tilted my head and watched while she tried to sidle her way closer. He moved back and tried to sidestep again, all to no avail.

I decided to take pity on him. Putting on a friendly smile, I sauntered over and tucked my hand in his arm. "Hi. I'm sorry, I think we met before but I don't remember your name."

The woman's expression fell. "Aimee."

"Nice to see you again." I searched for something I could compliment. Her earrings were the best I could do. But just because I didn't like her outfit, and quite honestly her whole vibe was trashy, there was no reason for me to be cruel to her. "Those earrings are pretty on you."

She touched her ear. "Oh. Thanks."

"You're welcome. Have a nice night."

Dex took the cue and led us away.

"How did you do that?" he asked.

"Just a little territory marking." I squeezed his arm. "Even someone as clueless as her can't ignore a woman who touches you like this."

"Should we hold hands again to drive the message home?"

I took my time, sliding my hand down his forearm, indulging in the soft touch until he clasped my hand with his.

"The neighbors are going to talk."

He shrugged. "I don't care."

That made two of us.

"Riley's going home with Katie after the dance," he said. "She doesn't have an overnight bag but Kristin said she can borrow some of Katie's stuff. I'll pick her up tomorrow afternoon."

"Which one is Katie?" I asked, pointing to Riley and her friends.

"The one in pink."

I watched Riley laughing and dancing with the other girls. She was having fun—and that was great. But I knew the strands of middle school girl friendships could be thin, at least until you found the right friends. I wasn't so sure about this Katie.

"Be careful with Katie," I said.

"Why?"

"I don't know. Intuition, I guess. And there's the question of how Ryan Hutchison got the photo of Riley sleeping.

Somehow I don't think she stole Katie's phone and raided her pictures."

"You think Katie did it on purpose?"

"Maybe, maybe not. It could have been perfectly innocent. She shared it with someone who shared it with Ryan. But girls can be mean at this age, even if they're normally sweet."

"Yeah, there were some girls Riley hung out with in sixth grade who seemed like good kids. But as soon as seventh grade started, they ghosted her. Or at least I think that's what happened. She never tells me very much."

My heart hurt for her. This could be such a tough age. It reminded me to tell my friends how much I loved them. "Hopefully Katie is one of the good ones."

"I hate that I can't protect her from everything. As soon as you said to be careful with Katie, my first instinct was to go cancel the sleepover. Sometimes I wish I could keep her in a bubble until she's twenty-five. Or maybe thirty."

Although Riley wasn't my daughter, somehow I understood exactly how he felt. I squeezed his hand. "It's a tempting idea, isn't it?"

He squeezed back. "I'm glad she has you to talk to."

I looked up and met his eyes. They were warm and inviting, his subtle smile sending a tingle down my spine. "Me too."

His gaze dipped to my lips. I couldn't remember the last time I'd craved a man's kiss with so much intensity. I wanted him to drag me outside, push me up against the wall, and kiss me until I couldn't breathe.

"Can I be honest about something?" he asked.

"Of course."

He moved in closer. "You're kind of killing me tonight."

"Am I?" I asked, my voice full of mock innocence. "I thought you weren't interested."

"Yeah, we both know that's not true."

"What are we going to do about this, Dex?"

He slid his hand around my waist until it came to rest on the small of my back. "We're going to dance."

I placed my hand on his broad shoulder and let him lead. The music was slow and we were probably supposed to be keeping kids six inches apart or something, but I figured the other chaperones could pick up the slack.

We moved to the music and I learned something else about Dex St. James that surprised me. He could dance.

The tattoo artist with a teenage girl. Who hugged his parents, drove a boring family car, and had taken care of his daughter on his own from the day she was born.

That man could also dance.

There was something deliciously old fashioned and masculine about the way he moved me around the dance floor. Subtle shifts of his feet, his hands gentle but strong. I didn't need to know where he'd move next. He guided me like an expert.

If he left me with all this unresolved sexual tension tonight, I was going to scream.

But there was something in his eyes—something different. It was as if he'd stepped around the boundary that had separated us. Dropped his defenses. Desire burned hot in his gaze and he didn't shy away from it. He owned it.

I had a feeling he was going to own me.

19

NORA

*T*he deejay switched things up and moved to a song with a faster beat. But Dex and I kept slow-dancing, as if the music didn't matter. I moved my hand from his shoulder to the back of his neck and he pulled me tighter against his solid body.

Without a word, he let go and took my hand. A second later, he was pulling me across the gym, away from the stage, lights, and dancing kids toward a door. He pushed it open and dragged me through, into the night air behind the gym.

The door banged shut. He pushed me against the wall and before I could so much as breathe, his mouth was on mine.

It was like he was a mind reader. Wish granted.

I welcomed him, grabbing his shirt to pull him against me, my back arching with the aching pleasure of his kiss. His tongue delved in, persistent and demanding. He was hard and hot and rough, setting my blood on fire.

My panties were going to be soaked.

His erection pressed into me and I almost gasped. Even

through his jeans it was impressive. I rubbed myself against him, reveling in the way he groaned into my mouth. Our kisses grew frantic as the tension between us unleashed.

An hour ago, if you'd told me I'd want Dex St. James to fuck me up against the wall behind Riley's middle school gym, I would have said you were crazy. Sure, I wanted him, but in some concrete alley? No, thanks.

Now? I wanted him inside me and I wanted it now.

I moved one leg to hook around his, desperate for pressure where I needed it. Dex didn't disappoint. Still kissing me, he slid his hand between us, his thick fingers delving beneath my panties.

My breath caught in my throat as he caressed my sensitive skin, his fingers trailing through my wetness.

"Yes?" he asked.

"Yes."

For a second, I wanted to guide him—tell him what I needed. But I didn't have to. Which was good, considering I probably couldn't have uttered another coherent word.

Groaning again, he plunged a finger inside me. I clung to him, biting the inside of my lip so I wouldn't cry out. Another finger slid inside and his palm pressed against my clit. My eyes rolled back and my knees almost buckled as sensation blazed through me.

How did he know how to do that on the first try?

His fingers curled and I was pretty sure his other arm was the only thing holding me up. He rubbed my clit, fingering me mercilessly. Harder and faster while I panted, rocking my hips with the motion of his hand.

He'd stopped kissing me, although I didn't know when. His eyes were locked on my face, his gaze intense. I gave in to the pleasure, letting him work his magic, taking me higher and higher.

"This is what you needed, isn't it?"

I could hardly form the words to answer. "Yes. Don't stop."

"You're going to come for me, Nora. Right here."

I nodded, practically breathless.

"That's it, beautiful. I want to watch you come."

He'd granted my wish. I was certainly going to grant his.

One more stroke and I came apart. My inner muscles clenched and released around his fingers and it was all I could do to stay quiet. He moved with me as I rode out my orgasm, the pleasure rippling through my entire body.

My eyes fluttered open. Dex's eyes were on me, his lips turned up in a subtle smile. He slid his fingers out and brought them to his mouth to suck my taste off them.

I reached for his erection, squeezing him through his jeans.

He grunted. "Later. I don't have a condom."

That simply would not do. "I have it covered. You need to fuck me right here."

His eyebrows lifted. My offer surprised him.

And I realized, he'd given me an orgasm just to watch me come, not expecting one in return. At least not right away.

Who was this man?

"Are you sure?" he asked.

"Positive. I'm on birth control and I know I'm safe. And I think we both know you are, too."

"No doubt."

I squeezed him again. "Dex, you better fuck me right now before we get caught."

He went for his zipper. "Somehow I don't think this will take long."

He unfastened his pants, lowered his zipper, and pulled

out his thick cock. My heart beat a steady refrain—yes, yes, yes—while he slid his fingers between my legs and rubbed my wetness on the tip.

Picking me up, he pressed me against the wall and I wrapped my legs around him. With a primal growl, he slid his thickness inside me.

I just about died.

His hips thrust once. Twice. Harder. His fingers dug into my flesh and he grunted low, as if he knew he needed to be quiet but couldn't help himself.

"Fuck," he said, thrusting again.

My thoughts exactly.

He slid easily through my wetness and much to my surprise, tension built deep inside me. For the love of everything, he was going to make me come twice.

"Yes. Fuck me, Dex." I whispered into his ear. "Fuck me hard."

As if he'd only been warming up, he tightened his grip and slammed into me. Again and again. In and out, harder and faster until the rough wall against my back ceased to exist. All I could feel was his magnificent cock ramming into me.

"I'm gonna come," he growled.

"Do it. Come in me now."

He sped up, thrusting all that manly thickness with fierce abandon. I watched as his orgasm took him. As he came undone inside me.

My body pulsed with his, my second climax more intense than the first. His cock throbbed as he spilled into me, his entire body quaking. Waves of pleasure washed over me, leaving me utterly breathless.

He stopped and blinked, as if he were coming back to himself. He let me down and glanced around while he tucked himself back into his jeans. "Are you okay?"

I smoothed my dress and ran my hand down the back of my hair. It was a mess. I was a mess. And I loved it. "I'm amazing, although I need a bathroom."

"Right, yeah. Sorry about that."

"Are you kidding? That was unbelievable."

One corner of his mouth lifted. "Yeah, me too."

"I could tell."

He buttoned his jeans and let out a long breath. If I looked half as dazed as he did, we were going to be incredibly obvious when we went back in the gym.

At least it was dark.

He started toward the door but paused, turning toward me. He touched my face and placed a soft kiss on my lips.

Somehow, being fucked against the wall wasn't nearly as intimate as that sweet kiss.

My heartbeat quickened as I met his eyes. He kissed me again, just a brush of our lips, and led me back into the gym.

I saw the sign for the restrooms and veered in that direction, touching the back of my hair to make sure I'd smoothed it out. I could almost still feel him—his thickness pulsing inside me, his mouth on mine. My legs felt wobbly but I didn't know if it was from the way he'd made me come twice—as if he were already an expert when it came to my body—or that little kiss before we'd come inside.

I took my time in the restroom, both to clean up—let's be honest, spontaneous sex against a wall was hot as hell but it made a mess—and to get my head together. I was glad he'd finally given in. And I loved the desperation. The fact that he'd dragged me outside, unable to wait. Unable to contain himself. That was what I wanted. Hot, frantic sex.

Because that could be *just* sex.

That kiss, though. That had thrown me off. I hadn't

expected that kind of tenderness from him, especially right after fucking me up against a wall behind a middle school gym.

I was probably overreacting. He'd been properly respectful of my consent and then fucked me like an animal.

It had been perfect.

I finished cleaning up, checked my hair and makeup in the mirror, and walked back out to the gym to find him. I didn't worry about whether the other adults suspected something. It wasn't any of their business and I wasn't particularly concerned about their opinions. I found him standing near the refreshment table with two bottles of water—one that he'd already emptied and another that he held out for me.

So thoughtful.

I took it with a smile. But I didn't tuck myself against him or drape his arm around me. I kept a little distance. Not so much that I'd seem aloof, but just enough that he wouldn't pull me in. I told myself it was just so we wouldn't be too obvious. We were supposed to be chaperones, after all. We needed to be the responsible adults.

I didn't want to admit that I kept those inches of space between us because Dex was scaring me.

I was Nora Lakes. Men didn't scare me.

Except I might have found one who did.

20

DEX

I'd lost my damn mind.

On the one hand, I felt fucking amazing. A bit dazed from coming so hard but my brain and body were swimming in a post-sex haze of awesomeness.

On the other hand, I'd just fucked Nora behind my kid's school gym.

It had been a long time since I'd done anything like that. Hell, it had been a long time since I'd had sex, let alone dangerous sex with a woman who was so hot I could hardly stand it.

Something about holding her close on the dance floor had made me lose it. I'd been holding myself back, trying to deny how much I wanted her for so long. And I'd snapped.

Now she stood next to me, sipping her water, looking for all the world like I hadn't just rocked her world outside. I wasn't fooled. I'd seen it in her eyes. I'd made her come twice—because hell yeah, I had—and she was impressed.

I just hoped Riley hadn't noticed us sneak out the back door. That could lead to some awkward questions.

"Hey, Dex?"

I turned to Katie's mom, Kristin, and gave her a friendly smile—and tried to get my brain to focus on dad stuff. "Hey."

"The girls are ready to go."

"Sounds good. Thanks for having her."

"Of course. I'll try to make sure they go to bed at some point."

"Good luck. I'll text you tomorrow when I'm on my way to pick her up."

We said goodbye and I wondered if I was doing the right thing. Was Nora right and Katie wasn't the nice girl she appeared to be?

Riley came over and I grabbed her for a hug before she could leave without one. She hugged Nora, too, and thanked her for coming.

I watched while the two giggling girls trailed Katie's mom and left.

"I hope she'll be okay," I said, my chest clenching with worry.

Nora touched my arm. "I bet she'll have a great time."

"I guess we can get out of here. Unless you want to make a song request."

She laughed. "I'm ready when you are."

I thought about taking her hand as we headed for the door, but she wasn't walking with her arm against mine. Was it my imagination, or was she keeping distance between us?

Maybe she just didn't want anyone to suspect what we'd done. I had to give it to her, she was cool as a cucumber about it. I could tell the difference but she didn't have a distinctive *I just had sex* look about her.

I probably did.

We went out to my car and left. I couldn't stop thinking about the way she'd tasted, the way she'd felt wrapped around me. I wanted her again but it wasn't the fire of lust that needed to be sated right this second. I wasn't about to pull over and hope she'd be into fucking in the car.

I wanted her in my bed, her hair fanned out over my sheets. I wanted to undress her slowly so I could savor her body. Kiss her soft skin and fuck her slowly. I'd come so fast behind the gym, it was almost embarrassing.

Although I was just happy I hadn't come in my pants when I'd had my fingers inside her. I'd been close.

I glanced at her out of the corner of my eye. She had her elbow resting on the window, her hand in her hair. Her long legs were crossed at the ankles, her body language relaxed and casual. She looked so breezy and free. Content.

I loved that I'd done that to her.

But I still wanted more.

I pulled into my driveway and turned off the engine but hesitated before opening the door. "Will you come in?"

Her lips parted, a flash of surprise passing across her features.

Maybe she needed more convincing.

I slid my hand through her hair and pulled her to me, taking her mouth with mine. I kissed her hard and deep, all traces of gentleness gone.

"Come in," I said, my voice rough. "I'm not done with you."

A smile played on her lips. "All right, Dex. I'll come in."

I got out and walked her to the door, already on fire for her. She brushed past me, into the house, letting her hand trail across my erection.

She thought she was in control. She had no idea what was coming for her.

I slammed the door behind me and unceremoniously picked her up over my shoulder. She squealed and laughed as I hauled her upstairs. We lost one—or maybe both—of her shoes along the way. I ignored them. One less thing for me to take off.

"Dex, what are you doing?"

I dropped her on my bed and stood over her while she rolled to her back and held herself up on her elbows. "Still yes?"

She bit her bottom lip and nodded.

Reaching behind me, I pulled my shirt over my head and tossed it aside. Her dress was already hiked up her thighs, revealing all that silky smooth skin. I didn't bother taking off my pants yet. I needed to touch her and we had plenty of time.

I started at her ankles and kissed my way up her legs. She tipped them open and I ran my mouth up her inner thigh, kissing and biting as I went. It was tempting to stop at her center and lick her into a frenzy—she tasted amazing—but I kept moving up. I unfastened her belt and took off her dress, leaving her in nothing but her bra and panties.

My hands roamed over her body, touching and caressing. She unhooked her bra and I pulled it off with glee, finally getting access to her glorious tits. They were full and round, her nipples darkening with her arousal.

I took one in my hand, kneading her gently, and licked her hard peak. She shuddered and gasped in a breath.

"Dex, you're driving me crazy."

I licked her again. "Good."

Her hips moved but I wasn't going to let her rush me. I nuzzled and licked and sucked, working her into a frenzy.

She'd teased me with these damn tits, I was going to make her pay for it.

Finally, I moved off her so I could take off her panties. I knelt in front of her, taking her all in. Her eyes were heavy, her full lips parted. Her tits glistened from my mouth. She had incredible curves, moving from her waist to her luscious hips.

She was incredible.

"You're really fucking beautiful."

Her mouth turned up in a smile. "You're not so bad yourself."

I took off my jeans and underwear, letting them drop to the floor while she watched, her eyes hungry. My cock jutted out, swollen and ready.

Pushing her legs open, I settled on top of her. The skin contact was electric, all my nerve endings firing. Without thrusting in—yet—I leaned down to kiss her. Our tongues slid against each other and she moved her hips enough to tease the tip of my cock with her wetness. I groaned in answer, letting her tease me.

It was fun to let her think she was in charge.

Without warning, I reared back and flipped her over. She tossed her hair over her shoulder and looked back at me, a mix of surprise and desire on her face. I grabbed her hips, lifted her ass higher, and thrust myself into her.

She cried out as I pounded into her, suddenly relentless. I drove my hips hard, my grip on her tight. I was going to fuck her until she couldn't breathe.

I reached out and grabbed a handful of her thick hair. She arched harder, moaning with every hard thrust. I had her right where I wanted her, in my control, her body surrendering to me.

"You want more?" I asked though clenched teeth.

"Yes. Harder."

I kept going, pounding her like an animal. Her taut flesh rippled and her tits bounced. Looking down, I watched my cock slide in and out and out of her hot pussy.

This was not a bad view.

But I wanted those tits again.

I pulled out, leaving her gasping for air, and rolled to my back. Manhandling her, I dragged her on top of me and thrust up inside her.

For a moment, her head dropped and she held herself over me, her hair trailing across my chest. When she looked up, her eyes were wild and her cheeks flushed. Her lips curled in a wicked smile and she rolled her hips, dragging my cock through her wetness.

But if she thought this meant she was in charge, she was wrong.

I grabbed her hips. "Sit up."

She obeyed.

"Good girl." I used my hands to move her, guiding her to ride my cock. "Now grab your tits."

Her eyebrow lifted. "You think you can tell me what to do?"

"You fucking bet I do." I thrust into her, harder this time.

She moaned and tilted her head back. "Damn it, Dex. How do you do that?"

I kept driving into her, gripping her hips so I could rub her clit against me. "I'm just that good."

Her hands slid up her waist and over her tits. She let her nipples slide between her fingers as she squeezed.

"That feel good?" I asked. As much as I liked watching her do it, if it didn't feel good to her, I wasn't going to make her keep going.

Clearly that wasn't an issue. She didn't stop. "So good. Oh my god, so good."

She squeezed her tits, pushing them together and teasing her nipples while I fucked her. Her hips moved with mine, our bodies in perfect sync. I growled and she moaned and it was a good thing my window wasn't open, or we would have given the entire neighborhood quite a show.

Her hands moved to my chest and she rode me harder. I let her have her way this time. Tension built in my groin as she slid up and down. Her eyes fluttered closed and her tits bounced, her moans and cries growing frenzied.

I could feel her heat growing, her climax coming fast. She was so fucking beautiful like this—flushed and wild and messy. I held her hips tight and drove into her, every thrust bringing me closer to exploding.

Her inner muscles clenched around me and she threw her head back. Her cries of ecstasy filled the room as she started to come. I let go, driving into her until I unleashed.

I grunted hard as I throbbed inside her, slamming her into me as I came unglued. I felt the pinch of her fingernails on my chest, the tightness of her pussy surrounding me, and the overwhelming surge of pleasure with every pulse.

She collapsed on top of me and I moved her hair out of the way. We were both breathing hard, covered in a sheen of sweat. Her body was languid and relaxed, like I'd just fucked the life out of her.

I couldn't help but smile in satisfaction.

I didn't try to move her. I liked the way she felt, her body draped over me, her skin warm against mine. For a long moment, I savored it—savored her.

Finally, she took a deep breath and extricated herself from me. I watched her get up, still admiring her body. A man could never get tired of looking at that masterpiece.

She brushed her hair away from her face. "Bathroom."

"Right through there."

I didn't bother getting up while she did her thing in the bathroom. Just put my hands behind my head and enjoyed the way I felt—tired and utterly sated.

She came out a few minutes later and grabbed her bra and underwear. I would have pulled her back into bed with me before she could get dressed, but I couldn't reach.

It was odd. Her expression was relaxed and happy. She looked how I felt. I had no motivation to move, so I didn't quite understand why she got dressed so quickly. She was already putting her dress back on.

"In a hurry?" I asked.

She smiled. "I'd be lying if I said that was anything less than fantastic."

"Agreed. Ten out of ten." Although I wondered why she'd avoided my question.

"I don't know about you, but I wouldn't be opposed to doing it again sometime."

"You know where I live."

"I certainly do." Her lips curled in another smile and her gaze moved up and down my body while she fastened her belt.

Apparently this meant she was leaving. I sat up. "I think your shoes are on the stairs somewhere."

"Don't get up. I'll find them."

"You sure?"

"Absolutely." She came over to the side of the bed and leaned down to kiss me. "I had a great time tonight."

"Me too."

"Goodnight, Dex."

"Night, Nora."

A confusing mix of feelings hit me as I watched her walk

out of my room. It had been a great night, the sex off the charts for both of us—clearly. Now it was over and she wanted to go home. Probably had a thing about sleeping in her own bed.

But I couldn't help but be a little disappointed because I wished she would have stayed.

21

NORA

*M*y shoes hit the pavement in a steady rhythm as I ran alongside Everly. She was dressed in a yellow tank top and black shorts, her blond hair in a ponytail. Sweet baby Ella—who wasn't really a baby anymore, but a toddler—was along for the ride in a running stroller. She wore yellow like her mommy, her wispy blond hair in two tiny pigtails.

We'd met for an early evening run, taking our old route out and back from the parking lot across from Brody's Brewhouse. Hazel was out of town at a conference and Sophie had plans with her mother-in-law, so it was just me and Everly and her sunshine baby.

I didn't mind. Although I tended to scoff—and maybe even complain—about the running habit Everly and Hazel had forced upon me years ago, I had to admit it was good for me. I'd never become a runner who loved the act of running. But I did like having completed a good workout.

And let's be honest, I needed something to counteract my love of dirty martinis. Especially because I was no longer twenty-five.

My brain chose that moment to remind me of the time that mover had called me ma'am. The nerve of him.

"Are you okay?" Everly asked.

"Do you ever get ma'amed?"

"I do, but I think it's a mom thing. It's only happened when I have Ella with me."

"Well that doesn't make me feel better."

"When did you get ma'amed?"

"It was a while ago, when I was moving. I don't know why I thought of it again."

Our finish line came into sight so we slowed to a walk to cool down.

"Don't let it get to you," she said. "Remember when we were in our early twenties? People in their thirties seemed so much older than us."

"True. And I don't feel like a ma'am."

"You don't look like one either."

"Thanks, my love. Neither do you. Even when you have our precious girl with you. You've never been prettier."

She beamed at me. "Thank you. Oh, before I forget, the foundation is putting on a black-tie casino night. You'll get an official invitation but I wanted to let you know ahead of time. I really want you to be there."

Everly was the executive director for a charitable foundation backed by the brilliant and exceedingly wealthy aerospace mogul, Cameron Whitbury. She absolutely loved her job, and her boss. I kind of wondered what that would be like.

"I can't wait. I love your events."

"I'm hoping you can help me find a great dress."

There were few things I loved more than helping style my friends. "I'd be offended if you didn't ask."

We stopped near our cars to stretch. Ella sang her

toddler version of the ABC song where every letter was P. She didn't quite get the tune right, either, but it was adorable.

"Do you have time to go in?" I asked, gesturing to Brody's across the street.

She checked her watch. "Sure. Let me just text Shepherd to let him know we'll be a little longer."

"Wouldn't want him worrying about his girls."

I unstrapped Ella from the stroller and picked her up, settling her on my hip. She played with my ponytail while Everly put the stroller in her car.

We walked across to Brody's and waited for the host to seat us. Once upon a time, we would have sat in the bar. But the little girl in my arms had changed that. It was amazing to think that Sophie wasn't far behind.

I was still ordering a martini, though.

The host seated us and brought a wooden highchair for Ella. Everly produced a wet wipe from her purse and wiped it down before letting me set her in the seat.

"These things are always sticky," she said.

Jake, my favorite bartender, came over to our table. He and I had always enjoyed a harmless flirtation. Never serious—he'd been happily married the entire time I'd known him—but he had a great smile. It was fun to get him to use it.

"Hi, ladies." He waved at Ella. "Hi, little squirt."

Ella held up the toy Everly had given her to play with.

"That's awesome," Jake said. "How old is she? Two?"

"She will be in July," Everly said.

"I figured. My daughter will be two in August, so they're close."

"How sweet," Everly said.

"Yeah, she's the best."

"What are you doing out here?" I asked. "I thought they liked to keep you behind the bar."

"Apparently this is what happens when you become an owner." He shrugged. "You wind up doing a little bit of everything."

"I didn't know you bought this place," I said. "Congratulations."

He smiled. "Thanks. It's kind of a dream come true, so I'm pretty excited about it. Anyway, what can I get you, ladies. The usual?"

"Yes, except iced tea for me," Everly said. "And she'll have the grilled cheese with a fruit cup."

"The usual for me."

"You got it."

Our drinks came out quickly and he brought some bread for Ella to snack on while we waited for our food. He clearly knew what he was doing when it came to toddlers.

"How's work?" Everly asked.

"More of the same." I sipped my drink. "Frustrating more often than not but it still has its good points."

"Really? I'm surprised."

"Why?"

"I don't know, you just seem like you've been in a really good mood lately. I thought maybe things at work were better."

She was right, I had been in a good mood lately. A great mood, actually. But it wasn't because April had suddenly decided to let me have my creative freedom.

It was Dex.

Specifically, the weapon of pussy destruction he kept in his pants.

I opened my mouth to tell her just that but I glanced at Ella. She didn't talk a lot yet, but she was learning, and there were probably things I shouldn't say in front of her, even if she couldn't understand them.

So I chose my words a bit more carefully. "A fling with my very hot neighbor has that effect."

She raised her eyebrows. "Do tell."

"Having him right next door is so convenient. I can just pop by and let him rock my world, then it's back to work."

The truth was, Dex and I had been slipping over to each other's houses, usually shortly after Riley went to school, almost every day for the last several weeks. Days I had to go into the office were trickier and weekends were usually out because Riley was home. Although he'd appeared at my back door late last Saturday night for a quickie before sneaking back to his house.

"Sounds great," Everly said.

"It is. He's..." I glanced at Ella again. "Extremely talented."

Jake brought our food and Everly cut up Ella's grilled cheese sandwich into small bites. "When do we get to meet him?"

My eyebrows drew in and my fork dangled from my hand. "Meet him?"

"Yeah. We'd all love to meet the guy you're dating."

"No, no." I waved my hand with a soft laugh. "We're not dating."

She met my eyes and there was an unusual seriousness in her expression. "Are you sure?"

"He doesn't take me out on dates, which I would say ought to be included in the definition of dating. It's just sex."

She pulled out her phone, scrolled to something, then held it up for me to see. It was a photo I'd sent of me with Dex and Riley at a French bakery I'd discovered. We'd gone for macarons.

"I sent you that because I wanted you to know about the bakery. It's divine. And it wasn't a date."

"Maybe not a traditional one, but how many times have you gone somewhere with them lately?"

I gave her a nonchalant shrug. "I don't know. A few."

Not quite a lie, but not exactly true, either. It was more than a few. He'd invited me to come with them to get Thai food one evening, plus there had been that Indian place we'd all wanted to try. Sushi, which had been my idea—Riley had loved it, Dex hadn't been a fan. He'd insisted on grilling steaks for us the next night. Then there was the shopping trip for a new swimsuit for Riley a couple of weeks ago and our runs around the neighborhood together.

But none of those were dates.

"It just seems like you spend a lot of time with him outside the bedroom," Everly said. "Half the time when we talk, you're with him."

"I probably do, but that doesn't mean we're dating. We're neighbors, of course we do things together."

"How many neighbors did you even know in our old building?"

"I knew you. And Hazel."

"That doesn't count, we were friends before we moved there. You weren't going out to dinner with people from next door."

"I wasn't sleeping with them either."

"Exactly."

Wait, was she winning this discussion? I had an unnatural urge to be right about this. "My relationship with Dex and Riley, as friends, is different from my fling with Dex. They're separate things."

"Okay."

I could tell by her tone she didn't believe me.

"I mean it. Yes, I spend time with him, and with his daughter. I like them. And yes, I'm sleeping with him, as often as possible, thank you very much. And fine, even if you want to classify some of our outings as dates, which they're not, that doesn't mean it's serious."

She tilted her head and there was a hint of sympathy in her eyes. "Would it be so terrible if it was, though?"

I took a sip of my martini to avoid having to answer right away.

Would it be so terrible?

Although that wasn't really the issue. Serious relationships weren't usually terrible in the beginning. It was where, and how, they ended that was the problem.

"You know that's not what I'm looking for. I like my life the way it is. And this arrangement is perfect."

"I don't mean to pick on you. I just want you to be happy."

"Darling, I am happy. Life is good."

She lifted her glass of iced tea and I clinked it with mine. "To living a good life."

"Cheers."

I was happy with the way things were. It was fun to spend time with Dex and Riley. As for the sex, it was incredible. The man was ridiculous. I liked having a steady source of orgasms right next door. We were both willing adults, there was nothing wrong with that. He didn't want a serious relationship any more than I did. It was part of what made him so perfect for me.

For now. Always for now. I couldn't risk anything else.

I finished my dinner, trying not to think about how complicated this could get when "for now" inevitably ended. Because it always did.

But Dex didn't seem like the type to get too attached.

He'd practically said so. He was too focused on his daughter. I was just a pleasant—and convenient—distraction, which was all I wanted to be.

The arrangement suited us both.

So I pushed aside the unsettled feeling that tried to disrupt my contentment. It wasn't something I needed to worry about.

22

DEX

I put my book down and pinched the bridge of my nose below my glasses. Insomnia had been messing me up lately. It would take me a couple of hours to fall asleep at night, which wouldn't have been too bad. But that had been coupled with an inability to sleep past three or four in the morning. I wasn't getting enough sleep and it was catching up with me.

I'd finished up with my clients early, and since it was a Saturday, I'd come home instead of staying to do admin stuff. It would all be there next time I went in. Fortunately, the shop was humming along. I had a great crew and business was steady. Lots to be grateful for there.

I glanced out the window. Riley had gone next door to see Nora about an hour ago. My mom was coming to pick her up for a sleepover, so I'd need to go get her if she didn't come home soon. Her moods had been up and down, as usual. Some days she seemed fine. Others, not so much. The emotional whiplash was getting old but I did my best to roll with it. I knew she wasn't trying to be a pain in my ass. She just had a lot going on in that head of hers.

Although I did wish she'd talk to me about it.

That was probably what she was doing next door. And to be fair, she usually came home from her visits with Nora in a much better mood. I needed to remember to thank her.

Okay, in a way I did thank her. Hard and often.

Taking off my glasses, I blew out a breath, then set them on the side table. Sleeping with Nora hadn't been the plan, but once it had happened, the inevitability of it had seemed pretty obvious. There had been heat between us from the beginning and we'd finally given in.

Over. And over. And over.

Still, it was fine. Simple. We took opportunities when they arose—namely, when Riley wasn't around. Once in a while, we made an opportunity. Like early this morning when I'd crept next door while Ry was still asleep.

All the sneaking around was hot, I couldn't deny that. Get to a bedroom, tear our clothes off, fuck like animals, get dressed and go about our business. Easy.

The *what comes next* question lingered in the back of my mind. I got up and pushed it aside because frankly, I didn't have an answer. And I didn't want to worry about it. Nora was amazing, her body was incredible, and the sex was fantastic. What more could a guy want?

A lot, but I pushed that aside too. Why make it complicated?

I went outside to find Riley so she could pack her bag for a night at Grandma and Grandpa's house. She and Nora were sitting on her front porch with what looked like iced tea.

"Hi, Dad." Riley smiled.

Definitely an improvement. "Hey, kiddo. Grandma will be here soon."

"Okay. I'll go get my stuff." She stood. "Thanks, Nora. I'll see you later."

"Bye, sweetie."

Riley ran across the yard and went inside.

"Is she okay?" I asked.

"She seems to be. I don't think she'll mind me telling you that she still hates PE and she's very excited for school to be out for the summer."

"I bet she is."

Nora stood. "I'm glad she came over. It was nice to chat with her."

I had the craziest urge to kiss her. Not because I wanted to see if we could manage another round before my mom got here. Because she was close and it would have felt good. In fact, it would have been nice to kiss her when we weren't banging the shit out of each other.

Which was exactly the kind of thinking that was going to get me in trouble.

She hesitated for a second, her eyes on mine. I had the weirdest feeling that she knew what I was thinking.

Did she want me to kiss her?

My mom pulled into my driveway, saving me the trouble of finding out.

She got out and waved. I felt a twinge of sheepishness, as if Nora and I had been caught. Doing what, I didn't know. Other than the first time behind the gym—which had been nuts—it wasn't like we'd been having sex anywhere other than a bedroom. And I hadn't indulged in that kiss I'd been thinking about, so Mom hadn't seen anything.

Still, she eyed us as we walked next door, as if she suspected something.

I told myself that was crazy. She didn't know. And it wasn't her business, anyway.

"Hey, Mom." I hugged her and kissed her cheek.

"Hi, baby boy." She gave Nora a hug. "Lovely to see you, Nora."

"You, too."

"Riley's inside getting her stuff," I said.

"That's fine, I'm a little early." Her eyes swept over both of us, that hint of suspicion still in her expression. "How have you two been?"

Nora's gaze flicked to me, then back to my mom. Had she noticed that too? The way Mom grouped us together as *you two*?

I was probably reading way too much into that.

"I've been well," Nora said. "How about you?"

"Good," Mom said. "Busy, of course. But I like being busy. Tonight's going to feel like a night off with just Riley."

As if on cue, Riley came out with her backpack hanging off one shoulder. "Hi, Grandma."

"Hi, honey. All ready?"

"Yep." She opened the passenger door and tossed her backpack inside. "Bye, Dad."

I hugged her. "Be good. And have fun."

"I will." She hugged Nora. "Bye, Nora. I'll see you when I get back."

"Bye, sweetie."

Mom eyed us again. I wanted to ask her what she was looking at with that smug expression. But I knew better. Whatever she was thinking, she wouldn't tell me.

Or maybe I didn't want to know.

"Bye, kids," Mom said as she went around to the driver's side. She winked at me. "Have a good night."

She backed out onto the street and drove away, leaving me alone with Nora.

"Want to go get dinner?" I asked.

Nora hesitated, looking at me like she was surprised. I didn't know what the big deal was. It was a little early but by the time we went to a restaurant, ordered, and got our food, it would be dinner time. And it wasn't like this would be the first time we'd had dinner together. The three of us had gone out to eat a bunch of times.

Only this wasn't the three of us.

But fuck it. I wanted to have dinner with her. "Come on. Eat a meal with me. It won't hurt."

She seemed to recover from whatever had made her pause. "Okay."

"What sounds good?"

"Just something easy. Takeout?"

For some reason—and I couldn't have explained it if I'd tried—I pushed back. That wasn't going to cut it. I wanted to take her out. "No, I want to go out. How about the wine bar on Main Street? Have you been there?"

"Once. It was good."

"I'll call and see if we need a reservation." I stepped close enough that I had to look down on her. But I didn't touch her. "I'll come get you in an hour."

She lifted her chin, her eyes flashing with defiance. But she didn't argue. "See you then."

I thought again about kissing her. Her lips were so close. But I decided against it. If anything, it looked like she expected me to. So I didn't.

Instead, I turned and walked away, leaving her standing there.

LUCKILY FOR ME, the wine bar had an open table. I took a quick shower, then changed into a fresh t-shirt and clean pair of jeans. That didn't take long—I was about as low maintenance as they came—so I went back to my book while I waited for Nora to get ready.

When it had been an hour, I went next door and knocked.

Nora opened the door and the sight of her just about knocked me on my ass. She wore a sleeveless black dress with a V-neck and fitted waist that accented her curves perfectly. The woman had legs for days and those heels? Kill me. Her hair was down and I wanted to kiss that red lipstick right off her.

She stepped out and shut her door. "Ready?"

I offered her my arm. "Let's go."

We drove to the wine bar and found parking out front. Every eye was on her when we walked in the restaurant and for good reason. She looked incredible. I kept a possessive hand on the small of her back, guiding her to our table— just enough to let everyone know this woman was mine.

Not that she was, exactly. But something deep inside me wanted to claim her.

We took our seats. Looked at the menu and ordered drinks, then dinner. Conversation came easy over our drinks and continued when our food came. We talked about Riley, laughed about our neighbor Phil and his continuing obsession with his shake weight. I told her—somewhat reluctantly—about my sister Maggie's insistence that she owed her for some of the things she'd read in her column. The way Maggie and her husband were going, they'd have another baby on the way sooner rather than later.

"How did you become a tattoo artist?" she asked.

"I got into art when I was a kid—mostly sketching and painting. I loved it, but growing up with a lawyer for a dad, it was more or less expected that I'd go to college for something either professional or academic. And when my brother Dallas went to law school, it felt like I had to go, too."

"You went to law school?"

"I dropped out of law school."

"What did your parents have to say about that?"

"They worried a lot and made sure I knew it. When I told them I was taking an apprenticeship in a tattoo shop, they thought I'd lost my mind. But ultimately, they were pretty good about letting all of us make our own choices, good or bad. We're the ones who have to live with them."

"No wonder you're such a good father."

That was probably the best compliment she could have given me. "Thank you."

"I mean it. You're amazing with her."

"I appreciate that." I shifted in my seat. "Lately I feel like I'm flying blind. She used to be so easy to understand. Now the little girl who loved to curl up in my lap and listen to stories before bed shrinks away when I try to hug her. I practically have to chase her down."

"Don't ever stop."

"What do you mean?"

"Hugging her, even if you do have to chase her to do it. I know it probably seems like she's pushing you away but I really think that's when you need to double down. Hug her more, not less. Keep showing her that you love her no matter what else is going on in your lives."

I nodded slowly. "That's good advice."

"I realize I'm not her mother. I'm not cut out to be anyone's mom. But I do know what it's like to be a self-conscious and sometimes confused teenage girl who really wishes she had a dad who cared enough to keep trying."

Damn. That hit me right in the chest. I didn't know what

to say, so I reached across the table and took her hand. Although, she was wrong about one thing; she'd make a great mom.

She looked aside and pulled her hand away, tucking her hair behind her ear. The waiter came back and asked if we wanted more wine. We decided to have one more glass and I talked her into sharing a tiramisu.

We chatted more, mostly about tattooing. I could tell she was steering the conversation away from herself but I let it go. She probably hadn't meant to share that about her father. Still, I heard her message loud and clear. It didn't matter how hard Riley pushed back, I was going to keep loving her like a good dad should. Even when that meant hugging her in front of her friends. I hoped she'd thank me for it someday.

After dinner, I took Nora to my place. Peeling that sexy black dress off her was even more fun than watching her wear it. I lost myself in her, enjoying her taste, her scent, the feel of her skin. She was beautiful and in these brief moments, alone in my room, she was mine.

But not for long. She didn't stay, lingering in bed with me. And spending the night seemed to be completely off the table, so I didn't ask.

I wanted that to be okay. But the more it happened—and the more time we spent together outside the bedroom—the less satisfied I was with our situation. Against my better judgment, I was falling for her. Which was not good. Relationships never worked out for me.

I'd known she was trouble the first time I saw her. But I hadn't realized how much. Now I was in over my head and I had no idea what I was going to do about it.

23

DEX

*R*iley hitched her backpack up her shoulder and I followed her into the house. I had to go back to the shop later—I had an evening appointment—but I'd been able to take off and pick her up from school. She had homework, so after grabbing a quick snack—and enduring a hug from her dad—she went upstairs.

She hadn't talked much but she also hadn't seemed sullen or upset about anything. I decided I'd take it.

Something made me glance out the front window. It was like I had a Nora radar. There she was, coming back from a run, her skin flushed and warm. I hadn't seen her in a few days—our schedules hadn't seemed to line up. I missed her.

I didn't want to. Not like this. Missing her body was fine. And I did. Just the sight of her through the window stirred my desire. But it was more than that. A few days without her and I was craving the sound of her voice, the scent of her skin, the simple pleasure of her presence.

That was dangerous.

Without thinking about it too deeply, I grasped for the lust that she evoked and pushed away all those inconvenient emotions. I'd keep it simple—go next door and fuck her senseless.

I glanced upstairs. Riley was doing homework and she'd probably stay in her room anyway. So I crept out the back door, shutting it quietly, and went over to Nora's.

She was in her kitchen, drinking a glass of water. I knocked on the glass door, softly so I wouldn't startle her.

Her smile gave me a warm feeling in my chest. She put down her glass and opened the door. "You must be a mind reader. I was just thinking about you."

I stepped inside and she shut it behind me. "Thinking about me or my cock inside you?"

"Maybe both."

"Good." I grabbed her ponytail and pulled her head back so I could take her mouth in a hard kiss. "Riley's doing homework but I really want to fuck you."

"I should shower."

"No. I want you dirty."

She was already breathless. "Upstairs. Now."

I followed her up, grabbing her tight ass the whole way. This made sense. It was purely physical. I wanted her, she wanted me. We'd both get what we wanted. Win-win.

She peeled her sweaty clothes off while I tossed mine on the floor, urgency driving us both. I grabbed her, pulling her against me, and kissed her again—hard and deep, savoring the hint of salt on her lips.

Her hand slid between us and she wrapped her fingers around my aching cock. I grunted as she squeezed, my hips starting to move of their own accord. Her thumb swept the tip and she slowly lowered herself to her knees.

She took me in her mouth and I almost came unglued. Her mouth was warm and wet, her tongue absolutely wicked. She didn't hesitate, plunging down on me mercilessly. I grabbed her hair and pumped my hips, watching my cock slide in and out.

Fuck, yes.

Her eyes lifted, making eye contact as she took me in deeper. I growled and my legs threatened to buckle.

I knew she'd finish—let me come down her throat. And sometimes that was exactly what I wanted.

But as good as this felt—and it felt really fucking good—I needed to be inside her.

I let go of her hair and pulled my hips back. "On the bed."

She slowed but didn't do what I asked immediately. Instead, she took her time, looking up at me while she let the tip of my cock slide against the roof of her mouth. While she held the base and licked, lavishing me with attention.

It was great. But I was going to make her pay for it.

I pulled out of her mouth. "Get on the bed. Now."

She held eye contact as she rose, still moving with deliberate—almost defiant—slowness. It made my blood run hot. She turned and stepped to the end of the bed but paused, looking at me over her shoulder.

I stepped closer, wrapping one arm around her so I could grab her chin. I tilted her head to the side while my other hand reached between her legs.

"That's my dirty girl. Nice and wet for me."

She moaned as I rubbed her clit and kissed her neck.

"Dex, please," she breathed.

"You need to come, don't you beautiful?"

"Yes."

I rubbed faster, working her into a frenzy. She arched her back and I pressed my erection into her, indulging in more friction.

"I need you inside me," she said in between breaths. "Now, Dex. I need you. I need you."

I'd give her everything she wanted. Everything she needed.

"On your knees."

Letting out a breath that sounded like relief, she climbed onto the bed. I got on behind her and grabbed handfuls of that magnificent ass. I lined myself up with her opening and plunged inside.

She cried out as I stretched her open. With my hands gripping her hips, I drove in and out, pulling her against me with every thrust. She was hot and tight, wrapping me in pure bliss.

Primal need drove me. I fucked her hard, grunting as I drove into her. I knew her body, knew what she wanted. I could feel the tightening of her inner muscles around me, knew she was close.

"Dex. Fuck. Dex."

I loved doing this to her. Fucking her so good she'd lose her mind. She gasped and moaned, arching back into my thrusts. I couldn't hold back. Couldn't stop. Her pussy clenched and I growled as all that heat and tension exploded.

She clamped down on me, pulsing as her climax swept through her. I spilled into her, growling as my cock throbbed.

Gradually, we slowed and came to a stop. I slid out of her, still breathing hard, and she collapsed onto the bed, as if utterly spent.

I had the strongest urge to lie down with her. Gather her in my arms and pull her close. I didn't really have time. I needed to get back before Riley realized I was gone, or worse, came over here looking for me.

But Nora didn't move.

I'd just stay a few more minutes. I could risk that much.

I dropped down beside her, hooked my arm around her waist, and hauled her against me. She didn't resist. Just exhaled, nestling her body into mine.

Tiredness washed over me. It was hard to keep my eyes open. I couldn't fall asleep over here. Had to get back home. But man, it was tempting. Nora's body was molded to mine, her scent all over me. I was relaxed and sated. Happy, even.

Just as my eyes started to close, Nora stirred. I let her go and she got off the bed.

"I need to clean up. You can take your time."

I rolled onto my back and rubbed my eyes. But the urge to sleep had already passed. And I really did need to get home.

I got up and found my clothes. Tugged everything on while Nora was in the bathroom. She came out dressed in a robe and offered me a goodbye kiss, just like usual. I smacked her ass, just because, and left.

Running a hand through my hair, I crossed our yards and went to my back door. Careful to be as quiet as I could, I opened it and slipped inside.

And came face to face with Riley.

I jerked back so hard I almost gave myself whiplash.

"Hey," she said, her voice betraying nothing.

"Damn it, you scared me." I rubbed the back of my neck. "What are you doing?"

She didn't answer and I couldn't read her expression. She just looked at me, like a scientist observing a specimen in a lab.

Finally, she spoke. "You're not going to break her heart, are you?"

I blinked in surprise. That was pretty much the last

thing I'd expected her to say. "What? No. That's not... I mean, we're not..."

"Dad," she said, and her voice reminded me of my mom. "I already know."

Oh, shit. "You know what?"

"That you and Nora are, you know." She shrugged.

My eyebrows shot up. I wasn't quite sure what she meant by *you know*. She was old enough to know about sex—we'd had the talk—but was that what she meant? And how did she know? I'd been so careful.

Damn, this was awkward.

"You don't have to hide it from me," she said. "It's not weird. I could tell you guys liked each other and you're grown-ups, you're allowed to have sex."

So fucking awkward. I raked my hand through my hair. "Ry, we don't have to get into that."

"I know. Gross. But I'm just telling you that it's okay with me. You don't have to sneak around and stuff. I know she's your girlfriend now and I think it's awesome."

My heart sank as the full import of what she was saying hit me. How could I explain this? Nora wasn't my girlfriend. We were just having sex. But I didn't want to say that to my daughter.

I wasn't happy about any of this.

"That's not exactly what's going on. It's more complicated than that. Or maybe it's simpler. I don't know." I took a deep breath. "But I'm not going to break her heart. You don't have to worry about that."

"I don't mean I think you're like one of those bad boyfriends from the movies."

"I know. I get it; you really like Nora."

She fidgeted with her hands, the way she did when she was nervous. "I know that you haven't had a girlfriend because of me. Mom's had lots of boyfriends but you never date anyone. And I just want you to know, it's fine. You should be able to have a girlfriend. And if you're going to, and it could be anyone, I'd really want it to be Nora."

I wasn't going to break Nora's heart, but my kid was going to break mine. I reached for her and pulled her in for a hug. "Oh, honey. It's not your fault. Please don't think anything about my life is your fault."

She relaxed into my hug and nodded against my chest. "I know it's not. It's just the way things turned out."

I gently held her arms and met her eyes. "Riley, you're the best thing that's ever happened to me. Don't ever doubt that. Things with your mom haven't been great and I know that sucks for you. But I'll never, ever regret it. I'll never regret having you."

Her eyes glistened with tears. "Really?"

"I promise. I'd give up everything a thousand times over for you. I don't regret anything."

She sniffed. I let go of her arms and she wiped her nose on her sleeve. It was a little gross but so endearing. Reminded me of when she was little.

"Do you have to go back to work tonight?" she asked.

"Yeah." I glanced at the time. "In about an hour."

"I was going to make mac and cheese. Do you want some?"

I brushed her hair back and kissed the top of her head. "Mac and cheese sounds awesome. I'll help."

Instead of the boxed stuff, she got out ingredients for my mom's homemade recipe. I grated the cheese while she cooked the pasta.

And despite how hard I'd been working not to, I faced reality.

Nora wasn't my girlfriend. But did I want her to be? Was

I willing to take that risk? Because, honestly, it scared the shit out of me. It was easier to push my discontent to the side and pretend all I wanted from her was sex. I'd been burned before and this time, it wasn't just my heart that was at risk. It was Riley's too.

She didn't just like Nora. She loved her. They'd bonded almost instantly and whether Nora realized it or not, she'd been fulfilling something Riley desperately needed.

Except maybe it wasn't just Riley who needed her.

I stood at the stove, stirring in the cheese, feeling like I was at a crossroads. I had a choice to make, and it wasn't just because of my daughter. This had gone too far for me to keep pretending I could do casual. That things could stay the way they were. There was too much at stake. I needed to be in or out, and when I thought about it like that, I realized it wasn't a hard choice at all.

I wanted in.

Whether Nora would agree was another story.

24

NORA

The office was quiet. I'd hit a block yesterday, trying to write an article about foreplay, so I'd decided to come in to the office this morning for a change of scenery. Whether or not it was helping was debatable. I'd written about foreplay before, more than once, and I was struggling to come up with an angle that was fresh.

Tala poked her head in with a smile. "Hey. Have a minute?"

"Sure." I closed my laptop with a sigh. "I'm not getting anywhere with this anyway."

"I hate that feeling." She sat down and crossed her legs at the ankles. Her burnt orange blouse looked great against her skin. "I don't have anything work related. I just thought I'd pop in and say hi."

"I'm glad you did. It feels like I haven't seen you in a while. What's new?"

"This shirt, for starters." She plucked at it. "I went shopping with a friend the other day. Tell me honestly. Is it too much?"

"Not at all. It makes your skin glow. Next time you might

pair it with lighter pants, though. The contrast would really make that color pop."

"Thanks. I'll try that." She tucked her long hair behind her ear. "By the way, I have to thank you again for your advice about that guy who was always on his phone. I said I wasn't going to but I went out with him again and it was more of the same. So I broke things off. Then the very next day, I met this guy at the pet store. He's kind of shy, but so cute. We've been out a few times and I think I really like him."

"That's so great. I'm happy for you."

"If I'd kept seeing what's-his-name, I wouldn't have met him. It's almost like you were a matchmaker without even trying."

"I aim to please."

"What about you? Are you seeing anyone?"

I couldn't help but smile. "Yes, and no. I'm having a hot fling with my neighbor."

"Ooh." She leaned forward and rested her chin on her hands. "Tell me more."

"At first I thought he wasn't my type. And I guess he's not. But variety is the spice of life, right?"

"What does he look like?"

"Tall, muscular, dark hair, blue eyes. And lots of tattoos." I picked up my phone and showed her a few photos.

She raised her eyebrows. "Hot."

I leaned back. "He's so hot. The attraction was immediate but we danced around it for a while. In fact, he turned me down at first."

"What was he thinking?"

I lifted one shoulder. "Who knows. Men can be so stubborn. It was easy to make him pay for it, though. I had plenty of opportunities to tease him."

"Until he finally gave in?"

"Something like that. Now it's great. He's right next door, which is so convenient. And he's, let's just say, very talented."

She pretended to fan herself. "Phew. Someone get a fan. You know, this would make an amazing article. How to have a fling with your hot neighbor. You should pitch it to April."

I opened my mouth to answer, but paused. How to have a fling with your hot neighbor wasn't a bad idea for an article. It sounded like something Nora Lakes would write. But I was reluctant and I wasn't sure why. It wouldn't have to be personal. I could leave out all traces of my fling with Dex and keep it generic.

Still, there was something about the idea that bothered me.

Before I could reply, April walked by, as if Tala had invoked her name like a summons.

"April," Tala said, twisting around in her chair. "Do you have a minute?"

"Hi, ladies," she said with a friendly smile. She was tall and thin with blond hair so light it leaned toward silver. Her beige pantsuit was tailored to her lean frame and her heels emphasized her long legs. "What can I do for you?"

"Nora has a great article idea." She turned back to me and widened her eyes, as if to say, *pitch her the idea*. "I think you should hear it."

"Great," April said. "Let's go to my office."

Tala stood, looking extremely satisfied with herself, gave me a little wave, and left.

I got up and followed April to her office, wondering what I was going to say when I got there. Irritation at Tala pricked at me. I knew she was trying to be helpful, and I hadn't had a chance to tell her I wasn't so sure about the idea. But still.

April's office was decorated with a sleek, minimalist vibe. Her desk had a marble top as did the credenza behind her. She had a few books and decorative items on a small bookshelf and modern art in gold frames on the walls.

We took our seats. She leaned back and folded her hands.

I made the decision in a split second. Crossing my legs at the ankles, I resolved to do what I did best. Own it.

Not the how to have a fling with your neighbor idea. I wasn't going to pitch yet another sex article, especially not that one. I was going to start taking back creative control of my work.

"I know we've talked a little bit about this in the past, but I'd like to expand my column beyond sex. *Living Your Best Life* used to be about all sorts of things that were of interest to women. Health, beauty, fashion, as well as sex and relationships. I feel like the hyper focus on sex is too limiting, both for me and our readers."

She paused, considering. "The problem is sex sells. Nothing else gets as many clicks. Clicks mean views and views mean advertising revenue."

"I realize that. But I think we risk my column turning stale if we don't offer our readers a better variety. Sure, maybe the sex articles will still be the driving force, but they'll keep coming back for all the other content that interests them. Besides, we both know women have interests beyond their vaginas."

Her lips turned up. "Fair point. How about this? Let's test it. Send me a list of potential ideas and we'll narrow it down. Then we'll sprinkle them in and see how readers respond."

Satisfaction bloomed inside me and I smiled. "Fabulous. Thank you, April."

I went back to my office feeling energized. My blog had been successful before it had been under Glamour Gal Media, so I knew expanding the variety of my articles could work. Women are more than their lady parts and I wanted to honor that—and entertain, inform, and inspire in the process.

The rest of the day went by in a flash as I did some cursory research and brainstorming. If I was going to truly convince April, I was going to have to nail this first non-sex article. It needed to be fun, engaging, and allow for a clicky headline.

It was almost six before I packed up my laptop and headed home. I was looking forward to a bath—thanks to a plumber, my tub was no longer leaking—and a glass of wine. I'd take a break, relax, and get back to work.

My phone buzzed with a text just before I turned onto my street. I swiped the screen to see who it was.

Dex: *Are you busy tonight?*

Bath, wine, and an orgasm? Yes, please.

I waited until I pulled into my driveway to reply.

Me: *I have some work to do but I'm flexible.*

Dex: *Will you have dinner with me?*

I hesitated, my thumbs poised over the keypad. My flight instinct was tingling. Why? Dinner with Dex wasn't anything unusual. Besides, I liked being wined and dined. Our fling had started with sex but why not let it morph into casual dating? In reality, it already had.

Telling myself I was being silly, I replied.

Me: *Sure. Anything specific in mind?*

Dex: *We could eat in. Takeout from the Thai place sound good?*

I rolled my eyes. What was I getting worked up about? He didn't even want to go out. Riley was probably at a friend's house or with her grandparents and he wanted company.

Me: *Perfect.*

Dex: *I'll order. Usual?*

Me: *Yes. I just got home so let me change. I'll be over in a bit.*

Dex: *I'll be here.*

I went inside and changed out of my work clothes into a loose V-neck t-shirt and joggers. Putting on comfortable clothes made me glad he'd suggested we stay in. It had been a long day and I was looking forward to curling up on his couch with some yellow curry.

After pulling my hair back, I slipped on a pair of sandals and went next door. Dex answered, dressed in a t-shirt and sweats. Seemed as if we'd both had the same idea.

"Hey." He kissed me. "Good to see you."

The hello kiss made my stomach tingle, my flight response flaring up again. Kissing between us was a sex thing, part of the urgency of it all. He didn't usually kiss me outside the bedroom—not unless we were on our way there.

"Is Riley home?"

"No, she's with my parents. I put our dinner order in but it'll be a bit before it gets here. I think they're busy tonight."

"That's fine, I can wait."

I thought that might be his segue into going upstairs but he didn't make a move to lead me to his bedroom. He grabbed two glasses of wine he'd already poured and took them to the couch. I followed, feeling unnaturally jumpy.

What was wrong with me? I was always in control of myself, always the one to set the rules. But somehow Dex was flipping things upside down and I didn't understand how.

"How was work?" he asked.

I settled onto the couch next to him. "It was good,

actually. I talked to April about expanding my column to cover a wider range of topics. She's finally open to the idea."

"That's awesome."

"It is. I feel good about it."

As we chatted about our days, I started to relax. I shared some of my article ideas with him and he told me about a tattoo he was designing for a new client. Riley's school year was almost over and her PE grade was back up to a B. I sipped my wine and the jittery feeling gradually melted away.

He set his empty glass on the coffee table and took a deep breath. "I need to talk to you about something."

My eyebrows lifted but I schooled my expression into stillness. "Oh?"

"Things between us have been great. Let's be honest, the sex is pretty mind-blowing."

"I won't disagree with that." My eyes flicked to his crotch. "You have quite the weapon there."

He gave me a crooked smile. "Thanks. You're not too bad yourself."

I smiled.

"Riley knows."

That surprised me. We didn't usually sleep together when she was home. "She knows what, exactly?"

"That we've been sleeping together."

I set my glass down. "I guess that was bound to happen. Is she upset?"

"Not at all. We actually had a good talk. She really likes you, so I think that makes it easier for her to accept. She brought it up so she could tell me she's cool with it and we don't have to hide."

"She's the sweetest girl."

"I know." He took a deep breath. "But talking to her about us got me thinking. About us."

I swallowed hard. "How so?"

"Yeah, the sex is great. But so is the rest of it. I like you, Nora. A lot. I've never just been attracted to your body, I'm attracted to you. So I'm just going to come out and say it. I want more with you. I want to give this a real shot."

My breath caught and my throat felt like it was closed tight. Panic made my stomach clench and my eyes darted around the room, as if I needed to find an escape route.

"Dex, I think I might have let things go too far."

"What?"

"I'm sure it's my fault. I thought I made my boundaries clear but obviously our friendship and our sexual relationship blurred together. I shouldn't have let that happen."

"So that's it? You just wanted my dick but the rest of it was bullshit?"

"I told you I wasn't looking for a relationship. And you weren't supposed to be, either."

He stood and swiped up our empty wine glasses. "Yeah, well a relationship happened, honey. Sorry to disappoint you."

I got up and put my hands on my hips as he stomped into the kitchen. "I've never been anything but honest with you."

"You're right. Get in, get fucked, get out."

"And you clearly hated every minute of it." I followed him into the kitchen. "I don't remember you complaining every time you came inside me. Or down my throat. Or wherever else you wanted to put it."

"You told me to come on your ass. I thought you liked it."

"I did like it," I yelled. "That's not the point!"

We stared at each other for a long moment. His brow was furrowed with anger, his eyes stormy.

Anger, I could take. But the hurt lurking behind it was going to break me.

I'd never wanted to hurt him.

"Dex, I—"

"Forget it. I shouldn't have brought it up. You're right, you made it very clear what this was and I was more than happy to go along with it."

I didn't know what else to say. I wanted to fix this but I couldn't give him what I didn't have.

And I didn't have it in me to be what he wanted.

"I'm sorry."

He nodded but wouldn't meet my eyes. "Me too. I'm not really hungry so I'll have the guy bring the food over to your place if you want."

"I'm not hungry either."

He didn't say another word. Just walked away. I stood still, as if I'd been frozen to the spot, listening to his footsteps on the stairs.

I squeezed my eyes shut to stop the onslaught of tears. I was not a crier, especially over a man. Not anymore.

Straightening my spine, I shoved all the hurt down— both what I felt and what I'd caused—and went home.

I PACED AROUND MY HOUSE, unable to keep still. My heart beat too fast and the mild sick feeling in my stomach persisted. Why was I such a mess? I hadn't been this unhinged since...

Since a long time ago.

I grabbed my phone but a knock on the door made me fumble it and I let it drop to the ground.

"Fuck me running," I muttered, leaving my phone where it was to answer the door.

"Hi." The guy on my doorstep held up a brown bag. "I have your order. The guy next door said it was for you. It's already paid for."

The last thing I wanted was the Thai food we should have been eating together. Damn it, Dex. We should have had a nice meal and a good fuck. What would have been so terrible about that?

"Thanks, but I actually don't want it. Why don't you take it?"

His eyes brightened. "Really?"

"Yeah, go ahead."

"I'm going to bring this to Jen."

I didn't know who Jen was but it looked like she was getting my dinner. And by the look on the delivery guy's face, probably my orgasm.

Damn it, Dex.

"Have a good night." I shut the door and went back to pick up my phone.

This called for reinforcements, although the way my night was going, my friends were probably all having hot sex with their husbands. Still, I sent a group text.

Me: *I have a problem. Are you all busy?*

Hazel: *What's wrong?*

Everly: *Are you okay?*

Sophie: *I'm here!*

Me: *You know how I've been having wild and strings-free sex with Dex? He wants to add strings.*

Sophie: *Is that bad? Sorry, I don't know why that would be bad.*

Hazel: *Nora doesn't engage in long-term, committed relationships.*

Everly: *She doesn't like strings.*

Me: *No, I don't. And I was perfectly clear about that.*

Everly: *Can you blame him, though? Of course he'd fall for you.*

Me: *Men do not fall for me. They enjoy our time together and move on.*

Hazel: *It would appear Dex isn't most men.*

That was certainly true. He wasn't most men. That was his charm. He was rough but soft, strong but gentle, with the heart of an artist in the body of a mountain man.

Everly: *What happened, exactly? Is he upset?*

Me: *He said he wanted more. But obviously I can't do that.*

Everly: *What if you could, though?*

That same sense of panic flowed through me again. Maybe panic was too strong a word. I wasn't about to go running out the door screaming in terror. But it was fear, just the same. A quiet fear. One I'd harbored for a long time.

The fear of being vulnerable again.

Me: *I'm scared.*

Hazel: *Admitting that is very brave.*

Sophie: *It really is.*

Me: *I just said I'm scared and by that I mean terrified. That's not brave.*

Everly: *Of course it is. You need courage to face this fear.*

Hazel: *And maybe it's time.*

I closed my eyes. I knew they were right. I'd just made a terrible, terrible mistake and instead of owning up to it, I'd let Dex walk away. I'd given in to my fear, let my flight instinct take over. I'd run.

Letting out a long breath, I opened my eyes. Hazel was

right. It was time I owned it. I didn't deserve Dex, but he deserved the truth.

Me: *I love you all so much.*

Everly: *We love you too!*

Sophie: *So much!*

Hazel: *You're the strongest woman I know. You can do this.*

God, they were going to make me cry. I swiped beneath my eyes, put down my phone, and went next door.

25

DEX

*T*he knock at the door made me roll my eyes. Seriously, dude, I didn't want the fucking Thai food. I'd told him to take it next door. Why the hell was he back? He could throw it in the trash for all I cared.

I opened the door, ready to give him an earful—I was not in the mood—but stopped. It wasn't the delivery guy. It was Nora.

She met my eyes without flinching, those gorgeous blues full of feeling. Why did she have to be so beautiful? This whole thing would have been so much easier if she'd just been average.

But there was absolutely nothing average about Nora Lakes.

"Can I come in? Please?"

I nodded and stepped aside, then closed the door behind her.

There was something different about her. She crossed her arms over her stomach, gripping her elbows, and there was no trace of her usual saunter.

I wanted to be mad—and I had every right to be—but

when she turned to face me, my first instinct was to scoop her into my arms and hold her.

The woman was killing me.

"I like you, too," she said with a tremor in her voice, as if admitting that scared her.

My brow furrowed. "Okay?"

"A lot. I didn't mean for that to happen, but you were right, it did."

I seriously did not understand her. "Then why tell me this was all just sex to you? That it didn't mean shit?"

"Because I'm scared."

"Of what? You don't have to be afraid of me."

"Yes, I do. You have the power to break me and I promised myself I'd never give that kind of power to a man again."

"What is this about? Is it because of your father? He cheated on your mom so now you figure that's what will happen to you?" I let out a frustrated breath. "I'm not him, Nora."

"I know you're not, and no, it's not about my father." Her shoulders slumped. "Okay, I'm sure he's part of why I am the way that I am. But that's not the problem."

"Then what is?"

She hesitated, as if she needed to work up the courage to speak. "I had a relationship with a married man."

I gaped at her. "What?"

"I swear to you, I didn't know. Please believe me. I would have never, ever been with him if I'd known. I was young and stupid and I should have figured it out, but I didn't. I own my part in it, but please don't think I'm a home-wrecker."

"Okay."

"I was twenty-two, just out of college. I took a job at an

advertising agency in Seattle and he worked in the same building. He was older than me, already in his thirties, and he swept me off my feet. He seemed so dashing and mature, the kind of man who makes you feel like you're the only one in the room." She shook her head. "I was so naïve."

I took her hand and led her to the couch. It seemed like we should be sitting for this. I didn't say anything. Just waited for her to continue.

"I fell head over heels in love with him, the way you only can when you're young and stupid. I thought he loved me, too. He said it all the time, showered me with attention and affection. He even bought me a ring, Dex. I thought he was going to marry me.

"I walked around with that damn ring on my finger for six months. I told my family, my friends took me dress shopping. He didn't seem to want to set a date but I didn't notice that or any of the other giant red flags waving in my face.

"I should have realized it all sooner. We never went to his place. Ever. He said he liked my apartment better. He almost never took me out to dinner unless we were out of town and when he did, it was always somewhere outside the city. He met my friends, hell, he even met my mom. But I never met anyone in his life. Not even his co-workers."

"How did you find out?"

"His wife." Tears glistened in her eyes and she looked away. "She suspected he was cheating so she hired a private investigator. She knew everything about me. My name, where I lived, where I worked. She confronted me in the lobby of the building where we both worked. She had photos of me with him. Dozens of them."

"Oh my god."

"I had no idea what she was talking about. But obviously she had no reason to believe me. She just started screaming at me and threw the photos in my face. It was the most humiliating moment of my life."

"That must have been awful."

"So awful. I'm ashamed to admit, it took me a long time to recover. I quit my job and even moved to a different apartment. I always felt like someone was watching me, waiting for me to wreck another marriage."

Whoever this guy was, I really hated him. "That was his fault, not yours. Surely his wife figured that out."

"I don't know what happened to them. I hope she left him. I did find out they didn't have kids, which was a relief. That would have been so much worse. I also wasn't the only woman he had on the side."

"To the surprise of no one, fucking douchebag."

That made her crack the barest hint of a smile.

"I didn't date again for a long time—a couple of years. I was too afraid of being played the fool. So when I did decide to date, I created a set of rules for myself. For starters, I'd do everything I could to find out who he was. I wasn't making that mistake again. And I'd keep it casual. I'd thought I was in love once and it had turned me into an idiot. I wasn't making that mistake again, either."

"But why always casual? You have to realize not every guy is going to play you like that."

"I know. But I didn't want to take the risk. It wasn't just that he was married or the trauma of the way I found out. I really believed I was in love. Deeply in love. And it made me completely blind. I thought I'd side stepped all the drama my mother put herself through with her marriages. I thought I'd found someone who was utterly unlike my father." She closed her eyes for a moment. "It turned out, he was exactly like him. And I didn't see it."

I reached over and took her hand. "So you went after

men who wouldn't ever put your heart at risk. Men who didn't want commitment or marriage."

"Yes."

"And I broke your rules."

Her eyes lifted to meet mine. "All except one."

It was my turn to crack a smile. "Yeah, I'm definitely not married. Look, I don't want to downplay what you went through. That's awful. But I'm not him. You can't punish me for the sins of some asshole with a god complex who couldn't keep his dick in his pants."

"That's why I came back." She squeezed my hand. "I'm sorry."

"You're making it really hard to stay mad at you."

"No, be mad at me. You should be mad."

I shifted closer. "How about I tell you to leave and then you get up and storm out. But you don't cry until you get home. Then you throw yourself face down on the bed and sob."

She stifled a laugh. "Oh, please. I'd at least down a shot of tequila before the sobbing began."

"Then what happens?"

"You realize you shouldn't have sent me away. That I meant my apology and risked a lot to be vulnerable with you. In your anger at yourself, you throw your phone against the wall and it breaks."

"Good one."

"It's rather cliché."

"Yeah, but I like it. Then I come after you and bang on your door. Obviously it's pouring down rain and I'm soaked."

"The rain is required."

"You come down and open the door for me and I'm standing there like a forlorn little puppy, dripping wet and sad."

"And I step out into the rain and I'm instantly as drenched as you."

"Is this from a movie we've both seen, because this is great."

She groaned. "No, it's not. It's awful. So cheesy."

I touched her cheek. "We're standing in the rain, both drenched. I cup your face and kiss you until you swoon."

"Swoon? Please."

"Oh yeah, you swoon and I catch you." I brushed her lips with a kiss.

"That's the worst."

"It's romantic. What's wrong with a big romantic gesture?"

"Big romantic gestures are overrated. Too easy to fake. Mess up my hair and ruin my lipstick instead."

I pulled her into my lap so she was straddling me. "That I can do. But first, you have to admit it."

"Admit what?"

"That we're in a relationship."

Her little grin was so sexy. "Fine. We're in a relationship."

"Good girl." I kissed her again. "Although we still have a problem."

"What's that?"

"I'm starving. Please tell me you have the Thai food over at your place."

"No, the delivery guy is probably already sharing it with someone named Jen."

I leaned my head back against the couch cushion. "Damn."

She draped her arms around my shoulders. "I'm sure I

have something I can throw together. Do you want to come over?"

"Sure, but only for dinner. No sex."

"Why not sex?"

"I'm kidding, I definitely want sex. But food first."

She leaned in and kissed me. I grabbed her ass and rubbed her against my erection. I really did want food first, but she was right there, and we were at risk of getting a bit too romantic.

Couldn't have that. Had to keep things a little dirty.

We went next door and put together a meal. I didn't even miss our Thai food. Afterward, I took her upstairs, and for the first time, we didn't fuck like animals. We made love.

Okay, we made love like animals. There was a very hot blowjob and spanking involved. Again, we couldn't let things get too romantic. It wasn't our style.

But this time, we didn't get dressed and go our separate ways. I pulled her back into bed and tucked her warm body against me.

And for the first time in ages, I slept like a fucking baby.

26

DEX

*S*leep retreated slowly. Only half awake, my eyes still closed, I reached for Nora. I hooked my arm around her waist and pulled her against me. She stirred, making a soft noise, then relaxed again. I breathed her in, enjoying her scent and the feel of her body.

I'd slept all night. Again. After years of insomnia, I seemed to have found the only thing that worked. Her. Every time we spent the night together, I fell asleep easily and didn't wake up until morning.

The woman was magic.

After a few minutes, she stirred again. "Morning."

I kissed her shoulder. "Morning."

"Is it Saturday?"

"Yeah."

She nestled her ass into my groin, making me groan. "Good."

I had to work, but not until later, so I kept kissing her neck and shoulder. We both needed to use the bathroom first, so we untangled before things got too heated. Then I pulled her back into bed.

We came together without any rush, our movements slow and indulgent. And quiet. Although Riley would probably sleep until noon, we didn't want to risk her hearing things she shouldn't. So we kissed and caressed, enjoying each other in a warm, intimate dance.

There were times for making love and times for fucking. We had room for both.

The rest of our morning was spent lingering over coffee. Then Nora went home—she had plans with her friends this afternoon—and I got dressed and went in to work.

My first appointment was a consultation with a new client, a woman named Brianne. I met her in the lobby and took her back to my station to chat.

She was mid-thirties, if I had to guess. Pretty with brown hair and dark eyes. She wore a hoodie and cropped jeans and had a wedding ring on her finger. I had her sit in the chair while I straddled my stool.

"Let's talk about your tattoo," I said. "What are you thinking?"

"To get straight to the point, a few years ago, I was diagnosed with breast cancer. It meant a double mastectomy." She glanced down at her chest. "I've undergone reconstruction, so I have boobs again, which I'm happy about. They actually turned out really nice. Anyway, I've been thinking about this for a long time and I want a mastectomy tattoo."

I smiled, the possibilities already coming to me like sparks of creative excitement. "I love that. I've done quite a few mastectomy tattoos and honestly, they're my absolute favorite."

"Really? When I called to ask about it, they were emphatic that I needed to see you."

"Absolutely. There's nothing better than celebrating triumph and survival with an amazing piece of art."

She tucked her hair behind her ear with a smile. "Okay, now I'm really excited."

"Do you have any ideas for what you want it to look like?"

"Kind of? I was hoping you could help with that. I just know I don't want it to cover my whole chest or anything. That's not really me. I'm thinking something a little more subtle."

"Do you have any other tattoos?"

"No, this will be my first."

I nodded, considering. After asking her a few more questions about her style, her likes and dislikes, and showing her samples, I had some ideas. I told her I'd get to work on a few designs and we could make changes from there, then sent her up to see Kari to book her next appointment.

Since I had some time before my next client, I went back to my office to take care of a few things and start sketching. I wanted something that would capture Brianne's journey and honor her warrior spirit.

I was really excited about this.

My phone rang. It was my sister, Angie.

"Hey, Ang. What's up?"

"Um, excuse me? You know what's up."

"No, I don't. What are you talking about?"

"I just talked to Maggie."

"Yeah, and?"

"She said you're dating Nora."

I didn't understand why she sounded mad. "So? I thought you liked her."

"I do like her. In fact, she made me the tiniest bit confused about my sexuality for a few minutes. Seriously, she's basically a goddess."

"Okay, so what's the problem?"

"When were you planning on telling us?"

"What do you mean? Was I supposed to make an announcement? Change my relationship status on our family group text?"

"Yes, you're supposed to make an announcement. You're such a guy. You haven't dated anyone in forever and now you're dating the most beautiful woman I've ever seen in person."

I grinned in smug self-satisfaction. "She really is, isn't she?"

"What's she doing with you? Are you sure she's not just slumming it a little?"

"Thanks, Ang. You're a great sister."

She laughed. "I'm teasing. But I shouldn't have had to hear through the grapevine that you're finally in a relationship."

"Sorry. I wasn't keeping it from you on purpose."

"What does Riley think?"

"She thinks it's great. She loved Nora already, so that makes a huge difference."

"Oh my gosh, I love this so much. I don't want to put any pressure on you, but I'm really rooting for this to work out. So is Maggie."

"Thanks."

"Speaking of Maggie, is there any way we can get her to stop talking about her new and improved sex life?"

"She's telling you too?"

She groaned. "All the time. I'm happy for her but I don't need that level of detail. It's getting weird."

"Thankfully I'm not getting detail. Tell her to call Tori. They can talk sex all day long."

"I'll try that angle. Or maybe we should just bring it up

in front of Mom and let the whole situation take care of itself naturally."

"Careful. That could easily backfire."

"You're right. Mom is way too willing to talk about sex. Speaking of, you better call her."

I winced. I did need to call my mom. She was going to be just as pissed off as Angie, if not more, that I hadn't made a formal relationship announcement yet.

"I will. Look, I'm trying to ease Nora into this. I don't need Mom casually leaving wedding magazines on my coffee table."

"That's fair. Here's the plan. Tell Mom. Then I'll have Dallas call her and talk her out of whatever scheme she concocts to try to influence your wedding and baby plans. He can get Dad involved if necessary."

That was a good idea. Mom seemed to listen to Dallas more than the rest of us. No wonder he was such a good lawyer.

"Perfect. I'll call her in a bit."

"Awesome." Her voice got quiet, like she was talking away from the phone. "Get off the table and why aren't you wearing pants?"

I grinned. Her kids were hilarious.

"Gotta go," she said. "Love you."

"Love you, too."

I went back to my sketchbook, finishing the first preliminary design concept. It wasn't bad but I'd need to spend some more time on it.

Kari poked her head in. Her red hair was up in a thick, curly ponytail and her piercings glinted in the light.

"What's up?"

"There's a group of guys out here asking for you."

That was weird. I didn't have any appointments. "Group of guys? Who are they?"

"They said they know Nora and they want to talk to you. I was going to tell them they need to make an appointment, but the one guy was oddly persuasive. He kind of scared me but also turned me on a little bit."

My brow furrowed. "I guess I'll come see what they want."

"Yeah, I think you should."

I wondered what this was about. Three guys who knew Nora? Who were they? Her father lived overseas, so it didn't seem likely it was him. She'd mentioned a half-brother, but if he was one of them, who were the other two?

Three men stood in the lobby. One waited with his arms crossed, a dark expression on his face. He had the polished air of wealth and wore a button-down shirt and slacks.

The second was busy looking at the piercing jewelry in the glass case. He adjusted a pair of black-rimmed glasses and in contrast to the first guy, his shirt was partially untucked.

The third was also dressed in a button-down and slacks, but his sleeves were cuffed and he stood with an air of casual confidence. He glanced around with an amused half-smile on his face.

Who the hell were they?

"Hey." I approached with a degree of caution, especially because the first guy looked like he might suddenly grow horns. "I'm Dex St. James. What can I do for you?"

"Shepherd Calloway." The angry looking one stepped forward and shook my hand in a firm grip. "This is Corban Nash and Camden Cox."

I shook Corban's hand. "Nice to meet you."

"You can call me Cox," the third one said in a slight Texas drawl as he offered me his hand. "Good to meet you."

"Is there somewhere we can talk?" Shepherd asked.

"We won't take too much of your time," Corban said. "But it's important."

Cox just grinned, like he was enjoying himself.

This was so weird.

"Sure." I gestured to the back of the shop. "My office is this way."

They followed me into my office and I shut the door. There wasn't a lot of space, and not enough seats, but that didn't seem to bother them. Cox took one of the chairs, making himself comfortable. Shepherd and Corban remained standing.

I sat at my desk. "What's this about? Did you say you know Nora?"

"She's one of my wife's best friends," Shepherd said.

"Mine, too," Corban said.

Cox raised his hand. "Same here, my friend."

This was starting to make slightly more sense. At least I knew who they were. Nora talked a lot about Everly, Hazel, and Sophie, although I had yet to meet them.

But what were their husbands doing here?

"It's come to our attention that you're in a relationship with Nora," Shepherd said. His low voice was almost monotone but there was an undercurrent of threat.

"Can you tell me something?" Corban asked.

A flicker of annoyance flashed across Shepherd's face.

Corban didn't wait for me to answer. "How did you get through Nora's defenses? I always knew Shep was locked up tighter than Fort Knox, but Nora has such an elaborate system of emotional protection. I'm fascinated to know how you got through it."

"Did he?" Cox asked.

Corban pushed his glasses up his nose. "What do you mean?"

"Did he get through all that emotional protection or is he still on the outside?"

"He must have. This is Nora we're talking about."

"Fair point."

They all nodded in agreement.

Strangely, I understood what Corban was getting at. "She tried to keep me out but I guess I was keeping her out, too. Although I don't know why any of this is your business."

"She's just such an interesting case of avoidant attachment," Corban said. "You see that more often in men than in women. And Nora really has her own spin on it."

Shepherd held up a hand. "Okay, Nash."

"Yeah, careful," Cox said. "Once Corban gets going on a topic, he'll tell you everything you never wanted to know. Don't ask him about lobsters."

"Lobsters?" I asked.

"Or penguins." Cox grinned again.

"The animal world has a lot to teach us about human behavior," Corban said, as if that were the most obvious thing in the world.

"Focus," Shepherd said. "Here's what you need to know. Nora is one of the most important people in my wife's life. That makes her one of the most important people in my life. And I will not tolerate anyone hurting her."

"Exactly," Corban said.

Cox raised his hand again. "Same, here."

I eyed them like they were all crazy. "You guys are kidding, right? This is a joke."

"Nope," Corban said. "Don't worry, I got the same speech. You're doing great."

"Same, again," Cox said, looking more amused than ever. He turned to Corban. "You're right, it is fun being on the other end of it."

"I told you."

"You really came down here to tell me not to hurt Nora?"

Corban and Cox nodded.

"If you do, I'll do everything in my power to ruin your life," Shepherd said.

The emotionless way he delivered that line sent a chill down my spine.

"This is crazy. You realize that, right? You're like a bunch of overprotective brothers."

"I had a feeling you'd catch on," Cox said. "And don't be fooled. Shepherd isn't kidding. He really will destroy your life. So my advice? Don't hurt Nora."

I kind of wanted to be offended at this display. They didn't know me. They didn't know how I felt about Nora or how she felt about me. Who did these guys think they were?

Then it hit me. They were her family.

All too often, I took mine for granted. My parents, who were still happily married. My siblings with their own crazy families, and continued insistence on being involved—sometimes too much—in each other's lives.

Nora didn't have that. She probably never had.

So she'd created it.

She'd told me plainly that she loved her friends more than anything. And faced with their husbands, who clearly cared about her deeply, I realized I was finally getting a window into another part of her life. Her family.

"You guys don't have to worry. I care about her. A lot. She's the one who balked when I said the word relationship. But we figured it out."

"I like him," Cox said, his amused grin never leaving his

face. "When he first came out, I thought we must have the wrong guy. But I get it."

"You liking him has nothing to do with it," Shepherd said.

"No, it does. He looks a little intimidating with all the tattoos and whatnot." Cox turned back to me. "And I certainly wouldn't have picked you out of a lineup for our Nora. She has pretty specific taste. But I'd say that makes you more likely to be right for her. The last thing she needs is another suit who just wants her for the temporary arm candy."

"That's a good point," Corban said. "Trust me, the fact that we're here is a significant development."

That was interesting. "You guys don't show up to threaten every guy she dates?"

"We don't show up to threaten any of them," Cox said. "Apparently you're special."

"The responsibility is yours," Shepherd said. "If she gets hurt, I'm blaming you."

I smiled again. "That sounds like a challenge."

"It's a threat."

"Okay, I get it. Like I said, you have nothing to worry about."

Cox stood and shook my hand again. "Dex, it's been a pleasure."

"Thanks. I think."

Corban shook my hand. "If you need any reference material on avoidant attachment, let me know. It might help."

"Um, thanks."

Shepherd didn't shake my hand again. He just shot me a cold glare and followed the other two out the door.

That had been interesting.

I wasn't mad that they'd come, not even that they'd threatened me. It made me feel good for Nora that she had good people in her life who cared about her enough to look out for her like brothers.

Hell, I even puffed out my chest a bit that I was the first guy they'd bothered to threaten like that.

Damn right.

27

NORA

*D*ex jogged alongside me, his breathing steady. The afternoon air was mild and the remnants of last night's rain pooled in easy-to-avoid puddles along the sidewalk and in low spots on the street. Birds chirped in the trees overhead and the pleasant suburban quiet surrounded us.

We turned onto our street and slowed to a walk.

"I told you I'd make a runner out of you," I said, nudging him with my elbow.

"I'm only in it for the view." He leaned back to look at my backside, then smacked it. "Worth it."

"Careful, big guy, you know how I feel about spanking."

He growled a little. "My dirty girl. You love it."

I shot him a wicked grin. "I really do. But later."

He smacked my ass again, then grabbed it for good measure. "What are we going to do when Riley's home for the summer?"

"We'll just have to be quieter. Or make sure she has plenty of sleepovers with Grandma."

"Good call."

"By the way, I met a few friends of yours yesterday."

"Really? Who?"

"Shepherd, Corban, and Cox."

I stopped. "Where did you meet those three?"

"My shop."

"Why were they at your shop? Don't tell me Corban and Hazel are getting matching penguin tattoos."

"No, they weren't there for tattoos. They were hoping to intimidate me."

I gaped at him, baffled. "What?"

He slid a hand around my waist and drew me closer. "They wanted to make sure I knew they'd ruin my life if I hurt you."

"Oh my god. They didn't."

"They did. It was pretty impressive, actually."

"I'm so sorry."

"Don't be." He kissed my forehead. "They care about you. I respect that."

"They've never done anything like that before."

"They told me that, too." He puffed his chest out a little. "Seems that I'm special, since I warranted a visit from the husband gang."

"Don't let it go to your head."

"Speaking of your friends." He took my hand again and we started up his driveway. "Can I meet them?"

"Of course."

"Can I meet them soon?"

"Sure, I'll invite them over. That reminds me, how do you feel about tuxes?"

"They're to be avoided at all costs." He eyed me with suspicion. "Why?"

"I have an event coming up. Black tie." I traced a finger down the center of his chest. "Will you be my date?"

He groaned. "What's the event?"

"Will that change your answer?"

"Probably not but I still want to know."

"Everly runs a charitable foundation. It's a black-tie casino night. It'll be fun."

He shook his head, like he couldn't believe I was talking him into this. "Of course I'll go. But if it involves a tux, I doubt it'll be fun."

I popped up on my tiptoes and kissed him. "You're going to look delicious."

We went inside and as soon as he'd shut the door behind us, Riley came running down the stairs.

"Hey, Dad?"

"Hi, kiddo."

"Um..." She stopped at the bottom of the stairs and fiddled with her hands. Her hair was in a thick French braid that I'd done for her earlier and she was wearing her favorite unicorn t-shirt and jeans. "Mom called."

The tension in the room rose. Dex stiffened, although I could almost feel him trying to hide any reaction.

My stomach dropped.

"Oh yeah?" Dex said carefully. "What did she want?"

"She wants to see me."

"When?"

"Tonight. For dinner."

Dex took a deep breath. "Do you want to see her?"

Riley nodded. "Yeah. I can see her."

"Are you sure?"

"Yeah, it's fine. I haven't seen her in a while, so I might as well, since she's free."

"Okay," he said. "If you want to, it's okay with me."

"She said she'll be here at six to pick me up. I'll text her back and let her know I can go." Riley turned and ran back up the stairs to her room.

I felt slightly awkward, like I'd just witnessed something very private. Dex didn't say anything, just stalked into the kitchen. I could feel the anger snapping off him like bolts of electricity.

Not sure what else to do, I followed him.

"She better fucking show." He slammed a cupboard door.

"Is that usually a problem?" I asked, my voice gentle.

"Sometimes."

I wanted to offer him something—comfort, reassurance, anything. But this situation wasn't my area, nor was it my business. I didn't know the first thing about dealing with an ex who was a sometimes-parent.

"Nora," Riley called from upstairs. "Can you come help me decide what to wear?"

I met Dex's eyes, looking for his guidance. Was this okay? I didn't want to intrude on a delicate family situation.

"It's fine," he said.

I went upstairs and for the first time, I felt out of my element with Riley. Helping her choose an outfit for the dance had been fun. And giving her advice on dealing with the social minefield that was middle school had come easily.

But when it came to this, I didn't know my role. Was I the lady next door? The mentor, willing to give fashion and friend advice? Or the woman who was now dating her father? Someone who spent more time with her—a lot more time—than her biological mother.

The reality of where I found myself hit me like too many shots of cheap tequila, making my legs wobble and my head spin.

I was dating a single dad. Which meant I was volunteering for a role that wasn't quite a mother, but was something a little bit like it. And now I was about to take center stage, charged with a part for which I'd never rehearsed.

Own it, Nora.

With a deep breath, I went into Riley's room. "Hi, sweetie."

She stood in the middle of her bedroom with her hands on her hips, surrounded by discarded clothing. "I have no idea what to wear."

One glance and had a feeling I knew where Riley's outfit anxiety was coming from. She wanted to impress her mom.

It broke my heart.

"I think the best outfit is one that makes you feel great," I said. "If you feel like a million dollars, you'll look like a million dollars. So let's narrow this down to your favorite pieces and we can go from there."

"Hmm." She looked around at the mess, then grabbed a shirt. "This one is cute."

"Good start. What else?"

She nibbled on her bottom lip as she sorted through her clothes. After picking up a few more items off the floor and bed, and digging through her closet, she laid out a selection of tops and bottoms.

"This is perfect, honey. Out of these, which top makes you feel the best? Which is the most Riley?"

She reached for a purple shirt I'd seen her wear before. Her instinct was spot on, it was very her. Cute and colorful without being loud, and it made her eyes pop.

But she put it down and went back to her closet. When she came out, she had a blue dress on a hanger. "I think I'll wear this."

I narrowed my eyes. There was nothing wrong with the dress. It was cute, the cut modern enough not to look childish but modest enough to be perfect for a thirteen-year-old.

The problem was, it wasn't her.

"Are you sure?" I asked.

"I think so. Why? Don't you like it? You wear dresses all the time."

I did wear dresses a lot. I loved the flirty femininity of them. "I do. And it's a nice dress. I like the color. I'm just a little bit surprised you'd choose it for tonight. When you grabbed the purple shirt, I was thinking that was perfect. Pair it with your distressed skinny jeans and those sandals we talked your dad into buying for you. It would be very cute and very Riley."

"Yeah." Still holding up the dress, she glanced at the purple shirt. "My mom likes me in dresses, though."

"I see. Well, the sandals will look nice with that, too."

She nodded again and smiled, her eyes so hopeful. "Will they?"

"They will. You'll look lovely."

"Thanks, Nora." She dropped the dress onto the bed and gave me a hug. "I should hurry. It's almost six."

I stepped around the discarded clothes. "Let me know if you need help with your hair."

"I'm going to leave it in the braid. But thanks."

At least she wasn't worried about what her mom thought of her hair.

Discontent ate at me as I went downstairs. Dex was in the living room drinking a beer. I hadn't seen him look this closed off since we'd first met. He glared at nothing, his eyes staring straight ahead, and he tapped his free hand on his knee.

"Is it going to be a problem if I'm here?" I asked.

He broke his gaze and looked at me, his eyes softening.

"No, it's fine. I'm sorry, Brooklyn just gets to me. I always second guess whether I should let Riley see her or just cut her off completely. Riley wants to see her, so how can I say no? Brooklyn is her mom and sometimes they have a good visit. But when it doesn't go well, Riley is so disappointed."

I got on the couch next to him and caressed his arm. "She seems to really want her mom to accept her. She picked a dress to wear because that's what she thinks her mom likes."

"See, that's what I mean. I hate that. If Riley wants to wear a dress, she can wear a dress, but not to make her mom like her."

"Should I have talked her into something else? I wanted to push back a little and tell her to wear what makes her feel good. But I wasn't sure if I should."

"It's okay. It's not about the dress. And that's the thing, it's something Riley is going to have to learn for herself eventually. She has to decide to be herself no matter what her mom says. Or doesn't say."

"I have to be honest, I had no idea parenting was so complicated. I should have. You're raising a small human and they come out not knowing anything. But this must be a lot."

"It is and it only gets more complicated as they get older." He checked the time. "She's going to be late. I just know it."

Riley came down the stairs wearing the blue dress and sandals. She'd put on a little makeup, like I'd taught her, and her lips were shiny with gloss.

"Do I look okay?" she asked.

Dex didn't miss a beat. "You look beautiful."

Her smile lit up her whole face. "Thanks, Dad."

She sat on the bottom stair and, resting her elbows on her knees, put her chin in her hands.

Minutes ticked by, painfully slow. Dex sipped his beer, the angry tension in his body increasing. Riley's expression went from hopeful to worried.

She got up and went upstairs. Dex didn't say anything. I waited on the couch next to him, trying not to watch the clock. Brooklyn was late.

Riley came back. Avoiding our eyes, she went into the kitchen. I didn't know what she was doing, but I suspected she was trying to fill the time and distract herself while she waited for her mom.

"How late is she usually?" I whispered.

"Depends." He cursed under his breath. "As long as she shows."

By six-thirty there was no sign of her. Riley was still in the kitchen. Dex rose from the couch, put down his beer bottle, and took out his phone. I stayed where I was while he stepped aside, closer to the front door, and made a call.

"What's going on?" he asked, his voice quiet. "Everything okay?"

He was silent for a long moment, listening.

"Then why did you call her?"

Riley appeared in the kitchen doorway. She wrung her hands together, watching her dad.

Dex braced himself with one hand on the front door, his back to his daughter. "You realize this isn't okay, right? You do get that?" He was quiet again. "No, that's bullshit. She's all dressed up waiting for you."

"Dad, it's fine," Riley whispered.

"No, you need to get your ass over here and take your daughter to dinner." He stopped and blew out a breath. "Fine. I'll tell her."

He ended the call but didn't turn around. Just lowered his phone and held himself against the door while he took slow breaths.

"She's not coming," Riley said.

"No." He turned. "Baby, I'm sorry. Something came up."

Surprisingly, Riley's eyes didn't fill with tears. Her features hardened and her jaw hitched.

She looked just like Dex when he was mad.

"That's okay." Her voice was oddly robotic. "I don't care."

I had a feeling she was on the verge of spinning around, running upstairs, and slamming her door. She was going to be hurt no matter what I did, or didn't do, but maybe Dex and I could ease the sting.

"Let's go out," I said, my voice decisive as I stood. "The three of us. I know it's not the same and it doesn't make this okay. But look at you. We can't waste this on a night in."

Riley's expression softened. "Should I wear this?"

I stepped closer and took her hands. "Honey, wear whatever you want. We'll go to that place that serves mocktails in martini glasses. Only my drink will be a real martini." I winked.

She smiled and my heart just about burst. "I'll be right back."

I let out a breath and turned to Dex. He gazed at me, a look of awe on his face.

"Thank you," he said. "I would have totally screwed that up and she'd be upstairs crying right now."

"Tears are probably inevitable, even with a strawberry lemonade mocktail. That kind of rejection isn't easy to bear."

"No, it's not." He came closer and drew me against him, wrapping his thick arms around me. "But this helps. You help."

Now I was on the verge of tears. I swallowed them back and slid my arms around his waist.

Riley came bounding down the stairs in the purple shirt, jeans, and sandals. She'd added a necklace of white and lavender beads that was the perfect complement to the outfit—and it was all very Riley.

I was so proud of her.

"I'm ready," she said.

I looked down at myself, realizing for the first time that I was still in my running clothes. "I should probably change. Give me ten minutes."

"You can get ready in ten minutes?" Dex asked. He clearly didn't believe me.

"Honey, I'm full of surprises."

He grinned at me with a look that did awful things to my heart. I gave him a quick kiss before going next door, full of a shocking truth I couldn't yet speak.

I was maybe, possibly, a little bit in love with that man.

28

DEX

*B*rianne didn't look the least bit nervous as I led her back to my station for her tattoo appointment. Her energy was relaxed and she had a smile on her face. She had her hair up and wore a black tank top and jeans. She'd brought her husband, a guy named Matt, and I liked him immediately. He looked at her with so much pride, as if to say, hell yes, my girl survived.

I got her situated on the chair and pulled a curtain to give us more privacy. Matt sat next to her, ready to hold her hand and offer comfort if she needed it.

"I have three different designs for you," I said. "Keep in mind, these are starting places. I can make any changes you want, combine elements you like, whatever you need. We won't start until you're one hundred percent happy. I blocked out the rest of my day for you, so we can take as much time as we need."

"Awesome, thank you so much," Brianne said.

I brought out the designs I'd created for her. One was floral, which was a common choice for mastectomy tattoos. The second looked like feathers blowing in the wind.

But the third was my favorite.

On one breast, the outline of a bird in flight, stylized, the lines delicate rather than heavy. It trailed flames and on the other breast, ashes with the remnants of the bird's fiery flight. A phoenix, rising from the ashes.

As much as I wanted to do the phoenix on her, I wasn't about to push. I let her look through the sketches and confer with her husband while I waited.

"This one," she said, pointing to the phoenix. "I never would have thought to ask for this, but it couldn't be more perfect."

"This is so her," Matt said. "I don't know how you captured her so perfectly after meeting her once, but you nailed it."

I grinned. "I was hoping you'd pick this one."

We went over the details of the design, making small changes until it was perfect. Then I got to work prepping everything I needed. I transferred the design onto transfer paper that would create a stencil on her skin and got the rest of my station ready.

"Okay, Brianne, we're getting close to the moment of truth. I'll have you take off your shirt for me so we can get the placement right."

She discarded her tank top and bra and handed them to Matt. Objectively speaking, her breast reconstruction did look great. Very natural.

"Your surgeon did a good job," I said.

"Oh my gosh, Dr. Reid was the best," Brianne said. "I thought he was kind of a jerk at first, but he grew on me."

"Dr. Weston Reid?" I asked.

"Yeah, that's him."

"Small world. I know him. Kind of. I went to school with

his sister-in-law, Mia. I ran into their family not long ago. Nice people."

"That's so crazy. Small world, indeed."

I transferred the stencil onto her skin and had her check the placement in the mirror. She was happy with it, so it was time to get to work.

My tattoo machine buzzed in my hand as the design took shape. I started with the outline, working first in black. Brianne barely flinched, even when I worked on areas that might have been more sensitive. She was definitely tough.

Matt chatted with her while I worked. I felt myself sinking into the zone, my focus sharp. The phoenix came to life, just like I'd seen it in my mind. Delicate black lines accented by areas of shading. Then the fire. Flares of orange and red, sparks trailing behind. It had movement and depth without overwhelming her body. It told a story without being the story. Tragedy and fear burned away to ash on the flames of her survival.

Hours went by in a blink, almost as if I was in a trance. I studied my work, checking for the smallest details. I made a few adjustments, filled in areas that needed more ink. Then it was finished.

Matt helped her up so she could see herself in the mirror. She stood still for a long moment, looking at her freshly inked skin. Tears sprang to her eyes.

"It's perfect," she said, her voice barely above a whisper. Her husband beamed at her.

I waited, giving them a moment. Then I got her properly wrapped and went over all the aftercare instructions. They left and I felt a buzz of satisfaction. There was nothing like creating something beautiful, a piece of art that would travel with a person throughout their entire life journey. And a client like Brianne, who'd overcome so much, was particularly special.

Kari helped me clean up my station. Then I said goodnight to everyone and left. Nora's friends were coming over tonight so I could finally meet them and I was glad I had a bit of time in between. Physically, I felt great. Thanks to Nora, I'd actually slept last night. But mentally, I was spent. I was happy for a bit of a break.

I was about halfway home when my phone rang. My mom.

"Hey, Mom."

"Hi, honey. How was your day?"

"Great, actually. I just did an incredible mastectomy tattoo. It turned out amazing."

"That's lovely. What a beautiful gift."

"Yeah, tattoos like that are really fulfilling."

"How's Riley? Is she holding up okay?"

I'd told my mom about Brooklyn's latest stunt. I still couldn't believe she'd called Riley and bailed on her an hour later. "She's been quiet about it. I'm hoping the fun stuff they're doing at school for the end of the year will take her mind off it."

"I'll hold my tongue, but you know how I feel."

"You're preaching to the choir. I'm furious. I'm just glad Nora was there. It was probably awkward for her but she did a lot to make Riley feel better."

"Are things getting serious?"

"With Nora?" I hesitated. Were things getting serious? "I don't know, Mom. Things are good. I don't want to jinx it."

"Don't be silly. You're not going to jinx your relationship."

"No, but I don't want to set expectations that are too

high. Don't get me wrong, she's amazing and Riley loves her."

"But?"

"But I don't know where it's going." I didn't want to explain that I already knew how Nora felt about words like *forever* and *marriage*. They weren't for her. "We haven't had that conversation, so let's just leave it at that."

"Fair enough. I don't mean to pry."

"Yes, you do."

"Fine, I do. But I'm your mother. I love you."

Prior to having Riley, especially prior to her entering adolescence, I wouldn't have understood that. But now that my own daughter was developing a life of her own, I had a similar urge to dig into what was going on with her—because I loved her.

"I know, Mom. I love you too."

We said goodbye and she ended the call. I shifted, stretching my back a little. It had gotten stiff while I'd been working. Like my reading glasses, it was an irritating reminder that I wasn't twenty-five anymore.

As much as I wanted to ignore my mom's question—were things getting serious—it had been on my mind. I wanted to be okay with where things were with Nora. We hadn't even been together that long, so why was I unsettled?

I knew the answer. I just didn't want to think about it too hard. Because I had a feeling I could already see where things were going.

Since becoming a father, I'd avoided casual relationships —casual sex. There had been times when a no-strings outlet would have been nice. And there had been a few women who would have been happy to have that arrangement with me. But I hadn't gone there. Partly because of Riley, and partly because, at the end of the day, that wasn't what I really wanted.

I understood why Nora avoided commitment. Being played by that douchebag had hurt her deeply. Her father had, too. But I wasn't sure where that left us. Sure, we'd gone from casual to something more.

But where did that road lead for her? Was she open to a deeper commitment or was she just along for the ride while it lasted?

The problem was, now that she was in our life, I didn't know what Riley and I would do without her.

Nora wasn't Brooklyn. Not even close. But I didn't know if she was interested in what we had to offer long term. If forever was even an option.

I pulled into my driveway and pushed all that aside. It wasn't the time for it. I had to be on my game tonight. I had a feeling the husband gang was going to bust my balls.

IF YOU'D ASKED me what I thought Nora's friends would be like, I probably would have assumed they were a lot like her. Women I'd dated in the past seemed to have groups of friends who had more in common than not—how they dressed, how they spent their time. Some of them had even looked alike. I wouldn't have expected a bunch of Nora clones, but I still didn't see this group coming.

Everly Calloway—pretty, blond, and all smiles. She had a lightness to her presence that was in stark contrast to her serious husband, Shepherd. I could see why Nora liked her. She was friendly and pleasant and her daughter was equally so. Little Ella Calloway made me miss Riley's toddler years.

Then there was Hazel Nash. If there was anyone who

was Nora's opposite, it was Hazel. Whereas Nora was fluid and graceful, Hazel had a nerdy awkwardness to her. She fiddled with her glasses and quoted studies and statistics in the course of normal conversation. The other girls just went with it, clearly used to her quirks. And her husband, Corban, had a similar intellectual vibe. Smart guy, kinda weird. I liked him.

And Sophie Cox. That sweet thing was a hot mess on wheels. She had curly hair and a contagious laugh, and her husband, Cox, was clearly well-practiced at handling her missteps. Nora had said she was a little accident prone. I took issue with *a little*. In the first half hour, she knocked over two drinks, spilled another, and almost tripped over her own feet. Cox just grinned as he kept her from hurting herself, always calling her "sugar".

Riley was enamored with all of them.

We hung out in Nora's backyard—I'd mowed the grass for her before I'd gone to work this morning—with snacks and drinks, and it wasn't unlike having my family over for a big get-together.

Because that's what this was. Nora's family.

I'd brought over my grill so I could treat everyone to steaks. I could admit I was looking to make a good impression. The girls had congregated around the umbrella table. They chatted and sipped drinks, and had even included Riley. I glanced at Nora as I brought the steaks from inside and winked.

Cox followed me to the grill and handed me a glass of whiskey from the bottle he'd brought.

"Thanks, man."

He nodded, lifting his glass. "Cheers."

I took a sip. It was good. Smooth with just enough bite to wake you up.

"This doesn't mean you're off the hook," he said. "Just so we're clear."

"Course not."

Over at the table, Sophie snort-laughed. Cox smiled, like he found her to be the most interesting and charming person in existence.

I kind of knew the feeling.

"How did you and Sophie meet?" I asked.

"Technically, in the fifth grade, but I don't like to dwell on that. I was something of a twit. The next time, she was climbing down from a second story balcony in a hotel."

"Seriously?"

"True story." He sipped his drink. "My sugar bug has a tendency to get herself into interesting situations. But it wasn't until we got drunk-married in Vegas that things got good. That was a hangover I'll never forget."

Was he kidding? I had a feeling he wasn't. "Drunk married in Vegas and things all worked out?"

"Eventually. She's certainly the biggest win I ever took home."

"Nora tells me you're having a baby. Congratulations."

"Thanks, my friend. Never would have thought this would be me. Married, having a baby. Didn't think that would be my life but damn, would I have missed out. Your daughter sure seems like a sweet young lady."

That made me smile. "She's the best. I know what you mean about almost missing out. Riley was a surprise. Totally changed my life. But I wouldn't change a thing."

Corban wandered over as I laid the steaks on the hot grill. "Can I just say, your tattoos are impressive. There's a cohesiveness to the designs that you don't always see with full-sleeves."

"Thank you. That was intentional. I designed them to coordinate so they don't look haphazard."

"How far up do they go?" He adjusted his glasses and tilted his head. "To the shoulder? What about your chest?"

"Maybe you ought to buy the man a drink before you ask him to take his clothes off," Cox said with a grin.

"I'm just curious. There's a lot of interesting psychology behind body modification."

"It goes up over the shoulder on the right." I lifted my t-shirt sleeve to show them. "Just partway up the arm on the left. I like a bit of asymmetry. What about you guys? Do you have any ink?"

"None for me," Cox said.

"I don't have any. What about Shepherd?" Corban nodded to where Shepherd stood by himself with his whiskey. "Think he has any tattoos?"

"That guy is a mystery," Cox said. "You never know."

"Not very friendly, is he?" I asked.

"You get used to him," Corban said. "At first I thought he was evil. But he grows on you."

"Shepherd is a great guy," Cox said. "He just doesn't like anyone to know it."

As if he could tell we were talking about him, he walked over to stand with us. He nodded to Corban and Cox. Glared at me.

Seemed about right.

I checked the steaks. They were nicely seared on one side, so I flipped them over. The scent of charred meat filled the air. I put the spatula down and glanced at the girls. Nora stood next to the table, holding little Ella on her hip.

My chest tightened. Damn, Nora looked good like that. It made me think about things I really shouldn't. I didn't know if that future was possible—if that was what she wanted.

If we were what she wanted.

Fucking feelings. Always making things complicated.

What was my problem? Nora and I were fine. There was no reason to rush. We were good together, Riley liked her, and that was all I needed.

For now.

As for the future, we'd have to cross that bridge eventually. And it was a bit disconcerting, not knowing what I'd find on the other side.

29

NORA

*I*t felt good to be excited about work again. My fingers flew across my keyboard, the words coming easily. April had given me preliminary approval for several topics, so I'd chosen the one that spoke to me—dating a single dad. It wouldn't be too personal; I'd reached out to several acquaintances to ask about their experiences dating single fathers, so I'd include their stories alongside my own. But I was in love with the topic and determined to do it justice.

It might not produce as many clicks as a sex article, but I was convinced it would put us on the road to happier readers who were even more excited to return for our content. And the fact that it gave me something totally new to research and write about was incredibly satisfying.

The morning had gone by in a blink. It was almost one, so I decided to take a break for lunch. I'd come into the office today and there was a nice café down the street that I hadn't been to in a while. The weather was cloudy but not raining, and a walk in the fresh air sounded good. I gathered up my things and headed toward the lobby.

Tala was waiting for the elevator, dressed in an emerald green blouse and dark gray pencil skirt. "Hey, Nora. Are you getting lunch?"

"I am. Have you eaten? Do you want to join me?"

"I'd love to." She glanced at my feet. "Those shoes are amazing. I love how you always look so put together."

"Thank you." I tilted one foot and admired my shoes. Simple black heels but they had a slight shimmer that caught in the light. "I love wearing these."

"I think I'd fall over in heels that high."

"There's a learning curve, but I'm used to them. And these are deceptively comfortable."

The elevator opened and we rode it downstairs. We chatted as we walked to the restaurant. When we got there, the hostess seated us at a table next to the window. After perusing the menu for a few minutes, we ordered lunch.

"How's everything over in editing?" I asked.

"Same as usual." She shrugged. "I just finished working with Jenna on her travel piece, which was kind of fun. Small towns of the Pacific Northwest. Now I have at least five new places I want to visit."

"That sounds charming."

"It was, although I'm not sure how much it will do toward our bonuses. I'm just glad I have your column to balance it out. Your articles always generate clicks."

"I suppose they do."

"Speaking of, what are you working on?"

I couldn't help but smile. "I talked to April about expanding my range of topics. I'm working on a piece on dating a single dad and it's so refreshing."

"Wow. I'm surprised she went for it."

"It's something of a trial run to see how the audience responds. We acknowledged that clicks might go down, especially at first. But I'm confident this will be good for us in the long run."

"It seems like a risk. I'm not trying to be critical, it's just that everyone knows your column drives a huge amount of the traffic we get."

"It does, but how long will that last when I keep recycling articles about blow jobs and multiple orgasms? It's getting harder to write about the same things in new ways."

"I can see that. But it must be a little easier since you're getting regular orgasms." She gave me a conspiratorial grin. "How's the hot fling with your neighbor?"

I smiled. "So hot. He's positively delicious."

"He has a daughter, doesn't he? Does she know?"

"We were trying to keep it quiet but she figured it out."

"Uh-oh. This just got juicier. How did she find out? She didn't walk in on you or anything, did she?"

"No, fortunately not. We were usually hooking up when she wasn't home. But there were a few times he came over to my place when he thought she wouldn't notice. Apparently she did and was smart enough to figure out what her dad was doing."

"Sneaking around with the sexy single dad next door? I love it."

"I won't lie, it's been fun. He's such a great guy." The server brought our salads and I placed the napkin in my lap. "What about you? Didn't you meet someone recently?"

She nodded. "I did and it's going well. I introduced him to Frannie and Freddie and they all got along."

I searched my memory. Who were Frannie and Freddie? It seemed like she'd mentioned them before. "Those are your..."

"Ferrets."

Right, ferrets. Not a type of pet I was familiar with, but to each her own. "I'm glad that went well. And that he's an animal lover."

"They're all so cute together. He can't have pets at his place so he loves coming over to mine."

"That's sweet."

"And they don't even interfere when we have sex, which is so nice. I mean, they watch, but they keep their distance."

I blinked, not sure what to say to that. "Oh. That's good."

"Yeah, it's so much better than with my last boyfriend. Now that I think about it, I'm pretty sure they were trying to tell me something."

I wasn't sure that I wanted to know but I also couldn't seem to keep from asking. "What did they do?"

"They were friendly to him most of the time, but sometimes when we were in the middle of sex, they would come up on the bed and nibble at his toes. They didn't bite hard or anything, but it always freaked him out."

"I can't say that I blame him for that."

She laughed. "Me neither. But they leave us alone, which I think is a sign of their acceptance."

"That's good for both of you. And your toes."

Suddenly I was glad April had never asked me to write an article about how to navigate having sex with exotic pets in the room.

Her ferrets liked to watch? Shudder.

Fortunately, our conversation turned toward topics less likely to make me cringe while we finished our lunch—mostly light office gossip. I treated her to lunch and we walked back together.

I went back to my article and made good progress. Shortly before five, my phone buzzed with a text.

Dex: *Just thinking about you.*

Me: *I like that. I'm thinking about you, too.*

I smiled and warmth filled me. Dex really was a great guy. I hadn't told Tala the half of it. I liked him for a million different reasons, the most important of which weren't even in his pants. Granted, I liked what he had there too, but there was more.

He was more.

It scared me because, in a way, I'd been here before. And I'd given my heart to the wrong man. Not just the wrong man, but a lying, cheating asshole who didn't deserve to be called a man. What I'd thought was love had clouded my judgment, making me blind to the truth.

I'd promised myself, never again.

But Dex wasn't him. He wasn't the man who'd ripped out my heart and humiliated me. And he wasn't my father, either. He was a better man than either of them could ever hope to be.

And it was possible that I was maybe starting to fall for him. A little. Not too much. I couldn't risk that yet.

Could I?

These were big questions and I was flirting with a word I'd never thought I'd use with a man. Forever.

I needed time to let this all settle in. My heart knew that Dex was different and maybe my iron clad rule about ultimate commitment didn't need to apply. That maybe I was going to keep letting him break my rules. But a part of me was still scared—afraid to take that leap.

Afraid to take that risk.

We didn't have plans tonight, and I wasn't sure how late he had to work. But suddenly, I needed to see him. Even if it was just for a minute and all I could manage was a quick kiss. I needed him.

I packed up my things and left the office, but instead of driving home, I headed for Dex's tattoo shop.

~

DEX'S SHOP SMELLED CLEAN. The lobby was decorated with prints showcasing various tattoo options—everything from flowers and butterflies to skulls and knives dripping blood. The L-shaped front counter doubled as a glass display case filled with piercing jewelry.

The shop went straight back, with several tattoo stations on each side. A guy with a long gray beard that draped over his round belly was busy tattooing a client's arm and behind him, a woman with dark hair pulled up in a ponytail worked on a client lying face down on her chair.

Behind them, I could see Dex.

He sat on a stool, his back to me, while he worked. I waited, enjoying this glimpse of him. Even from this angle, I could sense his concentration, his focus. He was deeply engrossed in his work and I realized how much I admired him. Law school dropout turned tattoo shop owner. He'd turned a dream into reality, and I was standing in it.

Suddenly, the shop took on new meaning. It wasn't just needles and ink, skulls and knives, butterflies and flowers. It was his work, his art, his purpose. His accomplishment.

A woman with incredible red curls, numerous piercings, and tattoos down both arms came out from a back room. She offered a friendly smile. "Hi, can I help you?"

"I'm actually here to see Dex. Just to say hi."

Her eyes widened. "Oh my god, are you Nora?"

"I am."

"Awesome." She looked me up and down. "Damn, he's right, you are hot."

"Thank you."

"He's with a client but he should be done any minute."

She glanced over her shoulder at the long-bearded tattoo artist. "Hey, Sonny, Dex's girl Nora is here."

Sonny turned and adjusted a pair of glasses. "You're Nora?"

I nodded with a little wave. "That's me."

"Damn. Dex wasn't kidding. Nice to meet you."

"You, too."

Dex didn't seem to notice what was happening at the front of his shop. He was too engrossed in what he was doing.

"I'm Kari," the girl said. "Feel free to hang out."

"Thanks."

She went to the back of the shop and disappeared around a corner. I waited up front, browsing the piercing jewelry in the glass case. The buzz of their tools and low conversation hummed in the air.

I moved down the counter so I could see Dex from a different angle. His client sat while he tattooed something on his upper arm. I loved watching him work, even from a distance. And a strange thought came into my mind.

What if he tattooed me?

Tattoos had never really been my thing. But since meeting Dex—and spending so much time up close and personal with his ink—I'd come to a new appreciation of them. They could be anything from beautiful body art to conversation pieces to a story of survival or honoring a loved one. There was so much variety, so much beauty in them. And Dex was incredibly talented.

It wasn't so much that I wanted a tattoo, rather that I wanted a piece of Dex's art—something that could be a part of me.

Finally, Dex stood and stretched his back. He talked to his client for a little while and Kari appeared again to help him bandage the new tattoo. I didn't mind the wait. It was fascinating to see him in his element, especially because he didn't realize I was here.

Kari said something to him and he turned. A slow, sexy grin spread across his face and my heart skipped as he came out to meet me.

He really did have a special kind of power over me. But strangely enough, it didn't make me want to run. Not away from him, at least. I wanted to run straight into his arms.

And maybe, just maybe, I could imagine staying there.

*S*eeing Nora unexpectedly at the front of my shop instantly turned a good day into a great one.

Dressed in a dark teal blouse, fitted skirt, and heels, she looked like she'd come straight from work. Her hair was back with a few tendrils framing her face and the way she smiled at me as I approached made me feel like I'd just won the lottery.

"Hey. This is a nice surprise."

"I thought I'd swing by. I hope you don't mind."

"Not at all." I went around the counter and placed a soft kiss on her lips. "Come on back."

I led Nora to my station and gestured. "This is where I work. I have an office through there, too, but it's not very exciting."

She took slow steps around the small space. "These are all Riley's paintings, aren't they?"

"Yeah."

She pointed to a sign that read, *I believe in unicorns.* "This looks like her, too. Did she get it for you?"

"For my birthday one year. I think she was around six. My mom helped her."

"So cute." She eased herself into the chair. "This is where the magic happens?"

"I guess you could say that. Although I feel like the real magic happens at home in my room."

Her lips turned up in a smile. "Do you have another client soon?"

"That's a good question." I checked my calendar on my phone. "Nope, that was it for today."

"What was the last one you were doing?"

"Here, I'll show you." I swiped to my gallery and showed her the pictures I'd taken. "He and his wife had their first baby last year, so he wanted something that represented his family."

The design incorporated a compass with his wedding date and the date of his daughter's birth. There was room to add to it as his family grew.

"This is beautiful. There's so much depth."

"Thanks. I think it turned out really well. He was happy, and that's the most important thing."

Her eyes lifted to meet mine and she lowered her voice. "Have you ever thought about tattooing me?"

Had I ever. I'd run my hands all over her silky smooth skin and imagined her as a canvas for my art. "Yeah, it's crossed my mind."

"What would you tattoo on me? And where?"

I straddled my stool and took her hand, stretching out her arm so I could caress the sensitive skin on her wrist. "Less would be more with you. Something delicate. Not because you're breakable, but because you're not. You're elegant and sophisticated, so a tattoo would need to reflect that."

"You'd put it here?" She gestured to her wrist as I continued to caress it.

"That would be an option. A dainty wrist tattoo would add just the slightest edge to your look."

"Would you like it?"

"It would be hot."

She smiled.

"But somewhere hidden would be sexy, too. Somewhere most people don't see."

"A secret only we share."

I groaned a little and lifted her arm to kiss the inside of her wrist. "Ink that's all mine. Can I show you something?"

She nodded.

I got out my sketch book and opened it. "I hope this doesn't freak you out. But I've actually designed several."

"For me?"

"Yeah. Not that I thought you'd want a tattoo. I know you have commitment issues." I winked. "But sometimes I'd get an idea, so I'd sketch it out."

I turned to my Nora page and showed her the sketches. There were four different designs, all inspired by her. Two were floral, meant for the upper back. One was a delicate wrist tattoo, a tiny moon and stars. The final design was also a moon and stars, but slightly larger, with more shading and detail. I'd pictured it high on her outer thigh.

"This one is beautiful." She pointed to the moon and stars. "They all are, but this one captures me."

"I don't know why, but the moon reminds me of you. There's an element of sensuality to it, maybe because it's usually visible at night. And how it's always changing—still the same moon, reflecting the same sunlight, but we see different aspects of it, depending on the day and the season."

"I really love this." She met my eyes again. "Will you tattoo this on me?"

A current of desire washed over me like an ocean wave. "Really? Where?"

"What about here?" She pointed to her outer thigh, up near her hip. Exactly where I would have suggested.

I groaned again. "It would look amazing right there."

"Is that a yes?"

"If you're sure, absolutely."

"I'm sure. Can we do it now?"

I grinned. It didn't surprise me in the least that she'd want to do it immediately. She was decisive. I loved that about her. "Yeah, why not?"

Nora waited while I finished cleaning up after my last client and prepped for her tattoo. The spontaneity of it had me buzzing with creative energy. I'd imagined what she'd look like with one of my designs adorning her skin but I'd never thought she'd actually go for it. Her trust in me made a sense of warmth fill my chest.

I adjusted the chair so it became a table and had her take off her skirt and lie down. Kari grabbed her a pillow to support her head. Although I appreciated the way she looked, lying on her side in her panties, those gorgeous legs on full display, I was too focused to be distracted by her body. And I didn't need to worry about the rest of my crew. They were professionals.

Okay, so I did cast a quick glance at Sonny, but he wasn't paying attention to us. I wasn't totally immune to feeling possessive of her.

"I'm going to clean the area first and then get the stencil ready." I cleaned her skin and took a closer look to see if there were any marks or moles that I'd need to work around. She had one little mole toward the front of her hip but it wouldn't be in the way. "Are you comfortable like this?"

"This is fine. Although I'm suddenly a little nervous."

I squeezed her leg. "That's normal. You're going to do great."

I prepped the stencil and placed it. I thought it looked perfect, but it was her body. She needed to be completely happy with it.

"What do you think?"

"I love it already."

"Is there anything you want me to change?"

"No, it's perfect."

I picked up my tattoo machine. "Okay. Are you ready for this?"

She met my eyes. "I'm ready."

I moved my stool closer and straddled it. Then I got to work.

For the first few minutes, I felt a tingle of nervousness. Not enough to shake my confidence. But I was aware that this tattoo was different from anything I'd ever done before. It was special, an act of intimacy and trust that I hadn't been expecting.

With every line, my focus sharpened. The design came to life on her skin, bit by bit, while the tattoo machine vibrated in my hand. She stayed still, her energy calm and relaxed.

"Still doing okay?" I asked.

"Fine," she said. "It hurts but in a way that's almost pleasant, if that makes any sense."

"Yeah, makes perfect sense." I wiped away the excess ink and checked my work before continuing. "Make sure you let me know if you need a break."

"No, keep going. I love watching you work."

I kept the lines delicate and used shading to create depth. The crescent moon seemed to glow and the tiny stars around it added the illusion of sparkle. I kept adding and adjusting until finally, it was finished.

"What do you think?" I wiped her skin again and let her look.

"I love it so much."

"Yeah?" It had turned out perfectly.

"Honestly, Dex, it's so beautiful. It's intricate without being overpowering."

I tilted my head and gazed at her. "I had the perfect canvas."

Leaning in, I kissed her lips. I didn't know how to express what this had meant to me. I was honored and I felt closer to her than I ever had before.

Maybe all my worry about where this was going had been a waste of time. I just needed to be patient and this would work out exactly as it was meant to.

31

NORA

*M*y tattoo was healing nicely after just a few days. I had to admit, I'd spent a lot of time admiring it in the mirror. Every time I got undressed, I'd gaze at it for a while, enamored. I loved having Dex's art permanently on my skin.

I'd also loved seeing him in his element. He'd been so focused, his hands so sure. I'd known he was talented but watching him work had been fascinating. I had a new appreciation for what he did for a living and the creative talent that made him who he was.

Tonight, though, Dex St. James was going to be out of his element, and firmly in mine.

The dress I'd chosen for Everly's charity event was deep red with a halter neckline and fitted waist. It was floor length with a high slit and paired perfectly with my silver open-toed heels.

My phone buzzed with another group text. My friends were all getting ready and we'd been sending each other pictures of our progress. But Sophie's latest photo almost sent me into a panic.

She was dressed in a loose-fitting dress with wide red and white stripes. It made her look like she was wearing a circus tent.

Me: *Sophie, honey, what is that?*

Everly: *Oh my...*

Hazel: *It's an interesting choice.*

Sophie: *I think I made a mistake. But the lady at the store said it was pretty on me.*

Me: *There are so many things wrong with this.*

Sophie: *What should I do?*

Me: *Take it off. Immediately.*

Sophie: *I was trying to find something that would hide my belly.*

Me: *Why would you do that?*

Sophie: *Because belly!*

Me: *Darling, you have a beautiful figure and it's no less beautiful now that you're pregnant. Don't hide it, show it off.*

Hazel: *Nora's right. You have beautiful curves.*

Me: *See, if Hazel agrees with me, you know I'm right. Do you need me to come over and help?*

Sophie: *You don't have time for that.*

Me: *I'll make time.*

Sophie: *Let me try a different dress first.*

I waited while Sophie changed. I wanted to find out where she'd bought that other monstrosity and call to complain. After a few minutes, she texted another photo.

This one was perfection. It was deep green and hugged her curves, showed off her little baby belly, and made her boobs look fantastic.

Me: *This is the one. You're a goddess in this.*

Sophie: *Are you sure?*

Everly: *I love you in this dress.*

Hazel: *Oh yes. Beautiful.*

Me: *If you don't feel good in it, that's one thing. But don't for a minute think you aren't stunning.*

Sophie: *I'm just self-conscious. We all know I've never been skinny but this baby is changing everything.*

Me: *Go show Cox. In fact, do it now so you still have time to get to the event.*

Sophie: *Why? We have plenty of time to get there.*

Me: *Not once he sees you in that dress. You're going to need time to fix your hair and makeup.*

Sophie: *Why would I... Oh! I get it.*

Me: *That's our girl. I'll see you all in a little while.*

I went back to styling my hair, putting it up with a few wavy tendrils around my face. Then I touched up my makeup and added bold red lipstick to match my dress. After one last look in the mirror, I decided to add a silver bracelet to complete the look. Then I grabbed a small black clutch, tucked in my phone and a few essentials, and went next door in search of Dex.

Riley's eyes widened when she answered the door. "Oh my gosh. You look amazing."

"Thank you, love." I gave her a hug and kissed next to her cheek.

"Can I see your hair in the back?"

I turned so she could look. "It's simple, actually. Just some twists and tucks, then a few bobby pins. I can show you how to do it."

"That would be so cool. This is so pretty."

"Is your dad ready yet?"

"I don't know. He's been upstairs for a while."

A moment later, Dex appeared.

It was official. Dex St. James in a tux was one of the most delicious things I'd ever seen.

He wore classic black with a crisp white shirt and bow

tie. It was timeless, bringing out his gentleman side, while the hint of his tattoos at the wrists made the look distinctly him.

So sexy.

If he hated the tux, or felt the least bit uncomfortable, it didn't show. He came down the stairs, moving as if he wore a suit every day—totally confident.

It was justified. He looked incredible.

His eyes were on me and the way he looked me up and down with barely disguised heat sent a tingle down my spine.

"Wow, Dad. I've never seen you look so nice," Riley said.

"Thanks, kiddo." He tugged on the lapels. "Well, what do you think?"

"I think you should wear a tux more often," I said.

"No." He eyed me up and down again. "Although if it means you'll wear that again, I might be persuaded."

I turned in a circle. "You like?"

"It's really not fair to everyone else who's going to this thing." He slid his hands around my waist and gave me a light kiss on the forehead. "You look incredible."

"I was just thinking the same about you."

He turned to Riley. "Are you all packed?"

"Yep, I'm ready."

Although Riley was old enough to be home alone, Gillian had arranged to pick her up so she could spend the night at their place. It was remarkable how much Riley's grandparents were involved in her life. I rarely saw my parents, let alone my grandparents. I'd never been close to any of my relatives. It made me admire Dex's family and I was grateful Riley had them.

"Grandma will be here soon." Dex hugged her. "I'll see you tomorrow."

"Have fun," she said.

He gestured toward the front door. "Shall we?"

We left and drove downtown to the Four Seasons. Dex led me to the ballroom with his hand on the small of my back, a light touch that was surprisingly possessive.

The ballroom had been transformed into a stylish casino, minus the noisy slot machines and sugar-laden cocktails. Guests milled around the tables sipping drinks, or tried their hands at the various games. Everyone was dressed to the nines, but there wasn't a man in attendance who looked as good as Dex.

I spotted Everly on the other side of the room, dressed in an exquisite black satin gown I'd helped her select. Shepherd stood with her, about a half-step behind, while she chatted with several of the guests.

Corban and Hazel were busy playing roulette. She also wore black, but hers was cocktail length with a flattering V-neck. Corban looked very dapper in his tux and bow tie.

Sophie's deep green dress was even more flattering in person. Her blond curls were pinned up and Cox leaned over to kiss her bare shoulder. The adorable parents-to-be watched a small group at one of the craps tables and I wondered if it reminded them of their wild night in Vegas.

We went to the bar for drinks—a dirty martini for me, naturally, and Scotch on the rocks for Dex. After a little mingling, and saying hello to my friends, we settled on blackjack.

It was fun, and I loved being out with him, all dressed up and sipping cocktails. But it was hard to stay focused on the game. My attention kept wandering to Dex in that tux. At the way his tattoos peeked out at the wrists, like he was hiding a dirty secret.

I wanted him to get me dirty.

After a while, he leaned in and spoke close to my ear. "I want to eat you alive in that dress."

A pleasant tingle burst between my legs. "Do you?"

"Oh yeah." His tongue flicked my ear. "You're driving me crazy."

That tongue flick held all sorts of naughty promises. I glanced around. We'd made our appearance and supported the cause. No one would notice if we slipped out.

"Should we go?"

"If you're ready. It's your thing, I don't want to pull you away too soon."

A sense of gratitude mingled with my desire for him to destroy my body. This wasn't his type of event, but he'd come for me. And instead of acting uncomfortable and taking the first opportunity to leave, he was willing to stay.

Luckily for him, I wanted him out of that tux, hot as it was on him.

"I'm ready. Let's go."

We left and the tension between us practically heated the air in the car as we drove home. I crossed my legs and recrossed them several times, trying to deal with the rising urgency.

He put his hand on my thigh and slid it up the slit in my dress, finding bare skin. His eyes flicked to me and the corner of his mouth lifted. "I can't wait to get you home so I can fuck you in that dress."

"Don't you want to take it off me?"

"No." His low voice sent a tingle down my spine. "I want to defile it."

My eyes rolled back. "Drive faster."

He squeezed my thigh and pressed on the gas.

We pulled into his driveway and I was even more grateful to Gillian for taking Riley for the night. He led me inside with that same possessive hand on the small of my back and shut the door behind me.

I stepped out of my heels as he peeled off his jacket and tossed it aside.

Without a word, he pushed me against the door and lowered himself in front of me. His hands moved up my thighs, beneath my dress, and he hooked his fingers through my panties. He slid them off and let them fall to the floor.

He lifted one leg and draped it over his shoulder. His lips trailed up my inner thigh until his mouth reached my center.

I was already familiar with the magic of Dex's tongue, but tonight, he was especially merciless. He licked and sucked like the expert he was, until I could barely stand it. I leaned against the door, my leg draped over his shoulder, gasping as he tortured me with bliss.

My other leg threatened to give out. I was spiraling toward climax already, the heat and tension building fast.

I cried out as my orgasm swept through me, the pressure exploding in a burst of sparks. He rode it out with me until I sagged against the door, breathing hard.

He lowered my leg and it was all I could do to remain standing.

"Don't think for a second that I'm done with you." He stood, discarded his tie, and started unbuttoning his shirt. "That was just a warm up."

I was too breathless to reply.

He moved me to the couch. I was putty in his hands, ready to do whatever he wanted. He positioned me on my knees and hiked my dress up over my hips.

"Fuck yes," he said, his voice a low growl. "I've been wanting to do this to you all night."

I looked over my shoulder while he unzipped his pants

and pulled out his thick erection. He took it in his fist and slid the tip through my wetness, up and down. Teasing me. Torturing me again.

"Dex, please." My voice was a needy whimper. I never begged a man for anything but once again, Dex seemed to effortlessly break my rules. "Fuck me."

"You want this?" He dragged the tip across my slit again.

"Yes. I want you inside me."

He slid his hand up and down his shaft and groaned. I watched as he rubbed faster. "Tell me again."

"Fuck me, Dex."

His hand jerked up and down his thickness. "You need to beg for it baby, or I'm going to come all over your ass."

"Please. Please, Dex. I need you. Fuck me now."

With a harsh grunt, he grabbed my hips and plunged inside me.

I arched my back, leaning into him. He drove in and out, holding me in a tight grip, growling as he fucked me. I closed my eyes, letting him have his way with me.

Without warning, he smacked my ass cheek. The sting heightened every other sensation in my body and I moaned.

"Again."

He smacked it a second time, right in the same spot.

"Harder."

His hand connected with a loud slap. I threw my head back and moaned while my inner muscles spasmed around him.

Grabbing my hips again, he drove in deeper. He thrust in, again and again, until I teetered on the edge of my second orgasm.

His rhythm changed and I knew he was close. I looked over my shoulder again. I wanted to watch him come.

Muscles tensed. His jaw was tight and he had a deep

furrow in his brow. He grunted and I felt his cock pulse, watched with awe as he unleashed inside me.

He was gorgeous.

The feel of him throbbing inside me and the look on his face as he came was too much to resist. I clamped down on him, my own pulses rippling through me. Our orgasms melded, peaked, and surged again. Waves of pleasure washed over me, like nothing I'd ever experienced before.

Finally, he stopped and slid out, then leaned down to kiss the spot he'd spanked.

My arms felt like jelly. I rolled onto the couch, too exhausted to even stand.

"What did you just do to me?" I asked.

"I meant to take you upstairs but I couldn't wait."

My eyes fluttered open. He stepped out of his pants and underwear and fell onto the couch next to me.

"Take the dress off."

"Dex, I don't think I can take anymore."

He grinned. "I just want to feel your skin."

With his help, I peeled off my dress. He shifted so he was lying down and drew me on top of him. His skin was warm against mine and the scent of him—clean and manly— surrounded me.

He caressed slow circles across my back. "See? This is nice."

"It's very nice."

It was. I loved the feel of his hard body beneath me. I relaxed into him, letting my eyes drift closed, my body warm and satisfied.

And there was nowhere else in the world I wanted to be.

32

DEX

*T*he shop was busy today. Every station was full and Kari had a steady stream of walk-ins wanting consultations. My last client had been a lot of fun. She'd wanted something to symbolize her love of books and reading. The vine sprouting books like flowers I'd come up with had turned out great. She'd been ecstatic, which was the most important thing.

I cleaned up my station and sanitized everything amid the buzz of tattoo machines and the low hum of chatter. Just as I was finishing up, I got a phone call from my sister, Maggie. I stepped into the back office to take it.

"Hey, Mags. What's up?"

"Hey. I need a small favor. And by that I mean a big favor that's going to inconvenience you."

"At least you're honest. What do you need?"

"Could you pick up my kids from day camp once or twice next month? I'll send you the dates. I'm just trying to make sure Mom doesn't do everything."

"I'm sure I can make that work."

"Thank you so much. How's Ry? Excited for summer?"

"She's good. Yeah, I think she's looking forward to the freedom. And the lack of a morning alarm."

"How's Nora? Are you guys still seeing each other?"

There was a hint of something in her voice. Doubt, maybe? "Yeah, why?"

"I don't know, her latest article made me wonder. But I guess if you're fine with it, it's not a big deal."

"What about her latest article?"

"Oh..." She hesitated. "You didn't read it?"

"No."

"She had to have told you about it at least, even if she didn't have you read it ahead of time."

"Maggie, what are you talking about?"

"It's just that it's obviously about you. She didn't ask you first?"

I had no idea what she was talking about. I'd read Nora's column but I didn't keep up with it on a weekly basis. What could she have written about me that had Maggie so concerned?

"I haven't read the latest one but I'll take a look."

"Yeah, good idea. Sorry, I hope I didn't make things weird."

"Don't worry about it. I'll talk to you later."

"Okay. Bye, Dex."

I ended the call with a strange sinking feeling in the pit of my stomach. Nora had written an article about me? Maybe Maggie was jumping to conclusions. It couldn't be that bad. After all, Nora's boss had agreed to let her expand her range of topics outside of sex. It wasn't as if she'd publish an autobiographical play by play of our bedroom activities. And even if she had, how the hell would Maggie have known?

Still, I was curious as to what had bothered my sister.

I found Nora's column and the headline for her newest article hit me like a punch to the gut.

A hot fling with a single dad

OKAY, I could see why Maggie thought that was about me. And I was surprised Nora hadn't mentioned it. Even if she hadn't used my name—which I was sure she hadn't—wouldn't she have at least told me before the article went live?

I wasn't sure how I felt about this.

When I started reading, the feeling got worse.

Not only was the article about me, it characterized our relationship as a meaningless no-strings fling. It gave her readers tips, based on her recent experience, of how to seduce a single dad while keeping the fling light and fun with absolutely zero commitment.

...IF HE'S NOT your usual type, even better. A fling—always temporary in nature—is a great way to try out a man you wouldn't usually date...

...TRY BEFRIENDING him first to see if you might be compatible. Friendship won't tell you everything you need to know about how he'll perform in the bedroom, but it will give you a basis for getting what you want from him...

·   ·   ·

...IF HE'S STILL RELUCTANT, tease him. Don't be afraid to use your assets to show him what he's missing...

...LET'S BE HONEST, ladies, single dads are the holy grail of hot flings...

...IF HE LIVES CLOSE, you're in luck. Convenience is one of the biggest advantages of neighbors-with-benefits. You can be in and out—happily satisfied—and back to your own life without any fuss...

...WHAT IS a girl to do when he wants commitment and you're happy with the arrangement as is? In my experience, you can let him think what he wants until the fling naturally runs its course...

...INTIMIDATED BY HIS KIDS? Don't be! The quickest way to a single dad's bed is through his kids. Befriend them, you won't regret it...

WHAT THE FUCK?

Even if the article hadn't been about me, it would have been shitty. Befriend a single dad's kids to get him to sleep with you? Let him think what he wants until the fling runs its course?

But it was about me. It was about us.

Was this what she really thought? Was this all we were?

And was this who Nora really was?

No wonder she hadn't told me about it. She was probably hoping I wouldn't see it.

Either that, or she didn't care. She'd have some excuse ready about her boss putting pressure on her to write another article about sex and this was the compromise.

I read it again, looking for a way out—looking for a way to not be furious. But the stuff about befriending a single dad's kids to get what you wanted stood out as if it had been typed in bold red letters. I couldn't stop thinking about Riley. About all the times Nora had invited her over for iced tea on her porch, or taught her how to do her hair, or helped her pick an outfit. Going to her art show, chaperoning her dance.

Had all that been part of the game? Did Nora use my daughter to get to me?

It didn't make sense. I'd called Nora out on this being nothing but a fling and yeah, she'd balked at first. But it had been an argument that had lasted all of an hour, if that. We'd been on the same page, even if it had taken her a little longer to realize it. She couldn't have been telling me what I wanted to hear just to keep the fling going.

Could she?

The problem was, I'd been waiting for this—waiting for the other shoe to drop. It always did. I had a miserable history of choosing the wrong women. Brooklyn was the last in a series of bad relationships. So much of why I'd mostly stayed single since having Riley was because of this— because what happened to my daughter when things went bad?

Damn it, Nora. Why did she have to make Riley like her so much?

The more I thought about Riley and her relationship with Nora, the angrier I got. My protective instincts pushed aside reason. A voice in my head tried to tell me to calm down and take a breath.

I didn't listen.

But why should I? She'd used my daughter as a way to get me to bang her and she'd only agreed to take things to the next level so I wouldn't stop. Where did this end for her? Where did she think this was going? Was it just a fling that would fizzle out and we'd go back to being nothing but neighbors?

It didn't help that she'd stung my pride. It wasn't just my sister who read her column. Kari did too, and so did a bunch of my clients. I'd told them to. And now they were all going to read about how Nora had played the single dad next door—me.

I got up and grabbed my keys. I had another client later, but I needed to deal with this now. My mom was picking up Riley from school and I wanted to make sure she didn't go straight to Nora's. Not until I could figure this out.

With my temper hanging by a very thin thread, I went home.

33

NORA

The article I was working on was making me happy. I was going from relationships to fashion, exploring fun ideas for first date attire, especially for my readers who were tired of the usual. No little black dresses here. I was all about fun, flirty tops, curve hugging bottoms, and shoes that added bright pops of color.

My fashion wish list was getting dangerously long. Job hazard.

A knock on my door pulled my attention from the latest trends in feminine footwear. I made sure my work had saved, then went to the front door.

I opened it to find Dex standing a few feet away, as if he'd knocked and moved back. Something was wrong. His brow was furrowed and his shoulders were tense.

"Hi. Is everything okay?"

"Can I come in?"

Not sure what was happening, I stepped aside. He came inside and I shut the door behind him. "What's wrong?"

He stood still, his back to me. "Were you going to tell me?"

"About what?"

"The article."

Had they published it already? "The single dad article? Is it out already?"

"Yes."

"That's so odd. It was supposed to be next week. I didn't even get the email that it went live."

He whirled around, his eyes flashing with anger. "Does it matter?"

I eyed him warily. I didn't understand what had him so upset. The article didn't use his name or any identifying details. "I suppose this means you read it?"

"Yes, I fucking read it. Maggie called me."

"And obviously you're mad."

He looked at me like I'd just said the dumbest thing he'd ever heard. "Um, yeah. And the fact that you're surprised by that tells me a lot."

"I knew the article was a bit of a risk but I didn't think it would make you angry."

"How could it not make me angry? Of course I'm fucking angry. You had no right to use our relationship like that and you really had no right to use my daughter."

"I didn't use Riley. What are you talking about? The article doesn't share any personal details."

He shook his head. "You know what? I'm glad this happened now. The longer this went on, the worse it would have been. I should have known not to get involved with someone who's fucking allergic to real relationships. And I never should have let you anywhere near my daughter."

I gaped at him, a mix of anger and betrayal practically choking the words in my throat. "How could you say that? Dex, I don't know what's in that article that has you furious with me but I swear, I didn't mean to hurt you and I would never do anything to hurt Riley."

"You already did."

His words hit me like a slap. I blinked in shock, the sting making my breath catch.

He didn't give me a chance to respond. He stormed out, slamming the door behind him.

What had just happened?

It took me a moment to recover but then I went straight for my phone. I needed to reread the article. What had I written that was so terrible? It had been more personal than I'd originally intended, but I'd included experiences of other women to balance it out. What was so bad about a love letter to dating a single dad? I'd wanted to reach other women out there who might be in a relationship—or thinking about a relationship—with a single father and show them the benefits. Encourage them to take a chance.

Why had that made Dex so mad?

I opened my column and my heart dropped through my toes, settling somewhere in the ground below me. A hot fling with a single dad?

This wasn't what I wrote. They hadn't just edited my article, they'd printed something entirely new. I hadn't written a word of this.

No wonder Dex was so angry. This article was awful. It was manipulative and fake, encouraging women to suck up to a single dad's kids to get him into bed. To tell him what he wants to hear—to lie to him and screw the consequences.

I never would have written this. Not even before knowing Dex. But especially not now.

I opened my door in time to see him leaving, his car racing down our street. Damn it. He was probably picking up Riley from school. Or from his parents' house. Or maybe just taking off to get away from me until he could cool off.

My blood burned with frustration. For a moment, I thought about following him. I didn't have his parents' address but I could try Riley's school. Catch up to him as quickly as possible and explain.

But I also needed to deal with my job. Fucking April. Not only had she lied to me, she'd published this trash under my name. For all I knew, she'd written it herself. Scrapped the piece I'd turned in and started over, all in the name of advertising revenue.

I was done. I had to quit, there was no other choice. I had no idea what I was going to do without a job, but I'd deal with that later. There was no way I could stay.

Still fuming, I sent Dex a quick text, telling him I could explain and I'd talk to him when I got home this evening. Then I grabbed my things and headed for my office.

The traffic on the way into the city did nothing to improve my mood. Finally, I made it to my building. I parked and got out, filled with determination.

I went up the elevator and marched in, past the receptionist and straight to April's office. From the corner of my eye, I saw Tala and another one of our editors wave, but I didn't respond. I had one purpose and that was to tell April exactly what I thought about what she'd done and let her know I was quitting. Immediately.

Fine, two purposes. Don't judge, I was flustered.

April looked up in surprise when I barged into her office. "Hi, Nora."

"I quit."

Her eyes widened. "Excuse me?"

"I'm not sure what else you expected after the article you published to my column."

"Maybe you should sit down." She gestured to the chair on the other side of her desk.

"I'll stand, thank you."

"All right. What's the problem with your article?"

Her soothing tone only made me angrier. "We could start with the fact that I didn't write it. That would be bad enough. But it's awful. It makes a complete mockery of my relationship with the man I care about and his daughter, who I also care about."

My hands trembled but I continued. "I want that article taken down immediately and a public apology issued, both to me and to my boyfriend and his daughter."

She looked at me with confusion. "Nora, I'm sorry, but I don't know what you're talking about. I admit, the article you turned in surprised me. I thought you wanted to write something a bit deeper. But I figured you must have your reasons."

"A bit deeper? The article I wrote was nothing but depth."

"Perhaps we have different definitions of depth. A fling with the hot single dad next door isn't exactly a multi-layered piece about relationships."

"I didn't write that article."

"What are you talking about? Of course you did."

"No, I didn't. I wrote about the surprising fulfillment of dating a single dad. About navigating the complexities of a relationship with not just a man, but a man *and* his child or children. You published a manipulative fluff piece that encourages women to lie and use a man's kids in order to get him into bed."

"Nora, I'm telling you, the article I approved and published is the one you turned in."

"And I'm telling you, it isn't. I didn't write it."

She opened her mouth, as if to keep arguing that I must have written it, but paused. She picked up her desk phone and dialed. "Can you come to my office for a minute? Thanks." She hung up. "We'll get to the bottom of this."

A moment later, Tala came in. "You wanted to see me? Oh, hi, Nora."

"Tala, there's some confusion over the latest article in *Living Your Best Life*."

She clasped her hands. "Oh?"

"Nora says she didn't write it. You edited her piece. Do you know anything about this?"

Her eyes darted between me and April and she kept fidgeting with her hands. "I'm not sure."

"Tala, what I wrote and what April published are two different things. We both know I didn't write that article. Where did it come from?"

She looked away and her shoulders slumped. "I wrote it."

"What?"

"The article you wrote was really sweet but no one was going to click on it. It was *too* sweet."

"So you rewrote it?"

"I swear, I won't do it again. I just knew that if your article tanked, all our clicks will go down. And I really need the traffic bonus this month. My credit cards are already maxed out and Freddie and Frannie caught colds and do you know how expensive it is to take animals to the vet? Plus they needed new harnesses so I can take them for walks with my boyfriend and they ran out of their special treats they love. It all adds up."

I stared at her, dumbfounded. "You rewrote my article without telling anyone so you could pay for treats for your ferrets?"

"And the vet bill. And there was the big Nordstrom sale a couple of weeks ago."

"You ruined my life for a clothing sale?"

She rolled her eyes. "Come on, I didn't ruin your life. My article is going nuts already. I probably saved your career."

I couldn't believe what I was hearing. "That article is awful. My boyfriend is furious and I don't blame him. You had no right to pass it off as mine." I turned to April. "And regardless of where it came from, you approved it. I realize I've written plenty on the subject of sexual flings but I'd never tell people to suck up to a single dad's kids in order to manipulate him into bed."

At least April had the decency to look uncomfortable. "I admit, there may have been a lapse in judgment."

I shook my head slowly. "You knew it would be controversial, didn't you? You knew this would stir people up. That's why you ran it—why you didn't question it. You were willing to sacrifice my reputation for clicks."

She waved that off. "Your reputation will be fine. No publicity is bad publicity."

"It is when it hurts people I care about." When I'd first walked in, anger had fueled my resolution to quit—anger that might have later cooled.

I wasn't angry anymore. I was hurt and betrayed. And I knew what I had to do. When I spoke again, my voice was calm. "I really am quitting. As of right now. And I want that article taken down."

April hesitated, her lips pressing together. "Fine. We'll pull the article."

I looked at Tala. "We women have enough to deal with in this world without making things harder on each other. Do better."

Then I turned around and walked out.

I'd have to deal with the details of leaving Glamour Gal later. Clean out my office, find out if I could get the rights to my column back. Professionally, I had no idea where this left me or what I was going to do.

Personally, I needed to put out this fire before it spread.

I checked my phone. Dex hadn't replied. I brought up his number and hit send. It went straight to voicemail. Either he'd turned off his phone or he'd immediately rejected my call. I tried again. Same result.

This time I left a message. "Dex, I didn't write that article. Someone else wrote it and published it under my name. Please call me back."

The traffic on the way home was torture. I sat on the freeway going five miles an hour, ready to scream. Suddenly road rage made a lot more sense. Who knew how many raging drivers were trying to get home to their significant other to clear up a terrible misunderstanding.

I tried his cell again. Voice mail. I tried Riley's. Hers seemed to be off too.

By the time I got home, I was jittery with pent up frustration. Dex's house was dark, his car gone. I went over anyway, just in case, and knocked. No answer.

I didn't want to keep calling him if he was just going to reject my calls. I didn't know where he was or when he was coming home. I was hurt and angry and overwhelmed. So I did the only thing I could think to do.

I called my friends.

34

NORA

*A*fter opening a bottle of wine, I promptly put the cork back in. I didn't want wine. I didn't know what I wanted. A martini? A gin and tonic? A good, old-fashioned shot of tequila?

Several, perhaps?

I glanced up at the kitchen ceiling. The holes Dex had drilled to drain the bathtub water were still there. And for some reason, that made me irrationally angry.

Tequila it was.

I got out a bottle and a shot glass and poured. The liquor burned as it slid down my throat. I thought about taking another but hesitated before pouring. Hangovers weren't exactly the mild inconvenience they'd once been. I'd pace myself.

The sound of a car outside caught my attention but it was just one of my neighbors—not my girlfriends, nor was it Dex.

That also made me irrationally angry.

Damn it, Dex.

He really thought I'd written that article. Instead of giving me the benefit of the doubt, or at least asking me about it and giving me a chance to respond, he'd thrown accusations in my face and walked out.

Of course he'd walked out. That was how he dealt with his feelings, apparently. And now he wouldn't even talk to me.

Asshole.

I reached for the tequila but I heard another car. This time, it pulled into my driveway.

Thank God. It was my beautiful, wonderful, loyal-to-the-end friends.

I opened the front door to greet them. They swept in, loaded down with... I didn't even know. Everly had shopping bags from a local grocery store. Hazel carried a stack of pink boxes and a bottle of wine. Sophie almost dropped both pizzas she was trying to balance. I grabbed one box before it slid off the other and onto the floor.

"We came with supplies," Everly said, characteristically cheerful.

"Since it isn't yet clear how dire the situation is, we brought some of everything," Hazel said.

"I'll be honest," Sophie said as she unloaded the pizza onto my kitchen counter. "I was craving pepperoni."

Everly and Hazel set everything else in the kitchen and started rummaging through the bag and boxes.

"Ice cream," Everly said, holding up a pint of chocolate. "I got four different flavors, so we can mix and match."

"Cupcakes," Hazel said, pointing to one of the pink boxes. "Also, croissants and donuts. I was tasked with procuring carbs."

"I see that," I said.

Hazel held up a folder. "I also took the opportunity to

print out some of your past articles on how to handle a break up. Then Everly reminded me that maybe you don't want your own words thrown back at you. But they're here in case you want to review them. Your advice is outstanding."

Everly kept fishing things out of her bags while Sophie put the ice cream in the freezer, then helped herself to a slice of pizza.

"I brought facial masks in case you've been crying and need moisturizing," Everly said. "Plus, they feel so nice. And chocolate, of course, if you need something other than ice cream. Hazel picked up a bottle of wine, because why not." She held up a colorful box. "Oh, and I brought hair chalk."

I eyed her with confusion and possibly mild disgust. "Why on earth did you buy hair chalk?"

"Just in case." She shrugged and put the box down. "If you're considering doing something drastic to your hair, we can use this instead."

"You haven't made a hair appointment in the last eight hours, have you?" Hazel peered at me over the rim of her glasses.

"No."

"Have you visited any animal shelters or adopted any pets?" Sophie asked.

"No, this isn't a cut my hair off or adopt a cat situation." I brushed my hair back from my face. "Although I did quit my job."

"Oh, my," Everly said. "It's really been a day, hasn't it?"

"What do you need?" Sophie asked around a bite of pizza. "Food? Chocolate? Alcohol?"

I threw my hands up in the air. "Honestly? I don't even know."

"That's okay," Everly said. "Just tell us what happened."

Another car drove by. Phil across the street. My tight grip on my emotions was beginning to slip.

"I turned in an article about all the positive aspects of dating a single dad. Tala, one of our editors, decided that it wasn't clickable enough for her liking, so she rewrote it and didn't tell anyone. The article they published, under my name, is awful. It's all about how to manipulate a single dad into bed. It even suggests using his kids to get to him."

"Oh, no," Everly said.

"Dex read it before I saw it. And instead of calmly asking me to explain, he marched over here, yelled at me and accused me of using him and his daughter, and stormed off before I could figure out what the hell he was talking about."

Hazel handed me the martini I hadn't realized she was mixing.

I took a sip. "I still can't believe Tala did that. Or that my boss approved it. She didn't even ask why the article was so different than the one I'd proposed. And she was perfectly happy to soil my reputation because she knew the controversy would generate traffic."

"Good for you for quitting," Sophie said. "They don't deserve you."

"Thank you. And this thing with Dex is just a stupid misunderstanding. But the big old jerk won't talk to me."

"Perhaps he feels the need to cool off for a period of time," Hazel said.

Everly nudged her. "We're supposed to be on her side."

"I am, I'm just being logical."

"No, Hazel's right." I set down my glass and stirred the olives around. "He probably does need to cool down. But it still irritates me that he walked away like that. And now he's who-knows-where, assuming I wrote all those things and they're about him. That I sucked up to Riley to get in his pants and I don't care about him beyond his ability to give me orgasms."

Another car drove by. Still not Dex. For fuck's sake, were all my neighbors coming home in the same half hour?

I took a big swallow of my drink and set the glass down. "Let's go out. I'm making myself crazy here. What do you think? Girls' night out? Can you all come with me?"

Hazel adjusted her glasses again. "It has been too long since we had a proper girls' night."

"See!" I pointed at her. "If Hazel agrees with me, you know I'm right."

"I'm in." Everly pulled out her phone. "Let me just text Shepherd and make sure he doesn't mind. Do you feel up to it, Sophie?"

"I've got second trimester energy," Sophie said and licked the pizza grease off her fingers. "Let's do this."

The logistics were slightly more complicated than in the days when Everly, Hazel, and I had lived in the same building. An impromptu night of clubbing once meant retreating to our respective apartments to get ready and then meeting in the lobby. Now it meant coordinating with three husbands, one of whom was home with a toddler, allowing time for them to go home and change, and then meeting up at a suitable club for our girls' night.

Still, we made it work. We picked Monkey Club, a place we'd frequented in the past. It was a weeknight, so we didn't anticipate a huge crowd. I was looking forward to having a few drinks and dancing off the stress of the day.

My friends left and I took my time getting ready, focusing on a once-common ritual of hair, makeup, and wardrobe. I took my makeup from day to night with a smoky eye and dramatic lipstick. For my outfit, I went all-in. This was no middle school dance. I paired a silver minidress with thigh-high black boots and silver bangles on my wrist.

I went outside to meet my Uber, not so secretly hoping Dex would finally be home. But there was no sign of him. His house was dark and my messages were still unanswered.

I teetered on the edge of angry and sad. I hated that he was mad at me.

But it was his own fault. If he would have just talked to me, we could have avoided all this drama.

So I chose angry. He didn't want to handle this like adults? Fine.

My driver took me into Seattle as the sun went down. When we pulled up to the curb in front of Monkey Club, my friends were already there, standing in a little knot near the entrance. Hazel looked adorable in her blouse and pencil skirt—her clubbing attire had always closely resembled her office wear. Sophie had chosen an A-line dress in a deep purple that accentuated her curves beautifully. And Everly wore a sparkly halter in her signature yellow paired with an adorable miniskirt and heels.

I thanked my driver and got out of the car, feeling fabulous. Or at least, I told myself I felt fabulous. I loved my dress and the boots were to die for. How long had it been since I'd dressed up and gone clubbing? I couldn't even remember. This was going to be perfect. Dex could fume or pout or complain about me or whatever it was he was doing. I was going to have some fun.

"Look at you!" Everly reached out her hands to clasp mine as I approached. "You look so hot in that outfit."

"Those boots are terrifying," Sophie said. "Of course, I fall in flats, so there's that. But they look amazing on you."

"You all look gorgeous," I said, hugging them each in turn. "Have I mentioned how much I love you? Because I love you so much."

"We love you too," Everly said.

We put our arms around each other in a big group hug.

"All right, let's go have a drink and shake our hot asses," I said. "Except for Sophie. Only ass shaking for you and that baby tonight."

She put her hand on her belly. "Baby and I are ready!"

I led the way inside and up the narrow staircase to the second floor. We paid the cover and went into the bar, taking slow steps to get the lay of the land.

Speakers pumped out loud music with a rhythmic beat and the lighting was low. A crowd of people danced on the dance floor but it wasn't packed and the line at the bar wasn't long.

"Drinks are on me tonight." I confirmed our order before heading to the bar—three dirty martinis and one lemonade.

I didn't flirt with the bartender even though he was objectively attractive. I handed Hazel and Everly their martinis wondering if I should have flirted. He had a cute smile. It might have been fun.

But I didn't want to flirt with the bartender, cute smile or otherwise.

I ignored the guy sipping whiskey at the end of the bar who gave me a thorough once over, openly appreciating what he saw. Once upon a time, I would have been pleased to see a man like him eying me as if he wanted me for dessert. He was attractive, well-dressed. After some conversation and exploratory dancing, I might have given him my number. Or even let him take me to his place tonight, if we really hit it off.

But all I could think about was Dex. How nice it would have been to spend the evening curled up next to him on his couch.

Now I was just being dramatic. This club was fun, my outfit was fabulous, and I was going to enjoy myself, damn it.

We sipped our drinks for a while and instead of talking about Everly's latest terrible date, Hazel's professional rivalry, or Sophie's awkwardly adorable mishaps, we chatted about pregnancy and babies and what to do about a husband who leaves his underwear on the floor right next to the laundry hamper.

My back prickled and I couldn't seem to stay still. Why did our conversation make me so jumpy? I wasn't married or having babies or worrying about a husband who seemed blind to the proper place for dirty clothes. And thank goodness for that. The last thing I needed in my life was the frustration of sharing my space with a man. Maybe it was good that things had blown up with Dex—even better that it was over something so silly.

I had my out, didn't I? No one would blame me if I said we were done.

"Let's dance." I was grateful the music masked the edge of panic in my voice as I grabbed Everly's hand. "Who wants to dance with me?"

Leaving our empty drinks at the small table, we made our way to the dance floor. Good music, great friends, a light buzz from the martini. Exactly what I needed.

Except it wasn't.

Dancing with my friends was fun, especially the way

they laughed and smiled. But none of it replaced the ache in my chest.

"Hey." A guy in a black button-down and fitted black slacks sidled up next to me and put a hand on my elbow. "Wanna dance?"

He had blue eyes and a peach fuzz attempt at a beard. His clothes looked expensive but they didn't hide the fact that he was probably ten years younger than me—at the very least.

Oh my god.

I looked around. Was there anyone else in here over the age of thirty? Or were we the only ones?

"No thanks," I said, trying to keep my voice even. "Girls' night and none of us are single."

"Damn." Shaking his head, he removed his hand from my elbow. "Let me know if you change your mind."

At least he hadn't ma'amed me?

Everly checked to make sure I was okay. I assured her I was. The song changed again and Sophie gestured toward our table. I checked my phone and tried not to be disappointed that Dex hadn't replied.

But I was. I really, really was.

Hazel met my eyes and raised her voice above the music. "Time to go home?"

Everly slipped her arm around my waist. "You need the ice cream now, don't you?"

With tears misting in my eyes, I nodded. "I'm sorry. We got all dressed up and we've hardly danced at all."

Sophie put her arm around me on the other side. "It's okay."

"We don't mind," Hazel said.

"Whatever you need," Everly said. "We've got you."

"Then let's go. I don't want to be here. I want to wallow."

We hugged again, holding each other for a moment in our sacred circle of trust. And I knew, no matter what happened between me and Dex, I'd always have my best friends.

And that meant a lot.

35

DEX

My head throbbed with a headache that nothing over the counter would touch. I'd spent the night in my mom's guest room, tossing and turning instead of sleeping—and regretting my decision to stay there and not go home. But if I'd gone home, she would have been right next door. I needed some space to cool down and get my head together.

Had it helped? Not really.

Riley knew something was going on, although I'd told her there was a plumbing issue at home which was why we were staying the night at my parents'. I didn't think she believed me. She'd given me a look when I'd dropped her off at school this morning that said she was concerned. Or maybe suspicious.

I didn't know what to tell her.

I'd hoped getting lost in work would help, and to an extent, it had. I had a client come in for more work on his half-sleeve, and while I'd been tattooing, my headache—and the reasons for it—had receded to the back of my mind.

But as soon as I'd finished, it had all come back with a vengeance.

My phone was still off. I knew I had messages from Nora but I hadn't replied. What was I supposed to say? What did you do when you realized the woman you were dating wasn't who you thought she was?

She'd called it the single dad article. Yeah, it had been about single dads all right. A handbook for taking advantage of them. It read like something Aimee Bachman, the neighborhood horny divorced mom, would have written, not Nora.

But maybe I'd been kidding myself about her. Seeing what I wanted to see. Because if that article was the real Nora, I hadn't known her at all.

"Hey, Dex," Kari said, poking her head in the back office. "There's a phone call for you. It's Riley's school."

"Sorry, my phone is off." I wondered if she wasn't feeling well. She'd seemed fine this morning. Hadn't she? To be fair, I'd been pretty distracted. I picked up the phone. "This is Dex St. James."

"Hi, Mr. St. James, I'm calling about your daughter, Riley."

"Is she okay?"

"Well, there was an incident in one of her classes. She started an altercation with another student. We have her in the principal's office and we need you to come in as soon as possible."

"An altercation? What does that mean? Is she hurt?"

"There were no injuries to either student."

I opened my mouth to ask what the hell she was talking about but decided to just get my ass down there and talk to them in person. "I'm on my way."

"Thank you. You can come straight to the office when you arrive."

"Will do."

Fuck.

"Kari, I have kid issues," I called up to the front. "I have to go."

"No problem, boss. I'll take care of it."

I grabbed my keys and left.

The sky was heavy with gray clouds threatening rain. After pulling out of the parking lot, I turned on my phone. It dinged with several messages. For a second, I thought about calling Nora. Which made no sense. Whatever was going on, it wasn't Nora's problem.

I had a text from Riley. All it said was, *I'm in trouble.*

Yeah, no shit, kid.

I couldn't believe this. Riley never got in trouble at school. She'd started an altercation? Did that mean she'd gotten in a fight? What a fucking mess.

By the time I pulled into the school parking lot, my head felt like it was going to explode and send my eyeballs popping out of my skull. I found a spot and took a deep breath. I didn't want to go in hot and make an already shitty situation worse.

Although Riley was definitely grounded until she was twenty.

I got out right as another car pulled into the lot. I had to do a double take. What was she doing here?

Nora parked and got out of her Jeep. She was dressed in a rumpled cardigan over a t-shirt, a pair of jeans, and her running shoes. On any other woman, I wouldn't have noticed the outfit. But on her, it screamed that something was off. Nora Lakes always looked perfectly put together no matter the setting—whether she was out for a run, lounging around the house, going to work, or out to dinner.

This outfit didn't match or coordinate or whatever the right word was. It was like she'd just thrown on whatever was closest and left the house.

But really, why the hell was she here?

She rushed over to me, her long ponytail so loose it was falling out. "I didn't get her text right away. What's going on?"

"Whose text?"

"Riley's."

Riley had texted her, too? I had no idea how to feel about that.

I also had no idea how to deal with the sense of relief that poured through me when I realized she was here to help.

Or how good it was just to see her.

Which was messed up. It had been less than twenty-four hours.

I shook my head to clear it. "I don't know what's going on. The school called and I'm here."

Her eyes met mine, a silent question in her expression. *Can I come with you?*

The decision wasn't exactly conscious. I just started toward the school office. "Let's go."

She fell in step next to me and we went in. The office manager checked us in and gave us visitor name tags. We followed the office manager down a short hallway to the principal's office.

The nameplate on the door said Janelle Teague. I'd seen her at a back-to-school night last fall but I hadn't met her in person. She sat at her desk, dressed in a light gray shirt. Her brown hair was pulled back in a slick bun and she had serious, no-nonsense air. About what you'd expect for a middle school principal.

Let's be honest, that's a tough age. I wouldn't have been able to do her job.

"Thank you for coming, Mr. St. James. Please, both of you have a seat."

Riley was slumped in a chair with her backpack in her lap. My first instinct was to look her over to make sure she was okay. Regardless of what the office manager had said on the phone, I wanted to know if she'd been hurt. But she looked fine. Miserable, but not injured or in pain.

My second instinct was to be furious with her. A fight at school? And at the very end of the school year? Yep. Grounded. Forever.

"This is Nora," I said as we took our seats. "What's going on?"

Principal Teague folded her hands on her desk. "Riley, why don't you explain."

Her eyes stayed firmly on the ground. "I got in a fight."

"You started a fight, Riley," Principal Teague said.

"What were you thinking?" I asked. "You've never been in a fight in your life. You know better than that."

Riley slumped lower.

"It was a free day in PE," Principal Teague said. "The students were outside on the field. According to the victim, Riley attacked her without provocation."

I stared at my daughter like I didn't know who she was. "What? Who was the other kid?"

"Katie," Riley mumbled.

"Katie? I thought she was your friend." I could practically feel my blood pressure rising. "This is insane. What were you thinking? You can't—"

Nora put a hand on my arm and I stopped short.

"Riley, what really happened?" Nora asked, her voice soft.

"She attacked another student during class," Principal Teague said, a hint of irritation in her voice.

Nora ignored her. "Ry, honey. What's going on?"

Riley sat up straighter. "I thought Katie was my friend. I told her about my mom and I thought she wouldn't tell anyone. But she told Ryan Hutchison and they made all these memes about me and sent them to everyone. They mostly say stuff about how my own mother hates me."

Red hot fury poured through me. I clenched my fists but Nora put a hand on my arm again.

"Honey, do you have any of these memes on your phone or know where we could find them?" Nora asked.

"She has my phone," Riley said.

Principal Teague hesitated, but handed Riley her phone. Riley tapped the screen a few times, then gave it to Nora. She swiped through the memes while I watched, each one feeding my rising fury.

Nora held up the phone. "These are just the memes. The comments are worse."

"Did the school know about this?" I asked through clenched teeth.

"We can't be responsible for policing every social media app," Principal Teague said. "But yes, we were aware that there were some inappropriate things being said online."

"And you never bothered to inform her father?" I asked.

"Dad, it's okay, the memes were stupid," Riley said. "Katie was doing it to be popular, and that's just sad. I decided to stop being friends with her because she wasn't ever my friend in the first place."

"Then what happened today?" I asked.

She took a breath. "I guess they got bored of making fun

of me because they started targeting someone else. Her name is Holly and she's super shy, I think because she has acne. The stuff they're posting about her is even worse than anything they said about me. I wish I would have said something about it sooner or told a teacher or something, but I was trying to ignore them. Then today in PE I heard Katie telling Holly that she was so ugly, she should commit suicide." She looked down again. "I kind of lost it. I ran over and smacked Katie in the face."

"Good," I said.

"Mr. St. James." Principal Teague's spine snapped straight and she shot me with a look that I was sure would freeze a middle schooler in their tracks.

But not me.

"I get it, you can't have kids brawling at school. But someone needed to stand up for that poor girl."

"We have a zero tolerance policy for violence," the principal said. "Riley is suspended for the remainder of the school year."

"And that's it? Katie tells a kid to kill herself and Riley is the one who gets punished?"

"Obviously we'll investigate the situation further and deal with Katie appropriately."

"You do what you gotta do." I stood. "But I'm proud of my daughter for defending someone who couldn't defend herself. You clearly have a bullying problem at this school, Ms. Teague. I hope you can figure out a better way of dealing with it."

Nora stood and Riley followed. I led them out to the parking lot, my blood still boiling, although my headache had become a dull throb behind my eyes.

I stopped on the sidewalk and rubbed the back of my neck. I had no idea what to say to Nora. We needed to resolve things one way or another but probably not in the parking lot of my daughter's school. And not in front of Riley.

"Thanks for coming," I said.

"Of course." She hesitated and I avoided her eyes. "I should get going. I'll talk to you later."

I didn't reply. Maybe I should have. But I just nodded.

She went to her car and Riley and I got in mine.

"What did you do?" Riley asked as she fastened her seatbelt.

"Excuse me?"

"What's wrong with Nora? Did you break up with her? Why would you do that?"

I turned on the car. "I didn't break up with her. There are just some things going on. It's grown-up stuff. You don't need to worry about it."

"I am worried about it."

"How about you worry about yourself. You're the one who just got kicked out of school."

"Me being kicked out of school is dumb and we both know it."

I sighed as I pulled out onto the street. "For the record, you shouldn't hit people. It's not a good way to solve a problem. But I am proud of you for standing up for that girl."

"I know I shouldn't have smacked Katie. I was just so mad."

"Of course you were. That was a terrible thing for her to say." I paused. "All this stuff with that Ryan girl and Katie... is that why you were failing PE? Mean girl stuff?"

"Yeah. They made fun of me sometimes so I sat out to avoid them. But I figured I shouldn't let them get to me."

"You're a pretty amazing kid, you know that?"

She smiled. "Thanks, Dad."

"But you're still grounded."

She groaned. "How long?"

"Forever."

"Dad."

"Fine, you have to go help your grandpa with his landscaping project until school is out. You don't get to sit around and paint when you should be at school."

"Fine. I can do that. Now tell me what's going on with Nora."

"It's none of your business."

"Yes, it is. She's part of my life too, you know."

How could I explain this? There was no way I could tell Riley that Nora might have become her friend just to get to me. She'd be heartbroken. But she was right, Nora was a part of her life and I owed her at least a partial explanation.

"Nora wrote an article about dating a single dad that was hurtful to me. It said a lot of stuff that I disagree with and made me realize our relationship probably wasn't what I thought it was."

"What did she say about it?"

"What do you mean?"

"When you asked her why she wrote it, what did she say?"

It started to rain so I turned on the windshield wipers. "We haven't really talked about it."

"So you don't know why she wrote that stuff? Or even if she did write it?"

"Of course she wrote it. It's her column."

"Dad," she said, her tone filled with exasperation. "She said they edit her stuff a lot and it bothers her because sometimes they make really big changes."

She had said that, hadn't she? "How did you know that?"

"When we had dinner at that place with the really good

noodles, she was talking about work. I remember because I said that it would be like someone adding colors to one of my paintings and she said that was exactly right. And we agreed that it sucked."

"Wow, you really listened, didn't you?"

"Yeah. Didn't you?"

I scowled.

"Sorry, but is that why we stayed at Grandma and Grandpa's last night? You had a fight with Nora?"

"Yes."

"This sucks."

"I know, kiddo. It really does."

Nora's Jeep wasn't in her driveway when we got home. But a car I didn't recognize was parked on the street outside my house. I parked, eying it with suspicion. Who the hell was here?

"Oh, shit," I muttered as three men got out of the car and walked up the driveway in the rain.

"Dad," Riley said.

"Sorry."

"Is that—"

"Yeah," I said, unable to keep the dread out of my voice. "It's the husband gang."

"What are they doing here?"

"I have no idea."

That wasn't exactly true. I had an inkling as to why they were here. I just hadn't thought their threats were quite this serious.

Apparently these guys didn't mess around.

I got out of the car and gave them a chin tip. I'd let them in, and hear what they had to say, but I wasn't about to be lectured by a bunch of guys who didn't know the full story.

"Hi there, Miss Riley," Cox said, nothing but friendliness in his tone.

She ran to the front door to get out of the rain, her backpack swinging off her shoulder. "Hi! Hurry, it's pouring."

I paused and motioned for the three men to follow her inside. Shepherd glared at me. No surprise there. Corban's brow furrowed, as if there were something about me he didn't understand. Cox just patted me on the shoulder as he walked by—a gesture with an air of condolence, rather than support.

With a resigned breath, I went inside and shut the door. "Gentlemen."

Riley watched expectantly.

Shepherd cast a glance in her direction, as if deciding whether to talk in front of her. "You know why we're here."

"Because of Nora?" Riley asked.

"She's a smart one," Cox said.

"I thought we made our position clear," Shepherd said.

"How about I make something clear." I crossed my arms. "This is between me and Nora. It's not anyone else's business and I don't appreciate you coming over here and acting like you can threaten me."

"It's not a threat," Shepherd said, his voice low.

Cox patted him on the back and took a step forward. "Maybe you let me take this one and we can cut through the bullshit. Dex, Nora didn't write that article."

"See!" Riley dropped her backpack on the floor with a thud. "I told you."

"Go to your room." I pointed upstairs.

She crossed her arms and stood still.

"What we have here is a misunderstanding," Cox said, as if Riley hadn't interrupted. "Trust me when I say I understand how quickly these things can spiral out of control. So let's not let that happen."

"Open communication is key to a healthy relationship," Corban said.

"It sounds obvious, but he's right," Shepherd said.

I stared at them, dumbfounded. She hadn't written it?

"I'm such an idiot." I didn't even need to hear the rest—how it happened, why an article she hadn't written had been published under her name. I knew Cox was right.

And I knew I'd messed up. Big time.

I pinched the bridge of my nose and started pacing around the front room. "She didn't know it had been published. That's what she said when I confronted her, and I didn't listen. Damn it. Why didn't I listen? Why didn't I give her a chance to explain?"

"This was easier than I thought it would be," Cox said, sounding pleased with himself.

"No, there's no easy," I said. "You don't understand, I really fucked this up. I don't know if I can fix it."

"Of course you can," Riley said. "You have to."

"You might be surprised." Corban adjusted his glasses. "Love can heal lot. We've all been there."

"And like Cox said, it's just a misunderstanding," Riley said.

I shook my head. "It's a big-ass misunderstanding."

"My wife got served with divorce papers," Cox said. "At work. That was a pretty big misunderstanding, but we got through it."

"Hazel and I started out hating each other," Corban said. "There was a lot to work through, but we did."

Everyone's eyes moved to Shepherd. He didn't move, his expression stony.

"Come on, Shep," Cox said. "You've got a feeling in there somewhere. You can let it out once in a while."

Shepherd glared at Cox, then cleared his throat. It was interesting to see him look mildly uncomfortable. Maybe he did have a feeling in there.

His voice was low. "I was in a similar position and I also didn't give Everly a chance to explain. At first." He held up a finger. "Once I realized what I'd done, I did everything I could to make things right."

My shoulders slumped. "So what do I do?"

"Calling her back might be a good start," Cox said.

He was right, I needed to talk to her. But not on the phone. And I didn't just need to talk, I needed to show her that I was sorry. Show her I'd do anything to make things up to her.

Show her I loved her.

Because, damn it, I did love her. That was why I'd over-reacted. It wasn't an excuse—I'd screwed up and it was up to me to make it right. But if I hadn't loved her I wouldn't have cared.

I did love her. I loved the hell out of that fierce, confident, beautiful woman. I didn't know if she'd forgive me but I had to try.

My back straightened, resolve pouring through me. I knew what I had to do.

I just hoped it would work.

36

NORA

*R*etail therapy wasn't helping.

I wandered through the store, idly brushing past the displays of summer clothing. A lavender floral dress caught my eye. It would look adorable on Riley.

After the incident at her school, I'd decided not to go home. Maybe I was the one walking away from the conflict this time but the visit to the principal's office had rattled me. I needed a little time to clear my head—to process what had happened.

I didn't want to make it all about me. Riley had been dealing with more than I'd realized—even more than she'd shared with me or her dad. And I was so proud of her. Not for slapping Katie, but for standing up for that poor girl being bullied. Riley hadn't let her experiences on the bad end of a mean girl situation close her off. Quite the opposite. It had opened her up to see someone else's struggle and she'd acted to help.

But I couldn't get over how natural it had felt to be there. To walk into that principal's office with Dex. To ask questions and voice my opinion.

Why had I done that? Who was I to Dex and Riley? Dex's neighbor? His girlfriend? I wasn't Riley's mother and really, there had been no reason for me to be there. I didn't belong.

And yet, I hadn't thought twice about going when Riley had texted to let me know she was in trouble and they were calling her dad.

I caught a glimpse of myself in a mirror as I wandered deeper into the store. Oh my god, what was I wearing? I rolled my eyes. I'd put on a t-shirt with a mismatched cardigan, jeans, and my running shoes. My ponytail was drooping and I hadn't bothered with makeup. I was a mess.

I thanked the sales associate and left, heading out into the rain. Buying a new outfit wasn't going to make me feel better. And I'd just quit my job, so needless spending wasn't a good idea anyway.

It had gone from cloudy to pouring rain. I didn't bother trying to shield my hair from the downpour. I was a mess already, so what did it matter?

I got into my Jeep and five minutes later, the rain stopped. Because of course it did. I drove home, wondering what I should do. I didn't want to call Dex again. The ball was in his court now. Although I did want to know if Riley was okay. I resolved to text her when I got home.

Dex's car was in his driveway. For a second, the clouds parted, bathing our houses in sunlight. The flowers he'd planted looked unnaturally bright and colorful, but the sight of them stung. This was why I'd avoided relationships for so long. This feeling. The hurt and disappointment. Granted, this wasn't nearly as traumatic as being confronted by a woman who'd hired a private investigator and finding out your entire life was a lie.

This was different. It was a quieter hurt. Dex thought I

was capable of writing that article, that I saw him as something to be used for my pleasure and that I saw his daughter as a means to that end.

I got out of my car and went inside, feeling restless. I sent Riley a text, asking her if she was all right and to check in with me when she could. Then I peeled off my damp cardigan, tossed it onto the back of the couch, and wandered into the kitchen.

Everly's box of pink hair chalk was still on the counter. After the club, we'd come here and gorged on cold pizza and ice cream. My friends had let me pout for a while. And I loved them for that.

Maybe I needed more pizza.

I went to the fridge to see if there was any left—Sophie's craving had been intense—but a muffled noise outside caught my attention. It sounded like music. Once in a while a car would drive by with music blaring but it came and went. This wasn't stopping.

There was one piece of pizza left, so I ignored the noise —it was probably just someone parked outside one of my neighbor's houses. Either that or Phil had taken to doing his shake weight workout on his front lawn.

That was something I didn't need to see.

My phone buzzed with a text. I abandoned the pizza, dropping the cold slice on the counter, and practically ran to my phone. Which was so dumb. I had more dignity than that. I was Nora Lakes and I wasn't going to let some man get to me like this.

Who was I kidding. Yes I was.

Because I was in love with him.

That thought hit me so hard and so fast, I froze. My eyes widened and my heart seemed to skip a few beats, leaving me slightly breathless.

It was true. I wasn't upset simply because of a misunder-standing with the man I was sleeping with. I was upset—this upset—because I loved him. And I didn't want this to be the end.

My friends had known. They hadn't badmouthed him or made plans to burn the things he'd left at my house or told me I was so much better off without him. They'd simply let me feel my feelings, knowing that I needed to process them. Knowing I was going to figure it out sooner or later.

Hoping against hope that Dex had finally texted me back, I checked my phone.

Riley: *Can you come outside please?*

Disappointment flooded through me. Not that I wasn't happy to hear from Riley. I'd been more than a little bit afraid that Dex wouldn't let her talk to me. Her text was reassuring, but I still desperately wanted to talk to her dad.

As soon as I opened the front door, music surrounded me. It was a love song from a movie and it wasn't coming from a car parked on the street, nor was Phil using it to power through his shake weight workout.

It was Dex.

He stood on the sidewalk outside my house, dressed in his usual t-shirt and jeans. The music had attracted a few of our neighbors. Phil came outside, as did several other people from down the street.

Dex held a stack of white poster boards in his hands. Another love song began, emanating from the Bluetooth speaker he used when he worked out—had he made a playlist? —and he began turning the poster boards over, one at a time.

Nora, I'm so sorry.

I never should have doubted you.

You're the most loyal, loving, badass woman I've ever known.

I know I don't deserve you.
But I'm asking you anyway.
Please forgive me.
I love you.

Tears gathered in the corners of my eyes and my throat felt thick. I stepped down from the porch just as the sky opened up and it started to rain again.

I didn't care. Fat drops splashed everywhere as I rushed to Dex. He dropped the poster boards and caught me in his arms.

Vaguely, I was aware of the applause of our neighbors. Dex held me tight, his face buried in my neck.

"I'm so sorry," he said, close to my ear. "I should have known it wasn't you."

"I forgive you."

He let out a long breath and moved back to look me in the eyes. "I love you."

Water streamed down my face and dripped from his hair. "I love you, too."

Cupping my cheeks, he kissed me. His lips were warm and wonderfully familiar. I sank into his kiss, my body melting against him.

"Did you just say you loved me?" he asked, the corners of his mouth lifting.

"I did." I glanced up, blinking at the rain. "Are we really declaring our love for each other while getting soaked in a rainstorm?"

He grinned. "We sure are."

I groaned. "Dex, this is the worst."

"I know." He kissed me again. "Don't worry, a little romance won't hurt you."

"Fine, but I'm not swooning."

"That's okay. I'll be sure to ruin your lipstick later." His eyes darted to the side. "But there's one more thing."

Down the sidewalk, Riley stood with a giant bouquet of red roses tucked in her arm and another poster board in her hands. She turned it over.

I love you, too.

With one arm still around Dex, I held my other arm out to her, laughing and crying all at once. She dropped the flowers and poster board and ran to us, throwing her arms around us both.

We stood in the rain, holding each other, just the three of us.

And it was perfect.

"I love you, too, sweetie." I sniffed and water dripped off the end of my nose. "I love you both so much."

"See, Dad? I told you she'd forgive you."

I laughed. "Maybe we should get out of the rain. We're drenched."

Dex brushed a strand of wet hair off my face. "Yeah, let's go inside."

"Sorry for dropping your flowers." Riley picked up the bouquet and her poster board. "I just got really excited."

I took the flowers from her while Dex picked up his speaker and the other poster boards off the sidewalk. "That's okay. They're beautiful."

"Dad said he didn't know if you'd be into flowers but I said it didn't matter. You'd love them anyway."

I inhaled deeply of the fresh, floral scent. "You were right."

Dex put one arm around me and the other around Riley, and led us inside out of the rain. His shirt was plastered to his body, as was mine. Riley had made out slightly better— she'd put on a hoodie—but her hair was dripping wet.

It didn't matter.

We dried off as best we could. Dex changed into a dry shirt and gave me one of his to wear. He didn't have a vase but I found a pitcher that was big enough and put the flowers in water. Riley winked at her dad as she excused herself to go upstairs and change. She seemed to be able to tell we needed a few minutes alone.

Dex brought me into the living room and pulled me onto the couch next to him. "I really am sorry. I jumped to a lot of very wrong conclusions."

"It did hurt that you thought I'd write that."

"I know. I shouldn't have assumed the worst. And I shouldn't have ignored your messages."

"Thank you."

"I'm also sorry for the big romantic gesture. But I had to."

I ran a finger down his chest. "You're lucky you're so cute."

He smiled. "What happened with the article, anyway?"

"One of the editors decided my article wasn't clicky enough and it was going to impact her bonus. So she wrote her own and turned it in as mine."

"No shit?"

"Unfortunately. So I quit."

He raised his eyebrows. "Damn."

"I know. Maybe it seems rash but my boss approved it knowing it was going to make me look bad. She didn't care because she knew controversy would generate traffic."

"I'd hate to see what kind of comments it's getting."

"They pulled the article already and I didn't look before they took it down. I don't really want to know."

He pulled me closer and I nestled against him. "It'll pass.

It's not like there's a shortage of things for people to be outraged about online."

"True. Now I have to figure out what to do about a job."

"We'll figure something out."

I sat up so I could look him in the eyes. "We?"

"Yeah, we. That's how this works."

He touched my chin, bringing my lips to his for a kiss.

We. I never would have thought that simple word could mean so much or feel so right. But it did. This wasn't temporary or fleeting. It wasn't a pleasant distraction that would run its course. Dex was so much more. He was everything.

And my heart whispered another simple word.

Forever.

37

NORA

*T*he backyard was chaos. Beautiful chaos.

Dex's nieces and nephews ran around with squirt guns, yelling at the top of their lungs, and jumped in the bounce house Gillian had rented. Their parents managed the pandemonium with practiced ease, all while sipping drinks. Smoke rose from the grill and the spread of food was impressive.

Corban and Cox stood chatting with Dex and his brother, Dallas, while Dex manned the grill. Shepherd was engrossed in conversation with Dex's dad, Joel. He held his daughter, a wary eye on the other kids, as if he were concerned she might get run over if he put her down.

Everly and Sophie chatted with Dex's sisters, Maggie and Angie, and Hazel had an in depth conversation with Dex's sister-in-law, Tori, and his mom.

We'd decided to invite everyone over for an end-of-summer barbecue and it was every bit as crazy as I'd thought it would be. But I loved it.

Somehow, I'd unofficially moved in with Dex and Riley. He'd started by inviting me to stay over every night. Soon, more and more of my things seemed to find their way next door. Now most of my wardrobe and personal items were in Dex's house, as was about half my kitchen—including my bar and wine glasses—and my entire home office. He'd cleaned out his spare bedroom and moved my office over when I'd taken Riley to the spa with my friends last weekend.

Sneaky.

Not that I was complaining. I loved sleeping next to Dex every night and waking to his touch in the morning.

And I had plans for my house next door. Eventually—probably sooner rather than later—my move would be official and I'd turn my house into a rental.

I brought a fresh tray of watermelon outside and set it with the rest of the food. The kids went through it like crazy. Within seconds, two of Dex's nephews had already grabbed slices and run off with them.

"You're welcome," I called.

"Thank you!" they both said, mouths full of melon.

Dex caught my eye and winked. I smiled back. I loved that man.

Someone touched my elbow. "Hello, darling sister."

"Jensen. You actually came."

My brother was dressed as if he were planning to take a woman out on a date, not come to a backyard barbecue. Suit jacket, no tie, the collar of his shirt unbuttoned.

He handed me a bouquet of multicolored flowers. "Of course I did."

"This is suspiciously nice."

"No suspicion necessary, love. And I know, you already told me, the women here are all married." He rolled his eyes. "You could have thought of me when you put together the guest list, but I'll forgive you this once."

"That's very generous of you, Jensen."

"I'm a generous man."

"You're a ridiculous man."

He grinned. "That too. How's work now that you're back to being an independent woman?"

I'd been able to get the rights to my blog back. *Living Your Best Life* was once more under my creative control. I was working on hiring a small team to help me run it and putting out more varied content to build my readership. Fortunately, the crappy single dad article had blown over. In fact, my love letter to dating a single dad had been the first article I'd published after leaving Glamour Gal and it had jump started my new venture in a big way.

Dex had framed it and put it on the wall in my new office.

"It's good. I have a few more interviews this week, but I'm close to hiring someone."

"Excellent." His gaze swung around the backyard and he gestured toward Gillian. "Who's that lovely woman?"

"Dex's mom."

"Perfect." His mouth curled in a grin. "Excuse me, love. I'm going to go have some fun."

I shook my head as he made his way toward Gillian. But I wasn't worried. She'd be able to hold her own. In fact, being the object of Jensen's shameless flirting would probably be fun.

Riley caught my eye. She had her phone to her ear as she slipped inside through the back door.

My instincts tingled. Something was going on. I followed her in.

She stepped into the living room and answered her phone. "Hi, Mom."

A sense of fierce protectiveness stole over me. Why was

Brooklyn calling her? For a second, I thought about running outside to find Dex. I didn't want to butt into a situation that wasn't my business.

But damn it, this was my business. Maybe I was just Dex's girlfriend, but Riley was important to me. If one of my friends had been in a difficult situation, I wouldn't have hesitated to be there for them. I'd do the same for Riley.

"We're having a barbecue right now, so it's busy." Riley met my eyes and shrugged.

I moved closer. If she wanted privacy I'd give it to her, but otherwise, I was going to stay with her.

She stepped toward me and slipped her hand in mine. My heart just about burst.

"Oh." She paused again, listening to whatever her mom had to say. "Actually, no thanks."

I couldn't hear what Brooklyn was saying but Riley squeezed my hand. I squeezed back.

"I'd rather not," she said. There was another pause. "Because I'm busy."

I kept waiting, holding her hand.

"You can if you want to, but when school starts I'll be busier... Okay... Talk to you later." She ended the call and met my eyes. "That was my mom."

"What did she want?"

"She wanted to see me. Tonight. I said no." She glanced down at her phone. "I'm not mad at her or anything, but I don't really believe her when she says she wants to see me. She doesn't show up. And I don't have to let her treat me that way. I can say no."

I pulled her in for a hug and she wrapped her arms around my waist. "You can absolutely say no."

"Thanks for being the one who always shows up."

Tears stung my eyes and I hugged her tighter. "I love you, honey."

"I love you, too."

She stepped back and tucked her hair behind her ear. "Is it okay if my friend Holly comes over? She lives right up the street, so she can walk."

"It's fine with me. Is this the Holly you slapped Katie over?"

She smiled. "Yeah. It turns out she's really cool."

"I can't wait to meet her."

"I'll go tell Dad." She ran out through the backdoor, pausing to glance over her shoulder. "Thanks, Nora."

With a smile, I followed her outside.

The women in Dex's family had all gravitated toward Jensen. He stood with them fanned out around him, eating it up like the attention-whore he was. I left them to it and wandered over to where Dex was busy grilling and slipped my arm around his waist.

He kissed my temple. "Hi, beautiful."

"How's it going over here?"

"Can't complain."

Hazel came over to get a drink out of the cooler, followed closely by Everly and Sophie.

"Hey Everly," Dex said. "Thanks for putting me in touch with Zoe Miles. We got everything squared away."

"Wonderful!" Everly said. "I'm so excited."

"Got what squared away?" I asked.

"Our wedding."

I extricated myself from under his arm. "Excuse me, what?"

"Our wedding."

"I heard you say those words the first time but since when are we getting married?"

"Since I booked the venue. It's next spring at Salishan Cellars."

I gaped at him for a moment. "What are you talking about?"

"The girls told me it's supposed to be there. I don't make the rules."

"Dex, we're not engaged."

A slow, sexy grin spread across his face. "I know. That's why I scheduled it for next spring. That should give you plenty of time to get used to the idea."

I blinked at him. I had no idea what to say to that.

He set the spatula down, then slipped an arm around my waist and pulled me to the side. His voice was low in my ear. "I'm going to marry you, Nora Lakes. That's just what's happening."

I will not swoon. I will not swoon.

"Is that so?"

His lips brushed my ear and his voice was a low growl. "You're mine."

My legs wobbled and he tightened his grip on me.

Okay, maybe I was swooning. A little.

"If you want a big romantic display, I can do that, too." He still spoke softly into my ear. "But I have a feeling I used up my one romantic gesture that day in the rain. And we both know this is it for us. We're a family."

He was right. I didn't want a big romantic display. That wasn't my style. I wanted honesty and loyalty, and I'd give it in return.

I also wanted a family. I wanted Dex and Riley and I wanted them forever.

"Yes. I'll marry you." I leaned in and brushed my lips against his. "But you better be planning to put a ring on my finger."

"Don't worry, honey, I have it covered. It's inside." He kissed me again.

"Did you really book the venue already?"

"I did."

"Does Riley know about all this?"

"Not yet. Should we tell her?"

With a smile, I nodded.

He took my hand and led me inside. He did indeed have a ring, hidden in a drawer in our bedroom. It was perfect—a classic emerald cut diamond with diamonds in the band.

"How long have you had this?" I asked.

"I bought it after the whole single dad article incident." He slipped it on my finger, then lifted my hand to his lips and kissed my knuckles.

"You knew then?"

He met my eyes. "I think deep down, I knew the first time I saw you. I knew you were trouble. And now look at us."

I held my hand out and admired the ring, not just for its beauty, but for what it represented. Nothing had ever felt so right.

We went downstairs and found Riley. She was in the front room, waiting for her friend Holly to arrive.

"Hey, kiddo," Dex said. "We have something to tell you."

I held up my hand so she could see the ring.

Her eyes widened. "Oh my gosh. Is that real? Are you serious?"

I nodded. "We're serious. We're getting married. Is that okay with you?"

"Are you kidding? Of course it's okay with me." She rushed forward and we caught her in a three-way hug. "I wanted you to get married so bad."

Her shoulders shook as she started to cry. Dex and I held

her. He glanced at me with concern, but I shook my head. It was fine. Sometimes a girl just needed to feel her feelings.

She stepped back and wiped beneath her eyes. "Sorry. I'm just so happy."

"I'm happy, too," I said and it was the biggest understatement of my life. I'd never been so happy.

Once upon a time, I'd thought I'd be forever single. I hadn't counted on the gruff, tattooed man next door breaking all my rules. But he had and I wouldn't have changed it for the world.

We were a family and we were going to be together forever.

EPILOGUE: NORA

The woman in the mirror couldn't have been me.

She wore a glorious form-fitting, floor-length gown with lace, a plunging V-neck, and a slight train. Her hair was in a chic up-do, showing off her neck and shoulders. No veil. Just a pearl clip with gold accents in her hair. Her makeup was soft and feminine, her nails manicured, and her gold heels positively fierce.

"I can't believe what I'm seeing."

Everly handed me a bouquet and I held it in front of me.

"Now I really can't believe what I'm seeing."

"You're the most beautiful bride," she said.

Hazel appeared in the mirror next to me and fussed with a lock of my hair. "She is truly stunning, isn't she?"

"So gorgeous," Sophie said. "I'm getting teary."

"Don't you start," I said. "If you start, then Everly will start, and the next thing we know, my mascara will be ruined."

The girls and I had decided on wine-colored bridesmaid dresses, each cut to flatter their body type. Everly's had spaghetti straps and we'd only had to have it altered slightly to accommodate her newly announced second pregnancy. Hazel had chosen a bold off the shoulder style that looked incredible on her. She'd been skeptical but I stood by my insistence that she try it on. Sophie's had an A-line skirt that did wonderful things for her curvy post-baby body.

Dex really had booked our wedding venue. At Sophie's wedding, I'd apparently told my friends that if I ever got married, I'd have it here, at Salishan Cellars, a winery in the Cascade mountains. I probably had said that—flippantly, since I'd been so convinced I was never getting married.

But Dex had broken my rules.

Now I was a bride. His bride.

Strangely, I wasn't nervous. A profound sense of peace settled over me as I gazed at my reflection. I hadn't seen this coming but sometimes the best things in life are unexpected.

Riley came into the bride's room already smiling. Her dusty rose dress complimented the bridesmaid dresses while allowing her to stand out. The scoop neck and A-line skirt were adorable and she'd chosen to wear her hair down in loose waves. She looked like a sweet little angel.

Little being a relative term. She'd grown another inch since the start of her eighth-grade year, and in her heels, she was almost as tall as me.

I handed Everly my bouquet and reached out to clasp Riley's hands. "Look at you."

"Look at *you*," she said. "Dad's going to freak."

Zoe Miles, the events manager, opened the door and came in. She had long, dark hair and wore a chic blouse and slacks. She'd married into the Miles family, who owned the winery, and had done an amazing job helping us plan the wedding. I'd liked her instantly.

"Are we ready, ladies?" Zoe asked.

"Ready," I said.

We followed her down a short hallway. A photographer snapped photos while we lined up for our entrance. This was it. I was about to get married.

Riley gave me a quick hug before she got in place in front of me. I had to take a few deep breaths so I wouldn't tear up.

When we were ready, Zoe opened the doors.

Our family and friends were seated in rows. To my surprise, my mother had decided to come, along with her husband. My father and his wife were also here—seated with Jensen on the other side of the room.

My new work colleagues had come, as well as a few friends I'd kept from my days with Glamour Gal. Corban sat next to Shepherd and Cox. Shepherd held Ella and Cox cradled his new baby girl, Isabel.

The rest of the room was filled with Dex's family.

There were Gillian and Joel, of course, beaming at me down the aisle. Dallas and Tori. Angie and Mike. Maggie—pregnant with the newest member of the clan—and Jordan. And a mess of nieces and nephews, most of whom looked like they'd kept their nice clothes clean.

So far. We'd have to get pictures with them quickly. It was only a matter of time before one of them spilled something.

But it wasn't the group of guests who caught my attention and held it.

Dex stood at the front, and for the second time since I'd known him, he wore a tux. And he looked every bit as delicious as the first time.

Sleek and handsome, with the peek of his tattoos giving him an edge.

I loved him so much.

Before I knew it, the girls were walking up the aisle, one by one. His brother and brothers-in-law took their places at the front with him and soon it was Riley's turn. Dex smiled at her, full of fatherly love and pride. When she got to the front, she hugged him and stepped to the side.

My turn.

Holding my bouquet, I walked slowly up the aisle. The guests all stood and there was probably music—we'd planned for it—but I didn't hear it. All that existed was the man waiting for me at the front.

The best man I'd ever known. I was so lucky he was mine.

Our ceremony was short but beautiful. And when it was finished, and we were pronounced man and wife, I didn't marvel over how unlikely it was that I'd just gotten married. I simply sank into his kiss while our guests applauded, hoping this feeling of perfect bliss would blaze in my memory for the rest of my life.

Who would have thought a woman like me would have fallen for a single dad and his daughter? I hadn't seen it coming. But now that we were a family, I knew I had what I'd always been missing. A love that would last forever.

~

BONUS EPILOGUE

Nora

*T*he last time I'd stared at myself in the mirror like this, it had been my wedding day.

I'd looked significantly better when Dex and I had said I do. Or at least, I'd looked more put together—hair, makeup, beautiful dress. This morning I was still in pajamas—it was a Saturday—I hadn't put on a stitch of makeup, and my hair was giving me the distinct message that dry shampoo was not going to suffice.

But just like on my wedding day, I looked at myself with a sense of awe and disbelief. Who was this woman, who'd once worn a wedding dress and become a wife?

And who now held a positive pregnancy test in her hand.

I looked down at the test again. Two lines meant positive and the second line had appeared almost instantly. There was no doubt about it. Dex and I were having a baby.

And I couldn't stop smiling.

There was a time when I would have laughed at anyone

who told me I'd be a mom someday. Marriage and family were fine for other people—like Everly, Hazel, and Sophie —but not for me.

Then that rule breaker, Dex St. James, had come into my life and he'd changed everything.

He'd made me a wife and a mom to Riley. And damn it, I loved him for that. He'd opened up a whole new world and given me a life I hadn't known I wanted. Now I couldn't imagine it any other way.

We'd settled into a rhythm as a family and life was full. We had a home, two busy careers, and a teenager with homework, friends, and activities. Were we crazy for adding a baby to the mix?

I put the test down on the counter and took a deep breath. Maybe we were crazy. But ever since our wedding a year ago, a feeling had been growing inside of me. For a while, I'd told myself it was just my hormones reacting to the other babies in my life. Everly had two, Sophie was pregnant again, and Hazel was pregnant with their first. Of course my ovaries had been twinging.

But then one night, Dex had whispered something in my ear, his voice low and soft.

"What if we had a baby together?"

Closing my eyes, I let the memory of that moment wash over me. I could still hear the gentle suggestion and the mix of love and possessiveness behind it. There'd been no pressure, no sense that if I'd said no, he would have pushed. But it had been something he wanted, something he'd been thinking about.

And I'd been shocked to realize I wanted it too.

Now, just a few months later, it was happening.

My hand strayed to my stomach. Was there really a little

life in there? A tiny person that was part of me and the man I loved?

Tears sprang to my eyes and I blew out a breath. Wow. So many feelings.

For a moment, I thought about marching into the kitchen where Dex was cooking breakfast with Riley and showing them the test. But this called for something special. I wasn't usually one for big romantic gestures, but this was a baby. I wanted to do something fun.

The question was, what? How should I tell Dex that we were having a baby together and tell Riley that she was going to be a big sister?

And should I do it before the St. James clan descended on our house for dinner later?

Ideas began to swirl. Dinner with the St. James clan meant people would start arriving shortly after lunch. I didn't have much time, and I had some shopping to do.

Dex

THE SCENE WAS FAMILIAR. My nieces and nephews ran around the backyard throwing water balloons at each other while the adults stood around chatting and enjoying beverages and appetizers. Smoke rose from the grill and the scent of burgers filled the air.

Riley had invited her friend Holly over to hang out. They both liked to paint, so they'd set up easels in one corner of the yard—as far from the water balloon battle as they could get. Both girls had blossomed since becoming friends. Riley said she and Holly had formed a circle of trust, and although I didn't know exactly what that meant, Nora had assured me it meant Holly was a good friend.

And there was Nora. My wife.

She stood chatting with my mom near the tables where we'd set out the food, dressed in a black tank top and fitted jeans. Her dark hair cascaded around her shoulders and that smile. It lit up the whole world.

The light caught on her wedding ring, a quick little sparkle. I didn't think I'd ever get tired of seeing my ring on her finger.

She glanced my direction and our eyes met. Smiling, I winked at her. She smiled back.

Life was good.

Actually, life was great. Business at the shop had never been better and Nora's business was thriving. Riley was doing awesome in school. Marrying Nora was the best decision I'd ever made.

What more could a guy ask for?

One by one, I took the burgers off the grill and set them on a platter. Then I took it over to the food table. After setting it down next to a huge package of buns, I slid an arm around Nora's waist and pulled her close. "What are you girls talking about over here?"

She nestled against me. "Nothing much."

"I'm prying into your life and hinting that it wouldn't be terrible if someone in the family gave me another grandchild," Mom said with a smirk.

"Gillian, I love your honesty," Nora said.

Three kids ran by, shouting a war cry. They seemed to have run out of water balloons and moved on to nerf guns.

"I don't know, Mom, we can hardly keep track of all the kids in this family as it is."

"There's plenty of love to go around," she said.

I smiled. I wasn't about to tell her that Nora and I had talked about having a baby. There was no guarantee it would happen and I didn't want to get her hopes up.

My sister Maggie came to the table and grabbed a paper plate. She paused, eying the food like there was something wrong.

"Who brought those?" She pointed to a platter filled with cookies topped with white chocolate Hershey kisses.

"Me," Mom said. "I made them this morning."

"Why did you make boob cookies?" Maggie asked.

"They're not boob cookies. What are you talking about?"

I looked at them more closely. They did look like boobs —each was a pair of sugar cookie circles stuck together, with Hershey kisses in the centers.

"They look like boobs," Maggie said. "Is it just me?"

"No, they do," Nora said. "I was just trying to be nice by not saying anything."

"They're not boobs," Mom said, sounding frustrated. "I put them too close on the baking sheet and they stuck. I figured they're small anyway, so I left them in twos."

"Which makes them into titty cookies," Maggie said.

"Maggie," Mom scolded. "Don't be vulgar."

"First the vagina slide, now titty cookies," I said.

Nora stifled a laugh.

Mom huffed. "I gave birth to you, and this is what I get?"

I put an arm around her shoulders and squeezed. "You know we love you."

She just sighed.

"Burgers are ready," I said. "Let's round everyone up."

"Kids!" Maggie yelled. "Dinner!"

"Hungry?" I asked Nora as my nieces and nephews started grabbing paper plates.

"In a minute. I need to go get something first."

She went inside, disappearing through the back door, while a line formed for the food. My siblings and their spouses helped the kids who were too small to carry their own plate. Jordan, Maggie's husband, held their youngest so Maggie could eat first. Dad wandered over, carrying one of my sister Angie's kids, and Riley and Holly set down their paint brushes long enough to get in line for their dinner.

Nora came back carrying two silver gift bags. That was odd. It wasn't anyone's birthday—just a random Saturday with good weather.

"Can I have everyone's attention for just a minute?" she said, raising her voice to be heard above the chatter.

Everyone paused and quieted down.

"I bought Dex and Riley a little something and I'm going to make them open these in front of everyone."

Riley came closer and stood next to me. She raised her eyebrows but I didn't know what was going on either, so I shrugged. Nora handed each of us a gift bag.

"What is this?" I asked.

She didn't answer. Just smiled, her blue eyes twinkling.

What was she up to?

"Go ahead," Nora said. "Open them. Both of you."

Riley pulled something out of her bag—it looked like a t-shirt—while I discarded the tissue paper in mine.

"This is a cute color," Riley said. "Thank you."

"Hold it up," my mom said.

My bag had a shirt as well. Riley's was lavender and mine was dark green. Riley unfolded hers and held it up against herself. I shook mine out and looked at the front.

Gasps and exclamations erupted from the crowd of family members gathered around us, but I hardly heard them. I just stared at the white lettering on the shirt Nora had given me.

Daddy X2

Did this mean?

My eyes flew to Riley's shirt. In big block letters it read, *Big Sister.*

"Oh my gosh, Nora!" Riley said, her voice heightening to a scream. She started jumping up and down, clutching the t-shirt to her chest.

I stared at my wife, my mouth hanging open.

She flashed that million-dollar smile. "Surprise, daddy."

I scooped her into my arms and held her tight. "Are you serious? We're having a baby?"

Her body shook with her laugh. "Yes. I just found out."

Riley's arms flew around us both and I drew her into our hug. The three of us stood there for a long moment, holding each other, while my family freaked out around us.

Finally, I let go. Nora's eyes were bright, her cheeks flushed. Riley had tears glistening on her cheeks and an enormous smile on her face. She'd already put her t-shirt on over her other clothes.

My girls. God, I loved them so much.

The ensuing scene was one of hugging and crying and hugging some more. Everyone was ecstatic at our news. The family—Mom especially—bombarded Nora with questions. She explained calmly, and with a smile that wouldn't quit, that she'd just found out she was pregnant, and although it was still very early, she simply couldn't wait to tell everyone.

Ten minutes earlier, I'd thought I was the happiest guy on the planet. Then this. I thought my chest might burst. That woman was the best thing that had ever happened to me.

Later, when the family had gone, Nora, Riley, and I curled up on the couch together. I wore my Daddy X2 shirt and Riley hadn't taken hers off. We talked about the baby and what it would be like to have a newborn in the house. Riley swore she'd babysit every day. And I knew that no matter what this new adventure brought, it was going to be great.

When I'd first caught a glimpse of Nora next door, I'd known she'd be trouble. She'd proved me right—but she was trouble of the best kind.

～

DEAR READER

Dear Reader,

It's been so much fun to return to our group of (sometimes reluctant) runners. I have LOVED writing about a group of women who are so unique, yet such fantastic friends. They're not the likeliest group of gal pals, but their fierce loyalty to each other is one of my favorite things in the series.

It probably didn't surprise you that Nora's story was last. I planned it that way from the beginning. It just made sense for her character. Unlike Everly, she wasn't hoping to find her Prince Charming. She was content to live her life on her own terms, letting men in as it suited (and pleased) her.

Interestingly, I had a very different story in mind for Nora when I originally outlined this series. I had what amounted to a synopsis for each book, a brief idea of what it would be about. And hers was not the book you just read.

What was it, you might be wondering? It involved her meeting a "men's expert" who teaches men how to score, essentially. He wouldn't have been any more interested in forever than she was, until a night with her.

It doesn't sound bad on the surface. Turning the tables on a serial manwhore is pretty fun, both from where I'm sitting behind the keyboard and as a reader. But honestly? The character I envisioned was kind of a male version of Nora. And there was something about that I just didn't like.

I find, as a writer and a reader, that pairing characters who are too similar can create a story that lacks intensity. Sure, it can have a fun/cute/interesting plot, but there's something missing.

Now, don't go emailing me with every WONDERFUL book you've read with a couple who are basically the male/female versions of each other. I know those books are out there!

But in this case, Nora didn't need a man who was similar to her. She needed the WRONG man. A guy who was nothing like the men she usually dated. Gruff, tattooed, a little rough around the edges. A far cry from the sleek, sophisticated men in suits she usually gravitated toward.

And low and behold, once upon a time, I wrote about a very handsome tattoo artist. If you didn't make the connection already, Dex appears as a side character in Hot Single Dad.

The truth behind that? When I wrote Hot Single Dad, I thought I might continue the series, so I added Dex as a side character, intending to use him as a future hero. I wound up moving onto other projects and never went back to that series. But apparently that was meant to be, because Dex was perfect for Nora.

And pairing Nora with a single dad has to be one of my favorite things ever. I just love how Nora and Riley's friendship blossomed and Nora was just what that sweet girl needed.

I hope you enjoyed this, and the rest of the Dirty Martini Running Club. It's been a fun ride!

Love,

Claire

ACKNOWLEDGMENTS

Thank you to everyone who helped make this book a reality!

Thank you Eliza for another great editing job. And to Erma for your proofreading skills!

To Lori for the absolutely adorable covers for this series. You've outdone yourself, my friend!

To my team for keeping things running so I can have writing time, for listening to my dramatic laments when I'm stuck, helping me brainstorm, and generally being the awesomest.

And definitely not least, to my readers. Y'all waited a while for our girl Nora, and I hope she was worth the wait. Your love and support continue to amaze me and I'm humbled and so grateful that I can share my stories with you.

ALSO BY CLAIRE KINGSLEY

For a full and up-to-date listing of Claire Kingsley books visit
www.clairekingsleybooks.com/books/

For comprehensive reading order, visit www.
clairekingsleybooks.com/reading-order/

The Haven Brothers

Small-town romantic suspense with CK's signature endearing
characters and heartwarming happily ever afters. Can be read as
stand-alones.

Obsession Falls (Josiah and Audrey)

The rest of the Haven brothers will be getting their own happily
ever afters!

How the Grump Saved Christmas (Elias and Isabelle)

A stand-alone, small-town Christmas romance.

The Bailey Brothers

Steamy, small-town family series with a dash of suspense. Five
unruly brothers. Epic pranks. A quirky, feuding town. Big HEAs.
Best read in order.

Protecting You (Asher and Grace part 1)

Fighting for Us (Asher and Grace part 2)

Unraveling Him (Evan and Fiona)

Rushing In (Gavin and Skylar)

Chasing Her Fire (Logan and Cara)

Rewriting the Stars (Levi and Annika)

The Miles Family

Sexy, sweet, funny, and heartfelt family series with a dash of suspense. Messy family. Epic bromance. Super romantic. Best read in order.

Broken Miles (Roland and Zoe)

Forbidden Miles (Brynn and Chase)

Reckless Miles (Cooper and Amelia)

Hidden Miles (Leo and Hannah)

Gaining Miles: A Miles Family Novella (Ben and Shannon)

Dirty Martini Running Club

Sexy, fun, feel-good romantic comedies with huge... hearts. Can be read as stand-alones.

Everly Dalton's Dating Disasters (Prequel with Everly, Hazel, and Nora)

Faking Ms. Right (Everly and Shepherd)

Falling for My Enemy (Hazel and Corban)

Marrying Mr. Wrong (Sophie and Cox)

Flirting with Forever (Nora and Dex)

Bluewater Billionaires

Hot romantic comedies. Lady billionaire BFFs and the badass heroes who love them. Can be read as stand-alones.

The Mogul and the Muscle (Cameron and Jude)

The Price of Scandal, Wild Open Hearts, and Crazy for Loving You

More Bluewater Billionaire shared-world romantic comedies by Lucy Score, Kathryn Nolan, and Pippa Grant

Bootleg Springs

by Claire Kingsley and Lucy Score

Hot and hilarious small-town romcom series with a dash of mystery and suspense. Best read in order.

Whiskey Chaser (Scarlett and Devlin)

Sidecar Crush (Jameson and Leah Mae)

Moonshine Kiss (Bowie and Cassidy)

Bourbon Bliss (June and George)

Gin Fling (Jonah and Shelby)

Highball Rush (Gibson and I can't tell you)

Book Boyfriends

Hot romcoms that will make you laugh and make you swoon. Can be read as stand-alones.

Book Boyfriend (Alex and Mia)

Cocky Roommate (Weston and Kendra)

Hot Single Dad (Caleb and Linnea)

~

Finding Ivy (William and Ivy)

A unique contemporary romance with a hint of mystery. Stand-alone.

~

His Heart (Sebastian and Brooke)

A poignant and emotionally intense story about grief, loss, and the transcendent power of love. Stand-alone.

~

The Always Series

Smoking hot, dirty talking bad boys with some angsty intensity. Can be read as stand-alones.

Always Have (Braxton and Kylie)

Always Will (Selene and Ronan)

Always Ever After (Braxton and Kylie)

~

The Jetty Beach Series

Sexy small-town romance series with swoony heroes, romantic HEAs, and lots of big feels. Can be read as stand-alones.

Behind His Eyes (Ryan and Nicole)

One Crazy Week (Melissa and Jackson)

Messy Perfect Love (Cody and Clover)

Operation Get Her Back (Hunter and Emma)

Weekend Fling (Finn and Juliet)

Good Girl Next Door (Lucas and Becca)

The Path to You (Gabriel and Sadie)

ABOUT THE AUTHOR

Claire Kingsley is an Amazon #1 bestselling author of sexy, heartfelt contemporary romance and romantic comedies. She writes sassy, quirky heroines, swoony heroes who love their women hard, panty-melting sexytimes, romantic happily ever afters, and all the big feels.

She can't imagine life without coffee, her Kindle, and the sexy heroes who inhabit her imagination. She lives in the inland Pacific Northwest with her three kids.

www.clairekingsleybooks.com

Made in the USA
Las Vegas, NV
06 February 2024

85261237R00225